OTHER CARSON BRAND NOVELS

STOLEN VALOR

DARK MOTIVE

REASONABLE SIN

ALSO BY CRAIG RAINEY

MASSACRE AT AGUA CALIENTE

THE ART OF PROFESSIONAL SALES

For Ryan, a Prouder Dad There has
Never Been

Within Anarchy lies a vacuum in which the state may not survive, and a people shall certainly perish.

—CRAIG RAINEY

PROLOGUE

MARK WILLIAMS KNEW HE WAS IN HIS LAST DAYS. It surprised him how easily he could admit it. Most of his life had been a series of way points, like steppingstones in a shallow pond. Like most people in his life as he moved along those points of dry safety, he endeavored to avoid falling from them into shallow waters.

Those waters were shallow because they represented no real danger, only sadness and pain. His human nature dictated he stay on the path for the rules' sake. The steppingstones of life were the chapters of life none of us want to read, but all of us must read. The pain of those chapters is the seasoning of a full life.

His steppingstones comprised those things in life he dreaded but knew were unavoidable. The first was the death of a pet. The next was moving with his parents from his childhood home, leaving his school and his friends behind. In his twenties his grandparents died. He wept uncontrollably at his grandmother's funeral. She had been as much a mother to him as her daughter. In his forties, Mark lost his father to COVID. His mother followed soon after. Tomorrow his steppingstones would come to an end. His life had advanced so far that the pond had become very deep, and he was a long way from shore.

As he grew older, he wondered how much time he had left. At forty-five, he guessed that number was no more than twenty of thirty years. Two or three decades seemed a short time, but manageable, easily ignored with the help of a busy work schedule.

When he learned he had only two years remaining, well that had come as a shock. His only consolation was that he had chosen the day and time of his passing.

Now that it was here, he couldn't help but question the wisdom of his decision made two years before.

His FBI salary was laughable compared to what Geo-Global Oceanic Partners offered him for the part-time job. He and Tammy could have lived extravagantly on the income alone from this second part time job. His new employer warned that maintaining his position with the FBI was a condition of employment.

It didn't take a genius to figure out that GGOP wanted access to someone high up in the Department of Justice. Mark was as high as you could go without being a cabinet official, and he was to be that contact.

He made the decision to take the job because he could not bear the steppingstone in his life which was his son. Justin was born with an incurable genetic mutation. He would live no more than a dozen years before his body deteriorated and he died a painful and horrifying death.

If his son's life had been the only criteria for Mark's decision to betray his country and surrender his life, it may have been more difficult. With clarity of the damned Mark recalled the moment at the breakfast table in their sunny suburban home.

Mark waited with his steaming coffee cup in his hands. His thoughts precluded any interest in the coffee. Tammy returned to the table after wheeling Justin to his room. She took her seat opposite him with the same deliberate care she had adopted since the day they brought Justin home from the hospital.

She was fifteen years younger than Mark, but their love was not what others imagined of a couple with so widely separate ages. They fell in love because of what they saw in one another. They married 10 years before. Justin was born the following summer.

They accepted their path. They would commit the remainder of their lives to the care and comfort of their only son, or until he passed. Tammy's measured manner was a learned trait created from the caution she exercised each day in caring for their son's special needs. One mistake could mean his life. She would not go down that road.

A moment after she settled in her chair across the table, waiting patiently for his news, he shared this new opportunity with her. He told her of the part time job with Geo-Global Oceanic Partners. He revealed the ridiculously lucrative salary.

Her puzzled expression prompted him to reveal his suspicions as to the true nature of the offer.

She shook her head as she was struck by the gravity of what this new employer would expect of her husband.

"It is out of the question," she said softly, with a tone she used around their son - firm but soothing.

Mark hesitated before providing her the last part of their offer.

He watched her closely as he said the rest.

"They have the cure for Justin's disease. They will provide it immediately if I accept their offer. He will be a normal healthy boy by the end of the week."

Tammy's reaction was hardly a reaction at all. If he had not watched her with the eye of a detective interrogating a perp, he would have missed the faint flutter of her eye lids, the quick intake of a shallow breath, or the hardly noticeable flush of her skin, which passed as quickly as it arrived.

The decision was made. Beneath the mask she created to hide the regret of the necessary hardships she would bear for the remainder of Justin's life, he saw her faulter. He saw hope.

He would give his life for his boy, but more accurately, he would give it for his wife. Tammy was still young, beautiful, and vibrant.

The life assigned her by Justin's condition would kill everything that made her the woman he adored. He could not reject an opportunity to save her and Justin, even if it was at the cost of his life.

He decided to keep to himself the part about his death.

That moment at the kitchen table was two years ago. After that day, he answered the calls, providing the information requested. He used the authority of his position to set actions in motion as his new employer demanded.

Much of the information he provided seemed to have little importance or relevance to a large petroleum conglomerate. Most made little sense to him. The innocuous appearance of what he provided soothed his suffering sense of duty and honor.

He experienced fear at the greater peril when he was required to initiate a 6-S edict on a DOJ contractor. The 6-S was a contract for a kill of an individual within the organization. He was not a mob boss, contracting hits on American citizens, particularly those committed to upholding the law. The information he provided; taking instructions and directives from a Chinese operative working here in the US was the last straw – at least he thought it was.

The most recent demand was more than he was willing to do. This was beyond illegal. What they wanted him to create ran counter to his oath of office, his moral code, and his principles.

He pledged to reject this last demand. They had saved enough money that Tammy would never have to work another day in her life. Justin was happy and healthy. He went to school like any other boy. He made good grades and had many friends. No, Mark would not comply. What could they do to him beyond the death he would meet in less than forty-eight hours?

The photo arrived on his phone via text message. It showed his son running on a field, a soccer ball skittering before him. He was at a soccer match with his little league team. The scene was contained in a circle with red crosshairs cutting the image into 4 slices. Mark recognized the circular photo with the crosshairs as a view of his son within the scope reticule of a high-powered rifle.

He wept as he texted his reply to the five-digit sender number.

"I'll do it. Don't hurt my boy."

Mark Williams contacted a man he knew would be right for the job. The phone rang once before it was answered.

"Yup," the voice said from the other end of the call.

"Steven," Williams said. "I have a special assignment for you. It is going to seem a bit outside of what I normally ask of you, but I believe you are the man for the job."

"Whatcha got, Boss?"

Williams conveyed the plan in broad strokes.

Considering the risks involved, Steven remained surprisingly quiet until Williams finished.

"I need you to fill in the details as you are able," Williams said. "Can I count on your discretion in this matter?"

"Of course, boss," was the reply. "This one is going to be expensive. It could get very messy. It will be almost impossible to cover the paper trail within the bureau."

"I know," Williams agreed. "This is the last one for me. I will arrange for the backing of internal channels to provide you whatever you need for the mission. You arrange the operation from the field."

Steven made no response for a long moment.

"Is there a problem?" Williams asked with a return to the authority of his office.

Steven cleared his throat.

Williams thought he detected emotional distress in Steven's voice.

"It's been an honor, boss," Steven said with genuine feeling. "It won't be long before it is my time to pay as you are doing."

The phone call went dead.

Williams sat frozen in place at his desk.

How many others were offered a deal by Geo-Global Oceanic Partners? Until that moment, Williams had no idea that their reach went beyond him. Steven's words confirmed his involvement, a separate deal made for his cooperation.

For the first time in more than two weeks, Mark Williams' dread of his final days was overshadowed by a new fear. He feared for the nation. What had he done? Was the conspiracy so large that it consumed the entire FBI?

He needed to call someone, to try to fix what he had done over the last two years. The image of his son in the crosshairs of a sniper scope stayed his hand for the moment.

Williams determined to see to his wife and son's safety, then he would expose the whole thing. His death, or the certainty of a conviction for crimes against the state, meant nothing compared to the danger he could help avert.

He packed his briefcase, leaving his office as quickly as possible.

That evening Tammy received a call from the state police. Mark Williams perished in a fiery auto accident as he drove home. Evidence on the scene and eyewitness accounts attributed the accident to him driving at high speed, losing control of the car, and plunging from the height of an expressway flyover.

1

BRAND KNEW THE FORMER SEALS would never accept him as an equal. None of them believed, with his limited military experience – six years in the Texas Army National Guard – he would successfully complete the Sovereign Services Advanced Course. When he did, only a spare few showed a small crack in their indifference with a slight arch of their brow, or a barely perceptible nod of approval. The others ignored the achievement, doubling down on their opposition, claiming privately he had gotten lucky, or he was not treated as sternly as he should have been. In short, Brand had achieved nothing which would impress them.

Brand was surprised when after only six months with Sovereign Services, Richard "Dick" Riser, CEO, invited him to his Virginia compound. *Sovereign Retreats*, as he called them, were fiercely coveted amongst the security operators in his employ.

An invitation was a rare achievement. He extended an invitation to only the top twenty-four operators in the organization. The current top ten members, of course, were invited along with top fourteen of the more than sixty remaining agents.

Among his minimum requirements to attend included BUDS SEAL school graduation and real wartime special operator experience or passing Sovereign's SEAL minicamp called SEAL PUP (Sea Air Land Practical Uptraining Program.) Although unspoken in public, and appearing in no company literature, he required wet or semi-wet real world practical experience. The candidate must be blooded. That is, he must have experience in the implementation of lethal force in a real-world environment. In other words, he must have killed in the line of duty.

It was unheard of for anyone without SEAL training and graduation from BUDS became a part of the Sovereign Twenty, so word of Brand's attendance set off a maelstrom of objections from the legacy SEAL contractors in the company.

It was obvious the new guy was a wet-behind-the-ears, weekend warrior, wanna-be super trooper. No one believed Brand had pulled the trigger on anyone, nor did they believe him capable of doing so. There was no effort made to mask their distaste for the new man. Boo's, angry slurs, and not so subtle behind the hand remarks greeted him wherever he joined the team as a group.

The leader of the Never-Brand movement was a former SEAL officer named Conolly. He was an unofficial leader within the organization and was highly revered within the ranks. Brand's understanding of the man marked him as a formidable warrior with a violent past.

He was rumored to be Riser's first recruit and was an unofficial member of the ownership and management of the company. Because of his nefarious acts in the field, it was said had he remained in the military he would have faced certain action by a military tribunal.

To Brand he seemed an unreasonable brute, even by special operator standards. Based upon his observations, every man in the organization feared him and gave him a wide berth. His closest ally was a black operator named Williams. He was a large man with a similar penchant for violence.

Conolly was the leader of four men, including Williams, who made it their private mission to wash Brand out of the organization. Their campaign had waged since the day Brand was hired.

All four were on the plane. Conolly was an existing *Sovereign Ten* member; the elite point of the spear which was the Twenty. The remaining three were a part of the Twenty.

Two of them, Lansch and Suarez, served as cadre members during his SEAL-PUP training. Their treatment of him had become so obviously cruel that Riser himself had intervened. The harsh treatment decreased but they dubbed Brand "Riser's Boy" - his pet dog.

By intervening on his behalf, Riser had done Brand no favors with the men.

Brand was seated at the rear of the aircraft and had a clear view of Conolly and his team. Conolly was front left. Next to him was the large black man, Williams. Across the aisle sat the remaining two, Lansch and Suarez.

They journeyed from a private airport just outside of Bethesda to a small private airstrip in rural Virginia. The Sovereign Gulf Stream G800 was modified to seat twenty-four. The flight was full. Two attractive attendants served coffee and soft drinks. Brand forsook his habitual Bourbon rocks for a cran-apple cocktail.

Deep jubilant voices filled the cabin with boisterous tales of past ops, war stories, manly-tales, and good-natured ribbing. Brand maintained the role of silent participant. He was not afraid or intimidated by the others. He felt out of place and unwelcome amongst these blooded warriors. He shared no tales. He did not join in their laughter. He kept away from the attention of the men, and he suffered no ridicule.

He had been with Sovereign Services for more than 180 days. By his estimation, he had earned his place amongst these men. They had sorely tried his will and tested his mettle - nearly to the limits of his abilities. He never allowed others to see how he suffered; nor would he ever share that information with anyone. He accepted that none of his companions would admit he had handled himself with unexpected strength or uncommon resolve.

Brand frowned at his thoughts. He looked up from his self-scrutiny towards the front of the plane.

At the head of the aisle near the cockpit bulkhead, Richard "Dick" Riser stood beside the bar. He surveyed his men mildly. He participated sparingly in his team's frivolity. He allowed himself only a rare occurrence of a quick smile, or an occasional nod when hailed.

As he often did while in his presence, Brand appraised the man. He recognized in him an indomitable spirit – an undefinable nature which set him apart as the most formidable of them all. He was without a doubt, master of any room he entered. He was six inches over six feet, and just shy of 300 lbs. Brand guessed his BMI at around 10%. Blazing blue eyes flared within a deeply tanned countenance and a closely cropped black beard. He wore jeans and a sportscoat over a tight black tee.

He ignored the openly fawning looks of the flight attendants as he focused upon his scrutiny of the men. Brand had fallen under his roving survey more than once during the flight.

Six months before, Brand met Riser for the first time in his downtown Bethesda office. Riser hired him immediately based upon the recommendation of Special Agent Dennis Moore of the FBI. During his onboarding with Sovereign, Riser had given him only one directive.

"Moore's recommendation got you in. It's up to you to stay in or I'll see you out."

By all indications, Brand was in. He was no longer a street brawling construction worker from San Antonio, Texas. He was a highly trained security operative, skilled in a vast array of tradecraft. He was no longer soft or out of shape. His endurance was far beyond anything it had ever been. He felt stronger than he had at any other time in his life.

Most notably, he was mentally tougher. Although the memories troubled his nights, he harbored fewer questions about those he had killed or injured. He recognized this violent and often lethal aspect of the job as consequential, an unavoidable sacrifice for a successful mission.

Much of his improvement, physically and mentally, was due directly to the SEAL mini-camp Riser insisted all non-SEAL personnel attend. He endured the training amongst others without SEAL experience. Most were former law enforcement or prior service military. A few were ambitious civilians trying to earn a higher position within the company.

Despite frequent claims from the instructors that minicamp was no more than a shadow of real SEAL training, the *Ring Out* rate was identical at sixty percent.

Brand was thirty-one years old, and he suffered. He completed the program by committing all he had towards completing the course. He barely got through it. The instructors openly displayed their surprise he had not joined the bell ringers.

The BUDS training was difficult, but his years growing up at Canyon Lake gave him a valuable leg up. Being a child of the water, he had worn fins most of his life and the hardship of swimming countless meters in the pool, then running exhausting miles immediately afterwards didn't torture his ankles as it did the other trainees. Many of the candidate's pulled the bell lanyard at that point in the training.

Whether from his general knowledge of how tough SEAL training was, or insight gleaned from frequent boasts from his instructors, Brand knew he in no way experienced the full brunt of BUDS/SEAL training. The training was intended to provide a basic understanding of the hardships the others had endured to earn their titles. It was a secondary benefit if the candidate gained a level of skill from the training.

Despite the belief that the training provided only a limited exposure to the punishing reality of BUDS, he gained valuable combat and arms skills from the techniques taught in the course. No matter what the other candidates or the SEALs thought of the course, he committed himself to learning all he could and worked to gain proficiency in any lesson presented in the course.

Brand emerged from his reverie and glanced around him. He was again impressed that against the odds, here he was amongst some of the toughest men on the planet. He didn't claim to be one of them, but he knew it took something special to occupy a seat on that flight.

The disregard from the others was annoying but not surprising. He never relied upon his military service for respect or credibility. Few military servicemen and women viewed National Guard service as legitimate military experience. *Weekend Warrior, Civil Super Trooper, Part-time Soldier, and Hobby Troop.* These were but a few of the names he endured.

The only reason any of the men knew about his military experience was his leaked employment application, which listed it under the military experience question. Despite the ridicule, he kept his head down and committed to the requirements of the job as best he could.

Brand's motivation to earn a place on the team was two-fold. The first was the lucrative six-figure salary and bonus structure within the compensation package. The second, he had nowhere to go where he was not sought by cartel sicarios or international hit teams. Simply, he reasoned where would he be safer than amongst the most highly trained and fiercely formidable fighting men on the planet?

No one including Brand would have given him one chance in a million of being invited to compete for a spot on the elite team. Being a "Twenty" meant working the top assignments and earning large performance bonuses exclusive to those assignments. Membership also guaranteed security operations work in the most demanding of high-profile situations. At that level, there was no following bankers around or driving CEOs to lunch. A lack of any kind of special op's experience usually excluded consideration for the post.

The jet touched down at the small airfield in Virginia. The Sovereign men deplaned onto the tarmac, carrying identical go bags. Passing a dozen luxury aircraft, Riser and his twenty-four men entered the opulent terminal facility like a military unit, headed to war.

Everyone inside watched the formidable looking group as they passed through from plush lobby to the street entrance of the terminal building.

Outside, they mounted a waiting charter bus and were soon underway on the last few miles to Riser's remote training compound in rural Virginia.

The bus wound through lush, wooded hills and rugged canyons. At the summit of one of the climbs they turned under a guarded, black iron gated entrance, and entered the *Sovereign Field Facility*. Despite the uninspiring name, the large stone and timbered architecture, and the wide welcoming entrance resembled an exclusive vacation resort.

Hidden within a thousand-acre wilderness was a cluster of stone and timber buildings comprising the main compound. The largest of the buildings was two stories, fronted by a sweeping porte-cochere.

Brand was last off the bus where courteous facility staff welcomed him. He entered the courtyard. Behind the main building was a pool area which reminded Brand of a hotel vacation resort complete with bar, restaurant cabanas, and private bungalows for overnight stays.

A bellman guided him to his private room on the second floor of the large building. His suite overlooked the pool area. Beyond, were a number of single-story buildings. The one farthest away, a long narrow metal structure, fronted what Brand guessed was a shooting range and weapons training facility. Surrounding the compound on all sides was a rugged terrain of heavy woods and rolling hills. The soft texture of turning tree leaves and matted forest floors was broken by rocky crags and deep ravines.

The bellman instructed him, Mr. Riser required his attendance at the *Poolside Café Cabana* at the top of the hour. The man withdrew before Brand could offer him a tip.

It was exactly 6pm when Brand took his place at one of the tables near the entrance to the café. When he arrived several members of the team were seated near a low side bandstand. They ignored him as they chatted amongst themselves.

With a band stand and a full bar in the back, the *Cabana Café* was more bar and grill than café. The motif was a continuation of the mountain resort style of the main building.

Within minutes the men of Sovereign Services filled the room. Other than those dark instances when their gaze fell upon Brand, they were raucous and in good humor.

Riser entered a few minutes later. He made his way to the back of the room where he stepped onto the wide bandstand. Conversations died away as he positioned himself in the center of the stage platform.

Riser scanned the men, making eye contact with each. These retreats were serious business. Except for the rigors of qualifying for the Twenty, the process seemed more recreational than functional to most of those who participated. Riser viewed these *Sovereign Retreats* as an integral method of locating and placing the most qualified of his men in the best assignments for his clients. The peripheral benefits of morale boosting, and team building were important, but less critical.

"Welcome to this year's Sovereign Retreat," he said with a sweep of his hand.

They greeted his welcome with applause and cheers.

"Many of you have been here before."

Riser pointed at the table of men who were present when Brand arrived.

More applause.

"Some, several times," he said with a glint of white teeth from within his dark beard. "Welcome to you rookies. I expect you to make the most of your time here, even if you are unable to earn a spot on the Twenty."

There followed a brief moment where the men searched out the rookies in the room, many glances falling significantly upon Brand. He studied the sweat beaded glass before him, weathering the critical looks.

"Listen up gentlemen," Riser continued. "For those of you who don't know, and I hope you are few, we are an organization which focuses on two things. The first and most important – because it ensures the second – is we retain the finest special operators at our highest echelons. The second is: our clients and those who wish they were our clients see us as the best and most admired in the business. In addition to the sixty plus credentialled special operators we maintain on our staff; we also deploy a street level security force of more than 27,000 commissioned security officers world-wide.

"From street level to the leadership within the Twenty, each of us carries the Sovereign label. Only twenty carry the coveted Black Card designation. You are graduates of formal SEAL training or in rare cases, you have completed our SEAL PUP course. Either way, we are a SEAL-centric organization."

The room erupted in cheers and yells.

Riser waited until the noise level waned.

"This weekend's exercise is the final evaluation of three required for admission into the Twenty."

The room once more erupted in cheers and applause.

"The first, as I mentioned, is SEAL experience."

More cheers.

"The second is the requirement of blood. You have taken a life purposely, aggressively, and in the line of duty."

Fewer cheers greeted the final criteria. Conversely, the men in the room grew soberly grim.

Riser raised his hands as if to ward off a criticism no one in the room felt.

"You are here because you have fulfilled the first and second of these requirements. The Retreat will determine your place in this organization."

Brand noticed a growing number in the room casting dark glances in his direction. He knew instinctively they doubted he had achieved the second criteria. Taking a life in combat was a part of the job description when you were full time active duty in a combat zone.

They knew his service in the National Guard would never put him in the position to do so. Weekend warriors deployed in the middle east guarded prisoners or provided other support services. They were in the rear with the gear, not in combat services. They were the epitome of the designation, *REMF – Rear Echelon Mother Fuckers.*

To everyone other than Riser, he was either a fraud, or a street thug who had pulled the trigger on a civilian.

Brand endured the looks with a hard glint in his eyes. His experiences on the matter were a sore subject with him, and completely personal, off limits to outside observers. He assigned no sense of accomplishment or misplaced self-worth to those he had killed.

His rage grew at the judgmental looks. It galled him that anyone would keep score in killing as he would reps in the gym, or laps swam in a pool. He had done what he had to because he had no other option. He felt no pride in it. He never asked for this life. It called him. He would gladly never been a part of any of it.

He was a regular guy, a construction worker, before the cartel killed his best friend and then his girlfriend, dragging him into an unforgiving world of kill or be killed. He viewed himself as lucky what was known of his deeds were forgiven by the feds as actions in the line of duty. Dennis Moore, his FBI friend, had arranged that – and this job. Treating a man as more because he had killed was repugnant.

Until that moment he had no idea Moore had revealed information to Riser about his dark past. The breach of trust left Brand feeling more than a little betrayed.

Riser noticed the looks and doubt in his men as they stole glances at Brand.

"Gentlemen," Riser continued. "Each of you is here because you deserve to be here. I selected you to be here."

Focus drifted back to their leader.

"This is the order of march. Eat a big dinner. Get some sleep. Tomorrow, we begin. Only twenty of you will make the cut. Four of you will return to Sovereign. Those who do not earn a spot in the Twenty will benefit from the experience and have the opportunity to return next year to earn your place amongst us. Goodnight."

2

THE MEN ASSEMBLED ON THE WEAPONS training grounds at dawn. Riser was dressed in forest camo as were his cadre, members of *The Ten*. The members of the current *Twenty* were dressed as the other candidates, in black combat uniforms. The Ten were the permanent party of the Twenty. The members of The Ten were selected from within the Twenty. Riser alone made the determination who was a part of his elite group.

Brand took in the brightening eastern horizon. The morning was cool. Dew soaked the well mown grass beneath his feet. His boots glistened with the moisture. He felt a pleasant elation as he waited for the exercise to begin. He relished the prospect of action. The Op would busy the others with something other than the unwelcome attention they paid him. Additionally, he experienced a small measure of nostalgia at the resemblance to past military training exercises when he was in the military. He compared his feelings to those he felt in Basic Training, AIT, numerous NCO schools, and most recently SEAL-PUP training.

Riser called for the attention of the troops.

"Men. We have created two seven-man teams for the two-day field exercise. The Ten and I will serve as OPFOR. Your weapons are live; the ammo are rubber rounds with reduced powder charges. The environment for this exercise is semi-lethal. The rubber rounds will sting a good deal but will not kill except in rare situations. No head shots men."

"Once you join your team, make your way to your individual primary rally points. I have selected your Squad Leaders. Team Alpha is Williams. Bravo is Lansch. They have the mission parameters. From this moment the Op is hot. The only easy days are the first and the last."

Riser held up a gloved fist.

"It pays to be a winner. Never out of the fight."

The team responded to the SEAL motto with a loud cry.

"Hooyah!"

Riser gave the rally sign.

"Good luck gentlemen."

Riser and his Opposing Force team gathered their gear and moved off into the woods beyond the shooting facility.

Williams and Lansch took positions before the remaining men.

Brand shook his head doubtfully. Both men were part of Conolly's Never-Brand club. Lansch had made his life miserable during SEAL-PUP training. Williams hated him, even going so far as to openly ridicule him at company training and in office meetings.

Williams glared at him now. He spoke first.

"Let's address the elephant in the room. Who gets the Weekend Warrior?"

Lansch interrupted him.

"He's with me. Get over here Warrior Brand."

Brand favored Lansch with a dangerous look, mastering his temper before he moved forward.

"Don't eye fuck me boy," Lansch warned him to the laughter of the others.

"Too bad," Williams lamented with genuine disappointment. "I wanted to lead the noob personally. I wanted to lend my personal touch to make a man of him."

Williams shrugged for effect.

"Your funeral John."

More laughter.

"Don't be so dramatic Davian."

Brand took his place before the group as the two wrapped up their fun. He gave Williams his full attention.

"Why don't you give that a try right here, in front of your audience, funny man?" Brand asked of Williams.

Williams appeared surprised that the typically silent Brand spoke, much less challenging him openly.

"Don't puss out now, big mouth," Brand urged him. "Conolly isn't here to back you now. Step up or shut the fuck up."

Lansch watched the interchange with an appreciative grin.

"Maybe I chose wisely," he said with a chuckle. "Don't pick on my team Williams – not if you don't want to be an early casualty."

Although Lansch's words were sarcastic and ridiculed Brand, they stung Williams. He was not willing to be insulted by the Nasty Guard rookie in front of the men.

"You just got lucky," he warned Brand. "I don't want Lansch to make excuses about why my team beat his. I'll deal with you when this thing is over, and you wash out."

Brand nodded.

"Every man here knows who's lucky right now," Brand said. "I expect you to keep your word when this thing is over, no excuses."

Silence fell on the group.

Finally, Lansch broke the spell.

"Call your team, Williams. The enemy's out there."

Lansch and Williams quickly selected their teams. Brand's team assignment was the only one they had not decided ahead of time.

Each team moved towards their designated rally areas. Lansch gathered his team in a tight circle.

"Listen up Bravo," he said, looking around for a sneak attack. "We are facing the Chief and his hand-picked crew. Every year, the story is the same. They eliminate every team in the fight. That is not going to be us. Each day has a different objective. Our objective today is a capture the flag Op at known point zero niner in zone kilo."

Lansch showed them their objective on a full color, coated map. Brand took note of the elevation indices and nearby terrain features of the objective.

"They call it the Kill Zone because it is exposed and presents the perfect ambush location. It is about three clicks to our north. We will have to traverse rough country. Noise discipline is critical. From here we creep. Remember your training. Brand, try to keep up. You will probably be our first casualty.

Don't take it personally. All the rookies die first."

Brand resisted the urge to knock out Lansch's teeth. Instead, he kept silent, his clenched fists gripping his weapon, an ATI Alpha-15 RIA, until it creaked in his hands.

"Brand, you take point."

The others on the team looked at one another. The rookie might be a target for their leader, but they would need the participation of every team member to win the Op. Sending the new guy to the front was risky.

Brand stepped out, headed north.

The team spread out, following him into the bush.

Brand kept to lower ground. Although it was certain Riser and his team knew the area completely and would anticipate their route, good field tactics required he follow the path that would least expose his team. They held no advantage against the Ten. Stealth and keen situational awareness would have to suffice.

After little more than an hour, Lansch lost sight of his point man. He edged forward, ahead of the others, watching for Brand. He advanced another twenty yards, but Brand failed to appear.

"Where the fuck are you?" he murmured under his breath.

Suddenly he was pulled to the ground. He found himself face to face with Brand.

Lansch was about to reprimand Brand when the other covered his mouth with a sweaty hand.

"Silence," Brand whispered.

He removed his hand from Lansch's mouth and pointed towards the east, motioning with a slight upward gesture. Lansch looked where Brand indicated. Hidden in a gap between two vertical rock shelves was one of the Ten. He scanned the trail carefully.

Brand used a hand signal to indicate the man was alone in his nest.

Lansch nodded.

Brand made a shooting gesture with his hand pointing at the sniper.

Lansch nodded again.

Brand took aim and shot the hidden man, stinging him with a hard rubber bullet. The sniper yelped as he searched the brush for the gunman, sweeping his rifle towards the sound of the shot. Brand shot him again.

He moved towards his kill as Lansch returned to the team with an update and modified marching orders. Brand was squatting next to the Ten team member as Bravo team arrived. His name was Watkins.

They chatted in whispers.

"You didn't have to shoot me twice," the man complained with humor.

"No," Brand agreed. "I didn't. Are you alright?"

"I'm good rookie. Nice work. I'll get you tomorrow."

Brand grinned and nodded.

"We'll see, Watkins."

Lansch kneeled near Watkins.

"It will take a while to live this one down, Henry."

Watkins shook his head.

"That's my best hiding spot for Kilo. If your man had gone another ten yards, I would have had you all pinned down in a bottled-up choke point. The rest of my team would have cleaned you up."

At the mention of the rest of Watkins' team, Lansch looked around sharply.

"Let's move out," he said. "Brand, you're still point."

The Ten's confidence in Watkins to eliminate Bravo team allowed the team to go after Williams and his Alpha team en masse. Brand led Lansch and Bravo Team to the edge of the clearing where a white flagpole stood atop a small rise. A red flag fluttered in the wind, beckoning them to take it.

Lansch spoke to his team.

"We will wait for nightfall to take Kilo-Niner. Until then we need to set up a perimeter around the flag. There are only seven of us so we will have to coordinate our fields of fire. Here's what we are going to do."

"Two squads of three will go in opposite directions. Clear the perimeter of the clearing then create a cordon around the objective. Once we root out hidden opposition during the day light, we will maintain the perimeter until after dark. I will ascend the hill and liberate the flag and we head back to the house. I'm buying at the bar."

"There are about a dozen things that can go wrong with your plan," Brand said. "Why not send a man up the hill? If he is killed, we will identify the enemy's location and we have a large enough force to assail OPFOR successfully."

Lansch shook his head, impatience twisting his lips.

"Why don't you leave tactics to the soldiers, rookie. You're with Suarez and Tate. Move out."

Brand considered Lansch for a moment before following the other two.

"Fucking weekend warrior," Lansch said to the remaining men. "Move out."

Brand took his position at the rear of his three-man team, following the edge of the hillock clearing, but staying far enough inside the woods to maintain cover and concealment.

Suarez, the senior man on the team hand signed his intention to investigate a cluster of rocks east of their position. He saw Tate behind and to his left. He didn't see Brand covering the right rear. He raised a hand with a closed fist, giving the sign to halt.

"Where's the noob?" he asked Tate in a hoarse whisper.

Brand sprinted to the edge of the tree line, crouching low as he entered the clearing at the foot of the hillock. The white flagpole beckoned, the red flag above snapping in the wind.

Lansch scanned the area around him, listening for movement. The sun would set in three hours. He settled into his hiding spot within a tight circle of underbrush, leaning against the twisted trunk of a long dead tree.

He waited cross-legged for some time. He heard no sound of a skirmish in either direction. Good. His teams had encountered no resistance so far. He relaxed against the rough bark of the stump, prepared for a long wait. He looked towards his objective, the white pole atop the hill where the flag waved…

'What the hell?" he thought.

There was no red flag atop the pole.

Brand was on his second Bourbon rocks when Bravo team arrived. The red flag lay on the bar beside him.

Lansch led his men to the bar.

"You broke with your squad and risked the mission," he said, slapping a hand on the bar with a loud smack. Why do you always have to be the outlier? You are part of a team. You left all of us exposed and vulnerable when you went out on your own. That's why you are unfit to be a part of our organization. You're not a team player."

Brand finished his Bourbon and waved his hand at the bartender for a refill.

"Give the boy scout shit a rest, Lansch. We are not a team. We work alone on our assignments. This exercise represents nothing about what we do. It is a field trip for a bunch of swaggering assholes, reenacting the good ole days when they were important and relevant.

"Watkins said it himself. OPFOR was certain he would clean us out, so they massed to the west on Alpha team. No one came to investigate the gunshots. No one arrived to clean up, as Watkins claimed. He was alone. We made good time to the objective. They had no time to engage Alpha and make it to Kilo Niner. If we had waited until nightfall, they would have had time to reach the objective. Many of us would have been killed following your plan.

"Either order a drink or get the hell out of here so I can finish mine. Here's you flag."

He tossed the flag at Lansch.

It was late the next night when Brand followed Lansch, right of his path line, giving him a ten-foot interval. The terrain was heavily wooded, and the going was slow.

Only he, Lansch, and one other team member, Strickland, remained of Bravo Team. With no radio communication allowed on the Op, the plight of Alpha Team was a mystery, although distant arms fire and pained cries indicated a guaranteed decrease in their number.

Riser's OPFOR team was silent and had been nearly invisible in the moonless night.

Two of Lansch's team had simply disappeared with no sound nor any trace.

Just after dark while Brand walked point, OPFOR assailed the team from behind. Hearing the attack, he returned, taking an arcing return route. The tactic saved his operational life. He spotted and took out one of Riser's team members laid in ambush for his return.

After the kill, Brand continued along his arc route where he came upon one of the *Ten* executing a perimeter attack on the survivors.

Brand tackled him, and after a short grapple, subdued the man, declaring him a casualty.

The perimeter skirmish alerted Lansch and Strickland of the attack, allowing them to escape.

Brand caught up with them a few minutes later.

They had eliminated a total of three OPFOR members. None of them were Riser or Conolly.

As per the rules, the Alpha team members were retired from the Op and Riser's OPFOR personnel returned to their team to continue on.

Brand returned his attention to the present.

Lansch creeped along before him and to his left. Further left was the edge of a jagged and sheer escarpment. Brand disliked following so closely to a limiting terrain feature. If attacked they would be left with only two directions of escape or evasion. Brand looked behind him where Strickland was a dark figure in the forest. He made no sound and seemed like a pursuing phantom in the murky darkness.

Brand dismissed the fantastical impression and continued his scrutiny of the area around them. The night was silent. Even the wild nocturnal creatures made no sound, as if they too watched the unfolding adventure with anxious anticipation.

Lansch slowed, small trees crowding to the very edge of the precipice, blocking their path.

Brand moved closer to the leader.

Strickland arrived seconds later.

"We have to find a way around this grove," Lansch whispered. "I estimate the objective is below and ahead about two clicks."

A twig snapped somewhere in the darkness of the woods behind them.

"They have our trail," Brand surmised.

"We need to get through this bramble," Lansch said.

"We should fall back as far as we can, and array along the cliff edge," Strickland said. "Set an ambush. We are trapped."

Lansch thought for a moment.

Brand moved carefully towards the edge of the cliff. In the darkness the granite face cast the wall in bold relief. There appeared little to cling to for a descent. Brand had seen the face earlier during twilight. The height was no more than a hundred feet. He spotted twisted, rough-barked bushes clinging to the face. They appeared to be strongly enough attached to the wall to use as hand holds.

He returned to the others.

They looked at him expectantly.

"What did you see, Trooper Brand?" Strickland asked.

Brand ignored the dig.

"I think we can descend the face."

"Not in the dark." Lansch disagreed. "This is an Op, not a life-or-death scenario."

Brand made no response. He was deciding how to make the descent.

They heard another sound on their back trail, but closer this time. It sounded like clothes brushing against a branch.

Brand turned without a word and returned to the cliff face. Lansch and Strickland followed noncommittally. They would go only so far as to take a look at the face.

Brand waited for them at the edge. They held back at a safe distance. It was obvious to Brand the others were reluctant to attempt the descent.

"I'll go first," Brand said as he eased over the edge.

His concern grew as he lowered himself. At first, he located no toe hold. Fully extended to arm's length, his feet struck upon a ledge. He tested the bush near his head. It clung strongly to the cliff, attached firmly by the roots in an unseen crevice in the sheer face.

He whispered to the men above.

"There is a ledge below me, and the bush will hold. Move it!"

Brand located handholds below the bush. He was relieved he could see more clearly than he had from above. It was a strange trick of the limited light and the shine off the cliff face.

He descended slowly but steadily as he located available toe and grip points. Small sharp stones and loose soil peppered him as Lansch lowered himself onto the wall. Strickland followed half a minute after.

Brand found the climb fatiguing but manageable. As he descended holds grew more plentiful. He guessed rain and winds had worn the top of the face more than the more protected lower wall surfaces.

He gripped one of those hardy bushes and looked below to assess his progress. He estimated they were halfway down. The assailants above must have paused to prepare for their attack because no one had reached the edge of the cliff above.

He held the bush with his left hand as he searched for a new hold for his right when he heard a sliding sound above him. He looked up in time to see Lansch dropping down the face, flailing to find a handhold as he struggled to save himself. He fell clear of the wall, dragging stones and loose aggregate with him.

Brand renewed his hold on the bush and leaned into the wall to avoid the impact of Lansch's falling weight dislodging him. The squad leader grunted with his efforts as he picked up speed headed down.

In a snap decision, Brand clenched his teeth against the effort he anticipated would be necessary and grabbed Lansch's left wrist as he passed him on the cliff wall. The weight was more than he had anticipated. His right foot slipped from its toe point, dislodging him.

Brand grunted with the strain. Lansch dangled below him, snatching at any hold he could see.

"Settle," Brand groaned under the strain. "I've got you, Lansch. Find a good hold – quickly please."

Brand felt the bush in his left hand give a fraction under the added weight.

Lansch collected himself and searched for a handhold. He located a secure point for his right hand. With a more stable posture he located small purchases for both feet. The stance was not ideal, but he was supporting most of his weight.

Lansch tapped Brand's forearm with his left fingers. Brand released him and Lansch found a grip with his left.

"Are you okay?" Strickland asked in a hoarse whisper.

"Keep going," Brand said as Lansch continued his descent.

Lansch made it to the ground safely. Brand dropped the last few feet, landing beside him.

They hurried from the cliff face to a stand of trees where they took cover from view of anyone who may look over the edge above.

Strickland dropped the last few feet onto solid ground and joined Brand and Lansch in the copse of trees.

It was a few minutes before they heard voices above. The conversation was unintelligible, but the tone was confused and flustered at the escape of their quarry.

"Where'd they go?" Strickland mocked in a deep voice.

Brand and the remaining members of the twenty-four gathered in the Cabana Café as they had on the first day. Although showered and changed, many in the group carried visible signs of the Op in the form of bumps, bruises, and contusions.

Brand rested on the edge of his chair, his aching muscles rebelling after the strain of holding Lansch's weight over the abyss. The pain in his shoulders and upper back were uncomfortable but were deemed temporary and self-healing by the medics who examined him.

Although their diminished number prevented Brand's team from winning the field problem event, within the ranks of the team his status was recognizably elevated. He even detected a smile or two from some of the others of the team. Even Conolly gave him a curt nod when he arrived at the cabana.

As they waited for Riser to appear, Brand counted quickly, confirming there were twenty-one remaining of the original twenty-four. Williams had been one of three who had sustained debilitating injuries and were unable to complete. Another missing from the room, Steve Payne, was one of the Top Ten and had retired from the event on the second day with a broken leg.

It was rare a sitting member of the current Top Ten lost his place on the select team. Payne had been a member of the Ten for three years. The replacement for Payne would be selected secretly from within the Twenty after the weekend event. His injury made his place available for a replacement.

With only twenty-one men remaining, the choice for the twenty left either Brand or another new man, Rosencrantz, to fill it.

Riser arrived, looking as fresh as the first day despite his participating throughout as an OPFOR team member. Brand had learned much about the man's toughness and skill during the field problem. He realized early how much he had to learn about tradecraft at Riser's hands. The man had eliminated Bravo team almost singlehandedly without firing a shot. Williams was injured in a hand-to-hand scuffle with Riser.

The rumor going the rounds detailed that after dispatching two of his team, Riser had Williams cornered and the latter ended up running into a tree as he fled into the night.

"Good work this weekend, men." Riser began. "As you are aware, we lost three to the field exercise. I will draw the new Twenty from the remaining twenty-one men remaining here. Nineteen of you are sitting members and shall remain in place.

"My decision for filling the spot for the final member was based upon a number of criteria, but most emphatically upon his ability to act within the Twenty as a strong and capable member. If the two men remaining were not up to the task, I would have held over the decision for the year, keeping Williams in place, providing he recovers from his injuries.

"The final member of the Twenty shall be Carson Brand of Bravo Team. Congratulations Mr. Brand, and welcome to the Twenty."

Brand was surprised at the applause following the announcement. The more vigorous applause came from the other six members of Bravo Team. The story had been told of Brand saving their team leader's life on the cliff. Strickland, and even Lansch, applauded and smiled.

Brand acknowledged the applause with a nod.

"Rosencrantz," Riser called to the final man. Pack your shit. Transportation is at the front. We will see you when we return. Good work. Maybe next year."

Rosencrantz left the group under good natured-taunts and jokes about being beaten out by a "leg" rookie.

As he made his way to the door, he covered his head against the pelting of table condiments and packaged sauces.

"The bar is open gentlemen," Riser announced with a grin. "Enjoy the next few days on us. Congratulations again."

After a hearty meal, Brand found himself at the cabana bar across from the café. He ordered his typical double Bourbon rocks.

He watched the celebration at the pool. The day was warming and many of the men thrashed about in the water. Several women in bikinis made the scene more interesting.

He turned in his seat to face the bar once more. Riser had appeared silently beside him, leaning against the bar.

"Bourbon rocks," Riser called to the bartender. He noticed Brand's deink. "We have something in common, Mr. Brand."

"Yes sir," Brand agreed, motioning to the bartender for a refill.

"You performed admirably this weekend," Riser said as the bartender handed him a filled glass. "Lansch was one of your biggest critics, yet you risked your ass to save him."

Brand drained his old glass and traded it with the bartender for the new drink.

He made no comment.

"You have come far since we first met in my office."

Thank you, sir," Brand responded.

Riser drained the glass while keeping an eye on Brand. His expression reflected entertainment at Brand's measured reaction to his words.

"Here," Riser said, sliding a business card sized metal object towards him on the bar top. "Keep up the good work."

Brand picked it up. It was a metal engraved card with the Sovereign Logo and the words "Sovereign Twenty" embossed across the top. The card was composed of a myriad of survival tools joined to form the card. He observed amongst the small mechanically joined items in the card, a fishhook, saw blade, knife blade, screwdriver blade, and other implements he could not identify. He had seen something similar on a survivalist web site.

"Cute," he told Riser with a smile. "Thanks."

"You're welcome. You earned it, son."

Riser moved away from the bar, leaving Brand alone with his drink and his thoughts. He slid the card into his wallet.

As Brand watched the big man move towards the pool two women passed, appraising Brand favorably. He nodded to them before returning his attention to his fresh drink. He swirled the amber liquid, watching the residue from the melting ice ball eddy and twist as it mixed with the booze.

Despite his small but remarkable increase in favor amongst his colleagues, Brand felt no desire to join them or encourage any further relationship with them. He suspected the women were hired help. He had no interest in feigned interest or impersonal contact with them. He drained the contents of his high ball glass. He turned to watch the pool area as the bartender refilled his glass.

His thoughts drifted to an unpredictable past which had brought him to this place. The journey astounded him. The line between the normal world he used to occupy and this new one was thin as tissue paper.

The new drink arrived.

Although thin as tissue, he thought sardonically, his church-based upbringing necessarily brought into question the dark actions he had taken on the journey.

What are the wages of sin?

A consequence of a successful Op, he thought sardonically.

Brand drank deeply from his glass.

With an effort, he extricated himself from the growing theological quandary, once more focusing on the festivities around him.

One of the women who had just passed him, a tall brunette with blue eyes, dropped her wrap and descended the stairs into the pool.

He appreciated her shape as the first wave of the bourbon washed over him. She glanced at him with a come-hither smile.

He felt desire replace his self-criticism. Maybe he was being hasty in his judgement of the hired help. She seemed nice.

3

MADISON BLAINE GILES LEANED BACK in her chair, stroking the stem of her wine glass. Her green eyes conveyed an adequate level of feigned interest in the unending diatribe from Alexander Strom, her boyfriend of three years.

"Father has no business in the matter," Alexander complained bitterly. "My life is my own. I have my own money now. My investments are growing. I require no assistance from him or his cadre of snoopy so-called financial experts."

Madison lifted the glass to her perfect lips. Her eyes remained locked on her boyfriend's face as she sipped her Château Lafite Rothschild.

"You are particularly quiet this evening," Alexander noted with an arch to his eyebrows. "Is something wrong?"

Madison lowered her glass halfway to the table. She surveyed her companion over the rim, suppressing a smile at the caution she saw there. He was immaculately turned out in his custom fit *Saville Row* navy blue suit. His manicured fingers drummed the table silently, dissipating what remained of his frustration with his father and his finances. She knew he was waiting for her to make her mood known.

Although he thought her oblivious of the constant flux of her changing moods and how they affected him, he was wrong. Her tools of the trade were numerous and intentional. Since childhood she had learned to get her way. Screaming and the stamping of feet were methods for children and the uninspired. With a glance or a shift of her position in a chair she could put another on the back foot. More often, a look and a catch of her breathing mid-inhale would do the trick. Much of the communication between people was non-verbal. Madison knew this and applied it expertly.

Alexander eyed Madison fearfully. He was wary of her silences. He was experienced with the disaster that could occur when he blundered onto her bad side. Almost anything could start the timer on that time bomb. Her trigger was slight and unpredictable. He sipped his champaign, searching her eyes for the danger he suspected lurked just within.

Even three years since their engagement the newness had not faded. She was exquisite. She was neither too thin nor too muscular. She was perfect. Her features were the classic composition desired in models and movie stars. She had a well-developed sense of humor, and most dangerously, she was highly intelligent.

"Enough about me," Alexander said hurriedly. "How was your day? Aren't you bound for the wretched woods?"

Madison smiled with a slight stretching of her perfect lips and the tantalizing revelation of perfect teeth. She enjoyed Alexander's discomfiture.

"Father is jetting to the west coast to close another deal. I'm hitching a ride as far as Mackinac Island."

"You are going to see Beatrice again?"

"Of course. She is my most adventurous friend. Is that a concern for you?"

Alexander frowned despite his efforts to remain impassive. Bea, as she liked to be called, was the daughter of a Wall Street billionaire and had a penchant for the intrepid. She recently purchased an old estate on Mackinac Island, on Lake Huron in northern Michigan.

"No bother," he assured Madison, who smiled like a cat at his poorly concealed efforts at self-control. "I miss you when you are away, particularly in so remote a spot as the Michigan wilderness. When will you return?"

"Father mentioned returning some time mid-month. I'm not sure."

"What of your responsibilities here?"

"Alex don't be a child. I am the daughter of a billionaire. What responsibilities do I need to attend to?"

"Dear, I've asked you not to call me that in public. What about your art? Don't you have a showing to prepare for?"

Madison sipped her wine. She placed the glass on the table then dismissed his concerns with a wave of her hand.

"I'm not interested in art anymore."

"What?" Alexander sputtered. "You have put so much time and effort into this showing. What happened?"

"I don't want to talk about it. Anyway, the matter is decided. I am going with father tomorrow."

"Of course, you are," Alexander stammered. "I just…I hope you have thought this thing through…the art, I mean."

Madison glanced at the hovering waiter who refilled her glass.

"There there, Mr. Worry Man, you will manage while I am gone."

"I have no reason to worry," Alexander disagreed with a touch too much passion. His tone moderated as her brows crept higher, a sure sign of danger to come. "I thought we might get together at the beach next weekend – just the two of us."

"It is too late in the season to enjoy the beach here. Bea says the estate has been fully renovated and I can't wait to see it. Besides, I haven't seen her for the longest."

Alexander covered his frown with his lifted Champaign flute. He drained the contents then shook his head at the approaching waiter.

"What was her crazy whim last time - and how did that turn out?"

"It was a ship and it sunk."

Alexander watched her silently, waiting for her own admission to reveal a self-evident truth.

Madison sipped her wine, watching him with a mischievous light in her eyes. She was enjoying his display of manufactured concern.

He realized with a flash of anger that one of the highlights of her reckless adventures with her friend was his pain and anguish.

"Well," he announced. "I have a thing in a few. I wish you a happy journey."

Madison relaxed, waiting for his mood to pass.

"You can't leave angry, my love. Tell me about your brother, Max. How is he getting along since the trouble?"

Alexander hissed under his breath at the subject.

"You know he has been disinherited with no chance for parole. There is nothing to talk about."

"How much have you loaned him, or should I say given him?"

"Madison, this is not proper table conversation. And to answer your question, I have provided Maxwell very little."

Madison cocked her head slightly.

"You don't believe me?" he asked. "Why do you always ask about Max?"

"No reason."

"I have always thought you a bit too interested in my brother for my liking."

"I have never guessed that. When did you grow jealous of your brother and me?"

"That's not what I meant."

"No? Then please tell me what you mean."

"Madison, why do you always have to gin up bad memories?"

"Oh Alex, try to control yourself. This is about my trip and nothing more. Max is a misguided spoiled brat who needed to see some hardship to appreciate what he is given. You could use a dose of reality yourself if one were to be honest."

"What's that supposed to mean?"

Alexander's concern for pressing her dissipated at the criticism.

"Weren't you just talking about having your own money and not wanting your father's financial experts to advise you on your business dealings? You have never earned a dime in your life that was not created or affected by your father's advice or influence. His efforts to protect his investment are only natural. You Strom boys could learn a lesson on enjoying your privilege without thinking you created it."

"I hate it when you use vulgar street vernacular. We are not *privileged*. We are more successful. There is a sweat component in there that always gets overlooked."

"The way you talk," She chided him. "Contemplate how much sweat, as you say, you contributed to the success."

"I am finished with this conversation," he said with finality. "Can we leave now?"

"Go ahead," she replied mildly. "I would like to finish my wine. I'll call for a car."

"Madison…"

"Really, Alexander. I could use a moment to settle my mind before I leave. I'll be fine."

"Are you sure?"

"My love, do I seem unsure?"

"So be it."

Alexander rose, dropping his napkin on the chair.

"Call me when you are in the air."

He leaned in to kiss her.

She offered her cheek.

He kissed her cheek then left her alone at the table.

Madison watched his back until he disappeared from view. She sipped her wine, looking out the windows at a breathtaking view of the New York skyline.

She chided herself for lacking the courage to break with Alex. She was not in love with him, and she suspected he felt similarly about her. They were comfortable with one another. Mainly, they were together due to a lack of suitable partners who occupied their station in society.

Wealth made strange bedfellows, she thought tritely.

Her thoughts wandered, returning to her new adventure with her best friend. Beatrice was refreshingly creative in devising ways to entertain her and take her away from her troubles.

She smiled as the prospect of a visit with Beatrice lightened her mood. The estate in upper Michigan was a mysterious prospect. The mansion and the grounds were one of the first built in the region in the early 1800's. It had remained vacant for years until Beatrice pressed her father to purchase it. There was a rumor it was haunted.

It seemed rather late in the season to plan a getaway to the summer resort island in northern Michigan. She knew little about Mackinac other than what she was able to find online. Apparently, the place rolled up the sidewalks and terminated ferry service early in the fall, opening again in the spring. It was early October and the only access to the island was by plane or private boat. All of this seemed very strange and mysterious.

Once more she entertained the childish possibility the mansion might be haunted. It would be just like Bea to take advantage of the rumors about the old estate and build on the macabre.

Madison smiled at the ridiculous notion. When Bea talked her father into buying a retired ocean cruise vessel, she had billed it as their own private cruise liner, complete with wait staff, crew, and on-board entertainment. The ship hadn't been haunted, but it now rested at the bottom of the Atlantic.

She finished her wine and stood from the table. There was packing to do, and she still entertained the idea of breaking up with Alexander before she left, although she doubted she would follow through and call him. She was reluctant to create unnecessary conflict just as she departed for her vacation.

4

THE LEARJET RESTED ON THE TARMAC. Brand waited outside near the folding stairs to the jet's doorway. A cool autumn breeze chilled by the restless Atlantic threatened the stubborn but failing warmth of the autumn afternoon. The sky was no longer the clear blue of summer. There was a noticeable pall to the sky's hue, and the clouds gathered earlier during the day rather than towards evening as had been the pattern until now.

This was one of Riser's first assignments for Brand since he joined the Twenty, with one of his most important clients. The client, Sabastian Giles, permitted no more than one security agent on his flights.

Brand recalled his conversation with Riser the previous day. The Chief had grinned at him throughout the talk, like a man poorly concealing a practical joke. The last moments of the briefing had been far from a joke.

Joke or not, Brand was not smiling now. He wore an expensive suit, tailored to hide his concealed weapons. He carried an MDP-9 in his leather attaché case. He preferred his carried Sig Sauer SP2022 nine mil, but the client rider stipulated he possess a fully automatic compact weapon.

A burgundy-colored limousine flanked by two black guard cars approached the aircraft at high speed. They ground to a halt near the aircraft. Men flooded from the guard cars, creating a protective cordon before opening the limo door for the client.

A well-dressed man of middle age stepped casually from the limo as if they had stopped carefully at a lush park rather than arriving like an assault team on enemy ground.

He was fit and tanned. His phone was to his ear, and he ignored everything other than the call. He approached the aircraft gangway with hardly a glance for Brand.

Brand remained at his post outside the aircraft until the flight attendant notified him they were preparing to depart. He climbed the stairs and took his seat at the front of the aircraft. He stowed his go bag under the leather chair and lay the attaché case with the MDP-9 in the seat next to him.

Giles concluded his phone conversation as Brand settled. He hung up and spoke to Brand.

"Would you tell the crew we need to wait a few moments for a late arriving passenger?"

"Yes sir," Brand replied, standing to carry out the request.

Brand moved forward where the flight attendant was belted in for takeoff.

"Ma'am," Brand said. "We need to wait a few minutes for another passenger. Can you let the flight crew know, please?"

The attendant smiled as she unbuckled her seat belt.

"Aren't you the gentleman," she exclaimed with an affected southern belle accent.

She smiled to expel any offense from the comment. This security man was polite and respectful, unlike most of those she had encountered. She was accustomed to swaggering tough guy types with overly indulged self-images. This one was attractive and polite.

"I'll notify the flight crew, sir."

"Call me Brand," he said with a smile in return.

"Thank you, Brand," she returned, emphasizing his name.

Brand dropped the stairs and returned to his post outside the aircraft. He waited several minutes before another limo approached. With none of the drama of the previous limousine, the car stopped smoothly near the plane. The driver hurried around the car, opening the door for the passenger.

Brand watched one of the most beautiful women he had ever seen step from the car.

She was blonde and lean.

Brand endeavored to maintain an impassive expression.

After his first glimpse of the newly arriving passenger, he kept his gaze neutral. Situational awareness training served him well here. He watched her while looking elsewhere, although a glimpse was all he needed to fully appreciate the newcomer.

Without a doubt, this was the daughter, Madison. She was tall but not too tall. Brand estimated she wore a year of his salary in clothing and accessories. Although lean, she was curvy in all the best places. Her features were striking but she was not a supermodel in the face. She was prettier than that. She was earthy but not predictable. Her beauty seemed to generate from an internal source, radiating as an aura, irresistible if focused upon for too long.

Brand endeavored to avoid that very thing as a mental image of a disapproving and admonishing Dick Riser filled his mind.

Madison made no effort to conceal her scrutiny of Brand as she approached. She appraised him from head to toe. He was just over six feet tall; his dark hair was well coifed. His blue eyes were striking in his tanned face. He appeared lean and strong in his well-tailored suit. Unlike the other security men she had encountered, he did not appear to be armed. She could always spot a man who carried a weapon. They invariably favored the side upon which they carried the pistol, making it easy to detect despite any special tailoring of the suit.

This man stood at ease, well-balanced. She knew he must be armed. It was his job. Her attention to detail was her strength, and this man was an impressive specimen. She decided to make him a project.

"Hi," she said to him as she climbed the stairs.

"Ma'am," he returned the greeting, with a professional nod.

After she boarded the aircraft, he climbed the stairs and pulled the door closed.

He returned to his seat as Madison settled across from Giles, her back to Brand and the front of the plane.

"You're late, Mads," Giles complained halfheartedly. It was obvious he held her in high regard.

"Of course, I am, Daddy. I have a reputation to maintain."

"I'm surprised Alexander let you go. He suffers so when you leave."

His expression was knowing, and his tone revealed a hidden reprimand.

"Don't worry about him," Mads assured her father. "Everything will work out as it should."

Brand removed a file from his attaché. He was familiar with the contents, but he reviewed the information about the client.

The meticulously organized dossier detailed billionaire Sabastian Giles, former hedge fund manager, whose corporate and personal holdings topped $400 billion. Giles recently purchased the most popular social media company on the globe.

Brand had seen his likeness continually on news shows, where the reporters and anchors claimed he would end Democracy with his radical views. His opinions during the few interviews Brand had seen, to his mind seemed reasonable and logical.

The newly crowned tech giant lived in New York but was rarely home. He traveled the globe frequently in one of his four private jets. The largest, reserved for trans-ocean flights was a modified *Dassault Falcon 900*. Domestically he flew Lear.

"I wish you would give him a chance," Giles complained. "He seems to be one of the good ones. You aren't a child anymore. You will eventually have to get on with your life."

She flashed her father a dangerous frown.

"Are you advising me to get on with my life, Daddy?"

Brand suppressed a smile.

Giles was about to step into a world of shit. She was dangerous. As a rule, women were dangerous. Brand couldn't keep count of the times he had found himself in trouble with Natalie, his late girlfriend, without knowing how he got there.

Reading more from the dossier, Brand glanced at the billionaire. He had heard about his kind of wealth, but this was the first time he had been personally involved with someone so successful. With Giles' coverage in the news lately, Brand realized he was in the presence of a globally famous figure. Based upon the popular outcry, maybe the word notorious was more accurate.

Giles and his daughter were oblivious to Brand's presence as their conversation continued. Brand overheard some talk about cutting her visit short if her accommodations were less than advertised, or the weather trapped her with no way back.

Brand shook his head.

He doubted she would be satisfied with the Ritz. He knew little about luxury accommodations, but he imagined her a spoiled rich brat who would probably complain no matter the level of luxury.

The daughter, he read, was Madison Giles, graduate of Princeton; deeply involved in her father's businesses. Giles expected her to replace him when he one day stepped down from his position as CEO.

Brand's focus on the dossier drifted as his thoughts returned to the end of Riser's briefing.

The big former SEAL's smile evaporated as he got down to business.

"This is one of my most prominent and important clients. Don't fuck it up," he had warned Brand with an uncharacteristic lack of equanimity. "Thus far every agent we have contracted to protect Giles has been shown the door."

He went on to explain Brand was one of three new men remaining at Sovereign who had not been blacklisted by the billionaire.

"What is causing the problems with this guy?" Brand asked.

"His daughter," Riser replied curtly. "She apparently enjoys placing security team members in compromising positions then reporting them to her father. No one has been able to resist her charms. I've never met her, but her photos present a stunningly beautiful woman."

"It's not going to be a problem for me," Brand claimed blandly.

He was no stranger to hot girls. He wasn't a lady's man, but he had a considerable experience with them. Based upon the actions he had seen, and the locker room talk he had heard, the men at Sovereign were swaggering warriors who, other than bar flies and prostitutes, had little real-world experience with the fairer sex.

Riser considered Brand doubtfully.

"Keep your dick in your pants, Mr. Brand."

Brand looked at Riser with poorly concealed contempt. The man knew nothing about what he wanted or needed. A fling with a hot heiress was not even on the list.

Lately, the future of the women with whom he had grown close was never long and always tragic. He once more experienced the pain of abject loss.

Natalie was murdered in front of him. Christina was reported killed before she returned only to betray him. Amy tried to murder him. She fell at his hand. Dehra was murdered in jail. All were beautiful. Each was precious to him. The pain of again losing someone he cared about was a powerful deterrent.

"It won't be an issue," he assured his boss firmly.

Brand emerged from his reverie with a determined shake of his head. He glanced at the billionaire and his daughter. To his surprise, both watched him intently. He considered them with waning interest before once more giving his attention to the dossier. He was growing suspicious they were co-conspirators in the entrapment of Sovereign security staff, and he had no patience for the game.

Madison seemed to sense the cold rejection from the new security man. As if confirming Brand's suspicions about the game they played, she turned to her father, speaking loudly enough to be clearly heard at the front of the plane.

"Dad," she said crossly. "You have a battalion of bodyguards at your LA offices and at the beach house. I really need someone to watch my back. You know how oblivious Beatrice can be about observing basic safety precautions. Remember the shipwreck. I don't anticipate a disaster, but the place is remote. I want him to stay with me while I'm there."

"Beatrice's sinking a ship with you on it is not helping your case for this visit, Mads. I am not amused. Do you think Beatrice is up to something other than a few days at an old house?"

"The house has been fully renovated and she has been planning this get-away for almost a month. You know how she is, Daddy."

Giles glanced at Brand who was making every effort to remain oblivious to their conversation. Brand gave his attention to the view beyond the near window and missed a small hint of a grin playing at the billionaire's lips.

"Mr. Brand," he called innocently.

Brand stood and approached them.

"Yes sir?"

"I will not require your services in Los Angeles. I want you to watch over my daughter, Madison. She will be staying with friends, and I am concerned about her security. Can I count on you to do this for me, and most importantly, to be discreet?"

Brand considered Giles and his daughter for a moment. It was apparent he was not pleased with the request.

"My rate for side work is more expensive than you are paying Sovereign. I recommend you arrange this through the company."

"Are you trying to be funny, son?"

Brand restrained himself as his mood soured at the obvious ploy to place him in a compromising position. He felt a growing certainty the rumors were true.

"No sir. Not yet."

Brand didn't smile, nor did he make an effort at humor. His answer was simply honest and direct.

Brand's glib remark disarmed Giles.

He took a closer look at the new man. Brand was completely at ease. The billionaire detected no guile or false intent.

His eyes widened in interest. He gave his full attention to the security man.

"Where are you from, son?"

"San Antonio."

"Texas?"

Brand made no reply.

"Mads, we have a Texas cowboy here." To Brand he said, "I expect you to be a gentleman as Texans are reputed to be."

"Yes sir."

Brand returned to his seat.

Madison's lips compressed into a straight line. She sat back in her leather seat, turning her head to watch Brand with an unflinching stare. She sensed his reluctance to accompany her. He knew about the demise of the security staff who had preceded him and obviously thought he could avoid a similar outcome by keeping her at arm's length.

She turned from him, facing forward again. Her tight smile and square shoulders conveyed confidence in her womanly prowess.

Challenge accepted.

The plane touched down onto the single airstrip under a dark and cloudy sky. The Lear taxied to the front of a single story, frame style, terminal building.

Brand stepped onto the tarmac. After a full visual sweep of the white terminal building and the dense woods surrounding the small airport, he took his position beside the gangway.

The flight crew withdrew Madison's bags from the cargo hold under the aircraft.

Brand spotted a horse drawn livery approaching the aircraft. Dressed in a limo driver costume under a long coat and a warm hat, the driver held the reigns of a team of four black horses pulling a large heavy carriage.

Brand grabbed the bags and moved towards the carriage.

Madison and her father stepped down the stairs and onto the tarmac.

"What's with the horse and buggy?" Giles asked of his daughter.

"A joke?" she replied uncertainly. "I read there are no cars on the island, but I thought it was a tourist thing."

"No joke," Brand announced as he returned to the plane. "Motor vehicles are outlawed on Mackinac Island."

He pronounced the name *Mackinaw* per the driver's insistence.

The carriage driver climbed down from his seat and stowed the luggage.

Madison shrugged, kissed her father goodbye, then moved to the carriage. She stopped outside the passenger door, eyeing

Brand impatiently. The driver was occupied with stowing baggage.

Brand collected his go bag then crossed the distance between them, He opened the door for her.

"Thank you. Get in with me," she told Brand.

Brand stowed his bag in the rear hold of the carriage then joined Madison inside.

The interior was cozy. Folded on a seat, a thick blanket was available to passengers for the cool weather travel. Madison pulled the blanket over their knees.

The roar of jet engines rose as the sleek aircraft taxied towards the runway for takeoff.

The carriage lurched forward. Brand ignored Madison as he looked out the window. The clip clop of horses' hooves added a strange but pleasant tattoo to the experience.

Madison gave her attention immediately to her new companion.

"What's your name?" she asked.

"Call me Brand," he replied.

"What is the rest?"

"Carson Brand," he added patiently. "Everyone calls me Brand."

"Carson is an unusual name. I would rather call you Carson."

Brand made no protest to her comment. He didn't want to make it a big deal for her to use against him.

"Are you afraid of me, Carson?"

"Do you know where we are going?" he asked, redirecting the conversation.

"The driver has the address. The Island is not very big. We shouldn't get too lost. How long have you been with Sovereign Services?"

"Ma'am, I would rather not discuss my personal life."

"My name is Madison, not ma'am. I need to know a bit more about you – Brand. We will be spending a few days together and I want to get off on the good foot. You are the help, but I make it a practice to be courteous even to the help."

Brand grinned in spite of himself.

"That's more like it," she said with genuine good humor. "This isn't going to get weird unless you make it weird."

Brand glanced at the beautiful Madison, then the carriage. It was already weird, although he didn't let it show.

"Tell me about San Antonio, Texas."

"Can we speak honestly?" Brand asked.

Madison's smile froze at this unexpected candor.

"Haven't we been doing that?" she responded, trying to maintain control of the conversation.

"San Antonio is great." Brand said impatiently. "I don't have family there, and only one person I consider a friend. My job with Sovereign is new and it is the only thing I have that is mine. You and your father have a reputation for chewing up agents and spitting them out. I would prefer not to follow suit. I am here to do a job and that is all. You are a client. That is all you are to me and that is all you are going to be to me. What are your intentions beyond that?"

Madison said nothing for a long moment. That she was surprised was obvious. It was also clear she was rarely surprised by much. Her expression transformed slowly as she assembled her thoughts about this new man. Finally, her features relaxed, then transformed into the warmth of a genuine smile.

Brand was immediately put on guard by her unexpected reaction to his admonition.

"My dad was right. There is more to you than meets the eye," she observed. "Okay. Let's speak frankly. No family: does that mean you are also single?"

Brand frowned, conveying his limited patience for further games.

"Yes, or no?" she pressed. "There is a point to this, I promise."

"I am single. Please get to the point."

"The others hung themselves because they lacked restraint; and they lacked strength of character. I see the opposite in you."

"Thanks."

"Wait a minute before you resort to sarcasm, please."

Brand crossed his arms, forcing himself to tolerate her efforts to justify his demise.

"My friend Bea, who you will meet, is my best friend. Her family is wealthy – old money. She holds the *nouveau riche* thing over my head like it is a pox. As a result, she is always trying to one-up me on everything from travel, to clothes, to friends.

"About a year ago she invited me out to LA for one of those lavish parties she is known for. She had a new boyfriend with her. He represented the beginning of her latest competition with me."

Brand looked at her sharply, discarding his resistant front.

"She tried to one up you with men? I don't see how anyone could match you on that ground. You probably have to beat back the guys at the country club with a bat."

"Country club?" she laughed. "How provincial of you. Thank you for the compliment. I thought that myself. I hope it doesn't seem too vain, but I could normally best her without trying. However, she crafted the rules in her favor. If the target man was a pretty boy or a high-profile social figure, I would own her. This new man – how can I describe him? He was not a Phillip, or a Biff, or a Sabastian. He was a salt of the earth, full-grown man. He was the type of guy who no longer exists amongst the men of our generation."

Brand shook his head.

His late best friend Bert used to talk at length about that very thing. He had been, and Brand was a part of the generation referred to as millennials. The previous generation did not see the men of his generation as particularly manly based upon the colloquial term.

"Do you know how hard it is to find a real man below the age of forty these days?" she asked. "The millennial male has even gone so far as to invent a new male personality type to pass himself off as a dominant male – the *Sigma*

Male. It is rumored the Sigma is better than the Alpha because he is not a mindless caveman."

As she continued, her tone modulated to a nasally imitation of a whining and wimpy man providing a sarcastic litany of sing song phrases.

"But rather, he is a quiet loner; a deeply thoughtful male, who is superior to all the others, even the Alpha, because of his inner strength and superior intellect."

She shook her head, abandoning her contrived manner.

"What a joke," she cried. "If you don't exhibit male traits, and your strength is based upon your ability to one up your male competition with smart remarks and snide comments, then you are not a dominant male."

"You've given this some thought." Brand observed with amusement.

"Do you disagree with my assessment?"

"I have heard another version of this before from a guy I knew. Where do you find this nonexistent real man?"

"I'd probably like the guy you're talking about."

"I am certain he would have liked you."

Madison shrugged off the compliment.

"You won't find this kind of man at the country club." She replied, mocking his reference to a bygone habit of a past generation. "I thought these apes assigned to my dad – these former Navy SEALS and super troopers - would be prime candidates. Don't get me wrong. They were true tough guys, but they did not behave well outside of the wild, so to speak. It was like inviting an out-of-control drunk frat boy to a black-tie affair."

Brand laughed at the description.

"Wasn't it obvious to Beatrice that you were recruiting from your dad's security detail?"

"Not as obvious as you might think. She presented some pretty rough characters for the competition. I couldn't tell these body guards the truth, but I coached them on what not to say and how to act."

"Let me guess," Brand guessed. "Those who didn't show their ass, fell in love with you going along with the game."

"Quaintly put, but yes, you are right."

Madison appraised this intelligent, considering, new man with fresh eyes.

She blushed at her thoughts about Brand.

"What do you want me to do?" he asked, uncertain why he was agreeing to go along with her childish prank. "To be clear, I am not your boyfriend and will not cross certain lines with you."

Madison nodded her agreement with his terms as she gathered her thoughts.

"I doubt Bea and her guests will believe I brought a security detail with me this trip. She will believe you are a new boyfriend. Can you handle that much intimacy?"

Brand experienced a keen sense of misgiving about playing the role of a client's love interest. The path he was about to walk was razor thin and hazardous. Riser would not be pleased.

Brand levelled a warning look at the heiress.

"I'll go along with this under one condition."

"What is your condition?"

"You promise not to get me fired and no games."

"You are safe as long as you play your part and don't get drunk and lay hands on me. As far as games are concerned, don't flatter yourself."

Brand nodded at her admonishment.

"You have a deal as long as you don't get drunk and lay hands-on ME. And don't flatter yourself either."

They laughed and shook hands on the agreement.

The remainder of their journey was spent taking in the beautiful scenery passing by as their carriage slowly rolled through the wooded countryside along the banks of Lake Huron.

5

BEATRICE MCDERMOTT MOANED under his weight. Everything about this man was big. My god how she loved it! He moved slowly above her. His ministrations of her body caused her the most exquisite excitement she had ever experienced. His body was heavily muscled, but he managed it with grace and the lithe movements of a cat.

His smell drove her mad. She wanted to bite a chunk from his huge shoulder. She instead, ground her teeth as he again brought her to a climax, exhausting her, and satisfying her to the depths of her deepest desires.

He followed her a quick moment later, his body tensing and throbbing over her and in her.

Finally, they unwrapped themselves from each other, spent and breathless.

She opened her eyes, and saw he was watching her with a broad smile, enjoying his effect upon her. She knew he realized his control of her, and she didn't care.

"Hugh, your dick is a magic wand," she managed to utter with a hoarse voice.

"Lunch?" he asked simply, ignoring the observation.

"I nearly forgot," she exclaimed, rising on an elbow. "You cook too."

"You didn't forget." He chided her playfully. "I'll whip something up."

He stood from the bed. He was several inches over six feet, tanned, and powerful looking. His long hair lay nearly to the center of his back. His beard was well trimmed. He looked like a cross between an oil field rough neck and a model from a Harlequin Romance cover.

She felt herself winding back up in response to his extraordinary physique.

As he pulled on his cargo shorts, she glanced at the bed stand clock.

"Shit," she cried. "It's nearly four."

"Yeah. It is," he agreed proudly. "I'll pivot to an early supper menu."

"Madison will be here soon. I have to get busy."

"That's today?" he asked mildly. "I thought she was coming on the weekend."

Bea jumped out of bed and scrambled for her clothes.

Hugh had a chance in turn to appreciate her nakedness. She was heavy breasted and curvy. She was voluptuous now, in her twenties. He guessed she would probably fight her weight all her days.

"Madison's life is a weekend," Bea said hurriedly. "I doubt she knows what day it is."

Hugh pulled on a shirt. He tucked it in as he watched Bea dress.

"The boat will be here in two hours," she cried, pulling on jeans and an angora sweater top.

Twenty minutes later she entered the kitchen. He had a full meal on the table. The drapes were drawn, and the view of a steel blue Lake Huron, tumultuous under a troubled sky, filled the room with the promise of dangerous weather.

She had been on the phone the entire time, texting at high speed. She hadn't seen Madison since last summer. She wanted everything to be perfect. Although they had never discussed it, Bea knew what was expected of her, and she never failed to deliver on that expectation.

"Hugh, it looks so good," she remarked about the food on the table. "Thank you."

"You're welcome, Beatrice. You deserve no less after last night, and this morning, and this afternoon."

She smiled and purred as she rushed over to him, kissing him over and over.

They sat and ate as she finished off her calls. Finally, she laid the phone on the table beside her.

"Will you stay for the party and meet her?"

Hugh shrugged his shoulders.

"I've got work."

"You told me your plans. Those don't include staying on the phone all weekend."

"Everything has to go perfectly. We can't afford any foul ups."

"You're right."

Bea was serious for only a moment. Her smile returned as she picked at the remnants of her meal.

"Mads will love you."

She shook her finger at him.

"Don't get any ideas," she warned him possessively.

"I'm a one-woman guy," he assured her with a loving squeeze of one of her breasts. "You suit me corner to corner and wall to wall. You are beautiful, smart, sexy, and in bed you make me feel like a real man."

"Oh my god," she exclaimed. "You've got that covered in spades. If you were any more of a man, I would likely be dragged around the house by my hair."

He laughed at that.

"I'll see what I can do," he promised. "But for now, Eye on the prize BB. Eye on the prize."

Hugh and Bea had cleared the dishes and were showered and dressed when Madison's carriage arrived. Bea led Hugh to the drive where Madison hurried towards them with outstretched arms.

Brand was at the carriage. He unloaded the luggage and tipped the driver.

"You are late, Mads," Bea said.

"Of course, I am," she agreed. "This time, however, it was car trouble."

She pointed at the carriage as they laughed at the jest.

The carriage departed and Brand carried the bags towards them.

"Bea, this is Carson. Carson this is Beatrice – call her Bea. Who is this big fellow?" Madison asked with an interested look at Hugh.

"Hands off, Mads," Bea warned playfully. "This is Hugh, my boyfriend."

Hugh moved forward with a welcoming smile. He hugged Madison and shook Brand's hand.

"Pleased to know you both," he said formally.

"How long have you been hiding this handsome fellow?" Madison asked Bea.

"Hugh," Bea asked. "What three weeks?"

"About that," he agreed, rubbing his hands together. "It's getting chilly. Won't you come in. We have mimosas ready if it's not too late in the season for that sort of thing."

"It's never too late in the season for Mimosas," Madison informed him, wrapping her arm in Brand's, leading him towards the large old house.

The mansion sat some distance off the road. It was constructed of red brick and roughhewn timbers. A long narrow side building stretched off to the left. The woods crowded up to the house on the right. Through the dense trees near the house, the lake water appeared in flashes. A rising wind shook the trees and swirled the falling leaves in tight eddies on the ground below.

They climbed the front steps.

Beatrice stopped, a hand on the door handle.

"Mads, this is probably the only time you will come in through the front door, but I wanted you to get the full effect."

Beatrice pushed open one of the tall wooden double front doors. It surrendered to her efforts with a groan of taxed hinges and mighty framing.

The others followed her inside a huge entry vestibule. The ceiling rose two stories above a long ornate staircase. Old portraits of long dead former occupants covered the staircase wall. Wood carvings displayed amongst antique furnishings filled the room near the edges. English paneling was the foundation for a rich wainscotting below period-correct wallpaper.

Brand dropped their bags at the foot of the stairs, taking in the elaborate construction of the old home. He followed the others to the rear of the house, then into the large kitchen. He looked over the intricate carpentry work and antique furnishings with a keen eye.

He guessed the place was built during a time long passed when craftsmanship was commonplace and cheap. Every detail was a relic of a remarkable carpenter's artistry. The polished wood flooring and intricate trim work was breathtaking. He inspected the kitchen area where tall windows overlooked a panoramic vantage of an unsettled Lake Huron bullied by gusting winds and a dangerous sky.

Bea brought him a Champagne flute.

"Where did you find this fine fellow," Bea asked Madison as she looked Brand up and down with interest.

Brand knew the game was on between these two highly competitive women. He returned Beas's searching gaze with a patient front. His role as a prize cut of meat did not please him. He was being paid for his time and he vowed to keep that in mind to sustain him during this inane contest waged by spoiled rich girls.

"He is handsome and brooding," Bea observed thoughtfully.

She stared into his face a few more long seconds.

"The strong silent type, I'll bet."

Bea turned to Madison.

"Where did you find this one, Mads? I think a bit of the beast lurks in those blue eyes."

"Carson is a friend of the family," Mads explained casually though obviously pleased with her friend's observations of Brand. "Texas oil family."

Brand weathered the huge exaggeration as well as he could. He was certain he would not survive much more of this petty game.

"I love Texas men," Bea said, wrapping an arm around Brand. "I will love you, Carson."

"Hands off," Madison warned. "Hugh, keep your woman in line."

"She is her own woman," he joked with raised hands and a wink at Brand. "When God handed out the vagina to women, he gave them ownership of the world. Women put us in charge to manage it. I know my place."

"Women own the world?" Madison asked doubtfully. "How do you support such a provocative claim?"

"With respect," Hugh continued with a furtive gesture of his raised hand. "There is not a warship sunk at sea, a battle waged, nor a hero who has died, that was not either directly or indirectly because of a woman. We men are born then die in the pursuit of women. Woman was created second, after God corrected what he had gotten wrong with man."

"Bravo," Bea said with a clap of her hands. "What say you, Madison?"

"I agree with most of what you claim," Madison replied seriously. "But you didn't finish. Man takes what he does not own or deserve and makes it his own. We women have to wage our own battle to recover nothing more than an equal seat at the table. With a continued fierce opposition to the male conqueror, we may once more own what is rightfully ours, according to your own words, sir."

Hugh raised both hands again in surrender.

"Touché," he said in supplication.

Madison raised her glass in salute to the big man's diplomacy.

He smiled and returned the flute salute.

"So, what is in store for us Bea?" Madison asked.

"We are hosting a small get together tonight - a special party planned in your honor."

Beatrice's manner changed from light and playful to the dark tones of a harbinger of foul deeds and dark forces at work.

"Tonight, when the guests leave on the private ferry, the only way to get off the island, our adventure begins.

"This weekend we are trapped in an ancient, haunted house, whose history is said to be plagued by strange noises, unexplained happenings, and unsolved deaths. This house is one of the oldest on the island. It is the only one left on this side of the island – now in the protected areas of the state park. It is rumored that because of the curse associated with the house, it was left untouched while so many other great homes were demolished by the park service.

"Local lore has it anyone who destroys or moves even a stone of this mansion or its associated structures from this site will be cursed to die by the most horrible means. Until my family purchased the place, it stood abandoned for some forty years. The construction crew refused to work after dark because they say an unseen evil presence haunted them even in daylight."

The other three said nothing as the strangeness of what they heard made an impression upon them.

Beatrice broke the spell with a laugh at their silent reflection, once more regaining her light humor.

"It has been too long, girlfriend," she said with a hug, dispelling the macabre gloom she had draped upon them.

Madison returned the hug with a nervous laugh.

"I read online the ferry service ceases after the tourist season. Is the airstrip closed too?"

"We chartered a boat from the mainland and every carriage on the island that has a driver is engaged for the evening. The weather is supposed to turn bad, so the boat will depart right after the party. The servants who don't live permanently on the island will be given passage back to the mainland with the guests. If the weather turns icy there is no airport access. The unpredictable and often violent weather changes are well known and common in this part of the world."

"So, we will be trapped here with no boat or plane off the island?" Madison asked with feigned concern.

"I'm afraid so, my dear," Bea confirmed with affected resignation. "Luckily, we are trapped here with two handsome manly men to protect us until we can be rescued."

All glasses raised.

They drank, absorbed in their own thoughts.

Brand took a more detailed notice of the developing weather outside the windows. He didn't know much about weather up north, but the threatening cloud buildup and the freshening wind caused him doubts as to whether anyone would be able to get off island tonight.

"Madison," Bea said. "Your suite is on the second floor right above the kitchen. Why don't you and Carson repair to your room and rest up from your journey. There will be no excuses for quitters tonight. Hugh, come with me you hunk of burnin' love."

"On my way," he said as he followed her through a large entry way. "I need to check in to work. I won't be a second."

Brand carried their luggage up the stairs to the second floor. He noticed another flight of stairs leading to a floor above. They crossed the second-floor landing and moved along a broad hallway, stretching to either end of the house. Their room was to the right of the staircase on the lake view side of the mansion.

Technically, Brand noticed, the kitchen was not immediately below their room. The kitchen was to the left of the staircase on the first floor. Their room was to the right of the staircase.

Madison pushed open the tall double doors to the suite, revealing a large room with a giant four poster bed and dark antique bedroom furniture. Floor to ceiling windows covered the back wall with a pair of large French doors in the center. A wide balcony was beyond, overlooking the lake.

Madison disappeared into the bathroom adjoining their suite. Brand stepped outside onto the deck. The air had cooled noticeably since their arrival. He heard Madison behind him. She had changed into warmer clothes and a fur-lined cap. Her blonde hair fell to her shoulders below the cap. Her green eyes shone with excitement.

Despite his vow, Brand couldn't help his loitering gaze.

She noticed his interest and spun in a tight circle.

"Do you like?" she asked unnecessarily.

Brand made no reply. He was liking more than he should. Riser's words returned. "Keep your dick in your pants."

"Walk with me by the water," she urged him.

Brand unzipped his bag and produced a jacket.

"If that's all you brought? We'll have to do some shopping for you," Madison commented as she looked disapprovingly at the wrinkled Gore-Tex jacket.

"Sorry," he explained. "I was expecting Los Angeles and warm weather."

They descended the broad staircase and left the house through the rear kitchen door. A stone courtyard created a semi-circle patio appointed with roughhewn outdoor furniture. Another set of steps led to the lake shore. Brand and Madison walked arm in arm along the gravelly beach. Brand cast a glance back towards the huge house. From the rear, he could tell it was a full three stories. The front roof line concealed the extra floor from view.

Movement caught his eye. To the right of the large kitchen windows, he could plainly see into the primary bedroom suite through the open French doors along the lower deck.

Despite the chilly air rushing through the open doors, Hugh and Bea were in the midst of a sex act, Bea on all fours atop the bed. Both looked at Brand and Madison as they moved together. Brand averted his gaze towards Madison who watched the lovers with an absent-minded smile.

She pulled herself from her reverie.

"Those two are incorrigible," she said in a tone that attempted to convey disapproval but fell short.

Brand did not reply, and his expression gave nothing away.

He was being paid for this, he reminded himself.

6

GUESTS BEGAN ARRIVING SOON AFTER dark. In their suite, Brand and Madison changed. Brand spent most of the time on the deck. Although chilly, he took comfort from the cool conditions counteracting his physical response to her appearance in bra and panties while she dressed.

Brand was dressed in his suit. He had only jeans and casual shirts in his bag. Madison insisted upon calling local clothing stores for him. To her dismay and his relief, they closed early. It was after Labor Day and the island was winding down for the season. Most of the residents had returned to the mainland. Those few who remained seemed to require no late-night retail access.

Brand occupied his time seated on a long bench, sipping a crystal tumbler containing his favorite bourbon rocks, from a decanter in the well-stocked antique bar near the entrance to the room. The French doors were open a crack so he could hear Madison without allowing too much cold air into the room.

Far out on Lake Huron, the sky flickered with frequent lightning flashes high in the clouds. They reminded Brand of the storms he grew up with in west Texas. These were far enough away the thunder could not be heard over the crashing waves.

"I'm ready," Madison called to him. "See if you approve."

He stood, draining the last of his drink. He entered the room and closed the doors.

Madison stood before him modeling her outfit. She wore a revealing dress that accentuated her positives. Her high heel strapped shoes showed off her long legs. Her hair was down but tied at the back. Brand had to pause for a moment to renew his resolve.

"That's what I hoped you would say," She teased him, satisfied with his reaction.

They descended the stairs where couples occupied the entry, waiting to greet newly arriving guests.

Madison stopped Brand a few steps above the lower landing above the main floor.

She smiled and nodded at the applause and the fawning comments over her grand appearance.

She nodded towards Brand for the crowd. Light applause rose once again. She looked him over proudly.

He looked handsome in his suit. It was well tailored and showed only faint wear from their flight. They descended the last of the stairs where Bea and Hugh made their way towards them.

"You both look amazing," Bea said with a huge smile and a hug for Madison.

Hugh kept at a distance but stared at Madison with relish.

Brand didn't blame him. Madison was stunning.

They made their way slowly towards the large living room where to make space for dancers, furniture had been pushed to the walls. From speakers concealed within the ceiling and walls, classical music filled the room.

Brand noticed the caterers and servants were primarily black. They rushed to complete the finishing touches on their wares for the evening. Only after he was served a drink and exchanged pleasantries with one of the waiters did he realize most of the staff were Jamaican.

Madison kept a reluctant Brand in tow for the first hour as she worked the room. She spent time with almost everyone in attendance. She was adroit at the art of small talk and connecting with the guests. She had a natural and infectious charm. Her appreciation of those with whom she spoke was unforced and genuine. She rarely spoke of herself other than to acknowledge others' comments, or to introduce Brand and provide a brief but completely manufactured explanation for him.

Finally, they took a seat at one of the large tables near the wall. She sat close to Brand, smiling at him like they had been in a relationship for months instead of having only just met.

Despite his caution, Brand allowed himself to enjoy her closeness and her intimate regard. She was beautiful. He had not been on a date with a woman in the real world in months. His love affairs lately had been bizarre and often tragic.

Madison was by no means a regular girl, but he relished the normality of being out with a girl with no ties to organized crime or targeted by evildoers.

He caught Bea's gaze as she surveyed them. She returned his look and smiled approvingly at him, possibly mistaking his enjoyment of the moment for a real connection.

Hugh occupied his time looking around the room with directed interest. He gave his surroundings his full attention. He acted as if he had never been to a social event like this one.

Brand found that surprising. His impression of the man was that he was accustomed to wealth and lived his life as one experienced in the social habits of the wealthy.

"Can I pour you a drink?" Madison asked at a volume where only Brand could hear her words.

"I'm not drinking any more tonight," he replied as gently as he could manage. "Help yourself."

She leaned closer to him.

"Carson," she said in his ear. "I want you to be in love with me tonight. You can despise me tomorrow."

Brand leaned back just enough to look into her eyes. He ground his teeth against his desire. She was intoxicating.

"I don't despise you," he whispered huskily. "I am your boyfriend tonight, as far as anyone knows."

She stared at him with a yearning look.

He surrendered with a sigh.

"I'll have a couple fingers of bourbon on the rocks."

"Thank you, Carson."

She called one of the servants who poured him a heavy portion of Bourbon with little ice.

Madison nodded at the Jamaican man with a smile.

Brand guessed she had coached him earlier on the pour.

He sipped from the glass, savoring the familiarity of the flavor and the burn. It was a comfort in this unfamiliar environment.

He glanced up to see Hugh watching him.

Brand raised his glass to the bearded man.

Hugh nodded in return.

Brand noticed Hugh was not drinking. He served Bea drinks as she required, but he drank only club soda and lime.

As if someone had changed the channel on the radio, the music changed abruptly from the droning background sound of classical music to thumping hip hop.

Bea leaped to her feet and pressed those at the table until they moved with her onto the dance floor.

Dancers packed the large room, filling the floor with bumping and grinding, swaying figures, and laughter.

Madison kept Brand on the floor for several songs. When they finally returned to their seats, Bea and Madison had added to their number new and old friends from the dance floor.

Soon their table was crowded with partygoers. Brand sat between Madison and a buxom Latina whose dress struggled to contain her bosoms. The table was abuzz with varied conversations. He remained mostly unnoticed in the din. Occasionally, to maintain civil discourse, a newcomer asked him an impersonal question. He responded amicably, but not with so much information as to encourage more conversation.

"Carson," a voice called from within the cross talk. "Excuse me…Carson."

Brand turned his attention from Madison, looking across the table.

A thin, well-dressed man sat across from him. He had spent much time and energy during the night trying to engage him in conversation. His name was Reggie, and he loved Brand's blue eyes and square jaw.

Brand thanked him for his compliments but had made a point to avoid any more awkward compliments or suggestive comments.

At the invitation of a jovial bearded man, the heavy breasted Latina stood from the table and moved to the dance floor.

Reggie acted quickly to occupy the vacant seat beside Brand.

"Finally," he said breathlessly. "We don't have to shout at one another."

Helplessly, Brand smiled and nodded.

Reggie began an enthusiastic interrogation. He asked where Brand worked and in which gym he trained.

Brand informed him he was from out of town. When pressed, he admitted he was from Texas.

Reggie nearly lost his mind at meeting his first real Texan.

Brand noticed Madison's amused expression as she clandestinely enjoyed his discomfort at the aggressive advances of the smitten Reggie. In a rare break in Reggie's fawning, she leaned towards him.

"Reggie is quite successful," she informed Brand. "He would make a fine partner for you. He is loyal, honest, and has great taste in men."

Brand favored her referral with an unappreciative frown.

She returned the look with a light in her eyes he had not seen before. She seemed genuinely interested in him.

He feared she was drinking too much. He decided to elevate his wariness and keep his distance.

A man in a sailor's uniform moved amongst the party goers, advising them to make their way to the carriages waiting to transport them to the boat.

The officer visited a loitering group near Brand's table.

"Big storm coming," he warned. "We can't wait any longer. Please say your farewells and move to the door."

Beatrice intercepted the uniformed man.

"Why didn't you just call? We could have been a bit more orderly getting people to the docks."

"We tried when we docked," he explained. "The phones are down on the island. The only cell tower on the island is offline. The dockhands tell us it is a regular thing when the weather gets bad."

"No cars and now no phones," Bea mused aloud. "Oh well. Let's get everyone on the boat."

Bea helped pass the word to the guests.

Madison leaned closer so Brand could hear her over the noise of the departing guests.

"Bea asked me an hour or so ago, but I wanted to wait to tell you. She and Hugh have been invited to an after party by a local couple – something intimate. Since the boat is early, I would like to go. Will you go with me?"

"Do you think it is a good idea? With bad weather blowing in I would feel better staying here at the house."

"I asked you to be my boyfriend tonight. Can't you play along a bit longer?"

"As the hired help," he said soberly. "I'll do what you tell me to do. As your boyfriend, I would try to convince you to come back to the room with me instead."

"Did I hear an offer to go back to the room?" Bea asked unexpectedly from behind Brand. "How can you pass up an offer like that?"

Reggie leaned back with a broad grin on his face. He hadn't heard the exchange, but he obviously agreed with Bea.

"I'll go back to the room with you if she won't," he said brightly.

Madison blushed and Brand leaned back in his seat. He felt off balance, unsure how to respond. He was uncomfortable with the sexual interest directed towards him. He didn't intend his statement as it seemed to be taken.

He blocked out the remaining flirtatious comments tossed about between Madison, Bea, and Reggie as he watched people drift to the front entry.

His gaze settled on Hugh. The bearded man watched them at a distance, talking with another couple.

With a brief word for his companions, he left them, making his way through the drifting crowd, finally arriving at their table. He took a seat next to Madison.

"Did Bea tell you about the after party?" he asked.

"We were just discussing the topic," Madison replied with an imploring look at Brand. "I think Carson has other plans for me."

"Come on Carson," Hugh urged him. "These are close friends of mine. They live on the island. Their place is not far. It will be fun. A nightcap and a late-night dip in their hot tub sounds just right to finish off the evening."

Brand remained silent for a moment.

"Carson is leaving it up to me," Madison said finally. "I think I'll take him up on his attractive offer. Sorry Bea. Rain check, okay?"

Bea rose slowly. She looked at Hugh. They exchanged looks for a moment. She seemed to recover some of her enthusiasm.

From the corner of his eye Brand saw Reggie shrink a bit in disappointment.

"Come on, baby," Bea called to Hugh, trying to cover her disappointment. "Come on Reggie. You don't want to miss the boat."

Reggie rose reluctantly, and after a sad goodbye to Brand, left the room for the door.

"Don't wait up for us, Mads," Bea called.

Brand watched them leave. It was clear Hugh was not satisfied. He acquiesced anyway and let Bea lead him from the table.

Doggedly, he paused at the doorway, halting Bea's progress. He searched for something to say that would change their minds. He surveyed Brand with a curious look before allowing Bea to drag him away.

Many of the guests bid them farewell as they left for the boat. Soon, only the servants and a few guests remained, awaiting the delayed arrival of returning horse-drawn taxis.

Brand watched Madison who stood at the entrance to the foyer, saying goodbye to a guest who headed for a waiting taxi. She returned to Brand with a fading smile.

"Sorry for cutting the night short," he said, standing from the table, "It's been a long day."

"How could I turn down your offer?" she asked playfully.

Brand looked at her squarely.

"I didn't finish what I was saying. I said if I was your boyfriend that is what I would do. The rest is, I am not your boyfriend. I am the hired help, remember?"

Madison crossed her arms.

"Is that how you see it?"

"See what?"

"See yourself, the hired help?"

Brand sighed wearily.

"I enjoyed the evening. I enjoyed our make-believe relationship. I'm also not blind. You are more than any man could imagine. I am not a suitable mate for you. I'm here because your father hired my firm, and I was selected to go. Most of the other Sovereign personnel have been barred from serving you and your family largely because they can't seem to resist you. I suspect you are not solely responsible. I suspect your father enjoys the game as much as you do. I am not a plaything to be used and discarded. I have a job to do, and I consider myself a professional."

"Are you finished?" Madison asked, her voice devoid of its former warmth.

Brand made no reply. Instead, he gave his attention to the last of the catering crew turning off the lights and leaving through the front door. With the overhead lights extinguished, only table lamps illuminated the corners of the room.

Crackling brightly in the tall windows, lightning flashed at frequent intervals, giving the room a cryptic appearance. The storm was close enough thunder now followed the lightning flashes. The storm was an imminent threat.

Brand faced Madison. He craved no fight with a woman with whom he had no stakes. No matter his attraction for her, by his estimation she was an ego-centric and spoiled brat who enjoyed using others for her selfish ends.

As he recalled one of his late best friends, Bert's, many sayings, and ill-advised comments, he swallowed a wry grin.

"Beauty is only skin deep," Bert often observed. "But ugly goes clear to the bone."

"What's funny?" Madison asked testily.

Brand realized she waited for an answer to her first question.

"Nothing is funny and yes, I am finished."

Madison watched Brand intently.

"You have quite a high opinion of yourself, don't you?" she observed as his rejection galled her and quashed her ego. "I guess you think you have it all figured out."

Brand recognized he had angered her and injured her pride. He made a note to avoid doing so in the future.

"What do you think life has in store for you, Carson? What are you waiting for? I am asking you because the first impression I got from you was you are holding onto something, and life is passing you by."

Brand felt a pang. She poked at him where he was the most tender. These days he struggled mightily to avoid introspective scrutiny. His life was a chaotic mess. He saw no benefit in analyzing it. He resented her curiosity and her insightfulness. Her observations struck too close to home for his comfort.

He hadn't given much thought to what he was holding to, but he knew instinctively she was right. He was holding onto something. He felt like it was a small part of what remained of himself and who he used to be. On good days he believed he feared nothing. On other days he knew that was a lie. He was afraid of losing himself to this new world of violence and death.

He looked at Madison. Her expression surprised him. She was no longer angry or frustrated. Instead, a warmth of understanding softened her eyes as if she were reading his very thoughts.

Her look was unexpected and disarming.

He shook his head sadly.

The Brand before all of this would have given in to the pleasure and the freedom being with her offered him, at least he would have ostensibly in his forbidden fantasy of her. She was the embodiment of the forbidden fruit. Even now his physical reaction to her reminded him of his powerful desire for her.

Like an icy wind on his bare flesh, he warned himself that caring for someone exacted a toll he no longer wanted to pay or wanted her to pay. He had lost so much of what he loved. The pain of loneliness sometimes visited him, but it was not as painful as losing someone he cared for. He couldn't bear to do it again.

"You can talk to me," she assured him, moving forward and laying a hand on his arm. "I make no promises I can help, only that I am willing to hear you."

She leaned in closer, her gaze searching his eyes.

He struggled to meet her eyes. She saw too much in him he wanted to remain unseen. He looked away.

"I have to admit you are a curiosity," she said with a studious preoccupation in her tone. "I have never met anyone like you."

"No?" he asked vaguely as he searched for something with which to divert her attention from him.

"I'm certain of it."

Madison bit her lip as she arranged her thoughts in a workable order. As a rule, she was organized. Missteps were not a part of her failings. Curiosity, however, was a big part of her make-up.

Brand endured her silent scrutiny for several moments until she spoke again.

"I want to ask you a question."

Brand shrugged, keeping his attention on the darkened view outside a nearby window.

"What do you think of Hugh?"

He resisted looking at her at this unexpected change of subject.

"I haven't given him very much thought," he replied, watching angry lightning flashes

"That is what I mean," she said, pulling him around to face her. "Every man here tonight deferred to Hugh as the Alpha – except for you. Reggie picked up on your strength, and he couldn't control himself trying to win your attention."

Brand looked at her vacantly.

"Describe Hugh to me. Tell me what you noticed, like I have never seen him before."

"Madison," he complained wearily. "I'm not interested in a psychological screening tonight."

"Fine. You work for me, and I need to know something. This is a test of your ability as my hired bodyguard. Is he a threat to me?"

Brand stood straighter, her words grabbing his attention. She was skilled at finding and actuating his triggers.

"Alright. I get it. Let me think."

Brand shook his head as he summoned his mental notes on the man.

"Hugh is about six-five, two-forty. He has long hair and a beard…"

Madison shoved him lightly, interrupting him.

"I have no training and I already know everything you are saying. This is supposed to be your field of expertise."

Brand looked at her crossly.

"As a rule, I keep these things to myself. The client has no need to know what I see. Knowledge can get in the way of my ability to protect you."

"Bullshit. Tell me about him."

Brand struggled against her authority. He had no desire to show her what lay behind the curtain. That was his domain alone. Her stubbornly set jaw and her steady gaze convinced him he had no choice in the matter.

He exhaled the last of his resistance.

"Madison, I don't trust him. He didn't drink anything other than club soda and lime but kept the booze flowing for everyone else. He exercised situational awareness the entire time, disguising it as innocent fascination - like he had never been to a party before. He is in shape but that could be a gym rat thing. He seems to have had some self-defense training."

"Karate?"

"I am not joking. He is well balanced when he moves. That requires training. When he laughs, it doesn't make it to his eyes. He is faking his feelings for Beatrice."

Madison stiffened at the idea.

"What does he want then?"

Brand shrugged.

"You," he replied simply.

"What?"

"I'm just guessing."

"I would never do that to Beatrice," she said impatiently.

It was apparent she was prepared to end the conversation as abruptly as she discarded the idea. She cocked an eye at Brand, suspicious of his motivation in making such a claim.

"Why would he carry on this act when he could easily call me or talk to me later?"

"My first guess would be money."

"Beatrice has little access to her father's money. She is trust funded until marriage and kids."

"I think it is your money he is interested in."

"What are you talking about?"

"You told your father on the plane that Beatrice has been planning your get together for nearly a month. She claimed she started dating Hugh three weeks ago. Hugh admitted he helped arrange the party. Two of his acquaintances live on the island, and showed up at a private party, and offered to take you to an after party at their home."

"You are a very suspicious man," Madison observed, unconvinced. "None of your suspicions and observations can be proved."

She considered him thoughtfully.

"You sound like a conspiracy nut," she said dismissively. "See many shadows in the dark?"

She laughed at her joke.

Brand did not.

"Just doing my job," he said. "Besides, he sized me up when we first met then later after we declined to go to the after party."

"Isn't that a male thing?"

"Maybe, but it is definitely a situational awareness thing."

"He invited both of us to the after party, not just me."

"I could be wrong. You asked me to tell you what I thought of him. I didn't want to talk about it."

"I admit I didn't expect your insight on Hugh to be as a professional sizing up a perp. My point is he is a healthy male specimen, and you were the only man in the room who was not either overawed or intimidated by him. Your observations tell me you watched him more closely than you appeared to."

"Sorry to disappoint you in hoping I was the manliest guy in the room. I guess you may lose your bet with Beatrice over this. I will always watch out for you: that includes sizing up your friends too."

To his surprise, Madison didn't bristle at the reference to the bet nor to his ridicule of her observation of him at the party. Instead, she studied him more closely.

"Like I said, I've never met anyone like you before."

Madison took a step towards the kitchen doorway leading to the stairs. She held her hand out to Brand. He accepted it and she pulled him along.

"Bedtime."

Brand stopped and regarded her doubtfully.

She shook her head at his reluctance, then pulled him towards the stairs.

Lightning flashed and thunder shook the house.

Madison started nervously and pulled him closer as she climbed the stairs.

Brand noted the storm was nearly on top of them. He wondered how the return boat journey was going. He hoped the crew had not underestimated the storm.

They entered the bedroom suite. Brand closed and locked the doors.

The electrical storm commenced in earnest, filling the room with stabbing light, casting stark shadows on the tall walls. Brand was impressed by the haunted house feel the storm gave the room.

Madison left him for the bathroom. She didn't bother to turn on the light as she melted into the pitch of the connecting rooms.

Brand guessed she was not so frightened of the storm and the old house as she let on.

She returned to the bedroom. She was completely naked and unembarrassed. She moved slowly to the bed so he would have time to see her, then burrowed under the covers, adjusting her position until she was comfortably situated on her back. She twisted her hair and clasped her hands behind her head. To Brand's relief, she was completely covered.

"Come to bed Carson," she purred.

He moved to the opposite side of the bed. He collected two pillows and an extra blanket folded on a trunk beside the bed. He moved to the settee near the glass doors and arranged the blanket.

He turned away from her so she would not see his body's response to her when he stripped to his boxers and rolled himself in the blanket.

"Goodnight Madison," he said, ignoring the physical effect she was having on him.

She exhaled her frustration as she extinguished the lamp.

Brand stared at the flashes on the ceiling and listened to the storm banging angrily outside the doors.

Madison stayed awake for a long time, tossing, and adjusting pillows and blankets.

Finally, he heard her breathing become steady and rhythmic as sleep took her.

Brand closed his eyes and was instantly asleep.

7

MADISON SAT UP IN BED. The room was dark, pierced by fewer lightning flashes. The storm was waning. Her internal clock told her she hadn't been asleep more than an hour or so. She remained stock still, listening intently. Something had awakened her, but she didn't know what. The house was silent.

She heard Carson's even breathing on the sofa. She could discern only a light breeze probing for access at the cracks between the old French doors. Nothing else seemed out of the ordinary.

She jumped as she heard a sound from upstairs. It was faint, but her nerves strung on pins and needles in her focus caused her a violent overreaction to the sound.

Why would someone be on the third floor of the old house? She and Carson had watched the last of the guests and the servants leave after the party. Beatrice and Hugh probably would not brave the violent storm to return from the after party. If they had, why would they be upstairs in the middle of the night?

She slid from the bed, crouching low as she hurried to where Carson slept. She touched his shoulder lightly. Like a bolt of lightning, he moved away from her, dragging her towards and under him. He had a hand to her throat when he regained full wakefulness. He removed it with a grunt. He noticed her nudity with something like begrudging appreciation.

He was about to scold her for sneaking into his bed when she placed a hand over his mouth. Her expression elevated his caution and provided him assurance she was playing no sexy game with him.

"Someone is in the house. I heard someone on the third floor above us."

He looked up, listening. She waited for his response, feeling his weight atop her. Finally, he lowered his head close to hers.

"Get dressed," he whispered in her ear. "Wait for me in the bathroom."

She disentangled herself from him and moved to obey.

As Brand dressed, he heard the sound of footfalls upstairs. A door slammed above them. He moved towards the door of their room. Madison emerged from the bathroom, fully dressed. She followed him.

"Wait for me here," he urged.

"I'm not staying here by myself," she assured him.

He shrugged at the futility of arguing with her.

"Stay behind me."

She nodded. Her expression conveyed worry and fear. He gripped her arm with an assuring pressure before he turned once more to the door.

He opened one of the tall doors, supporting as much of the door's weight as he could to prevent it from squeaking. He was only partially successful. The hinges protested slightly despite his efforts. He pulled the door ajar until the opening was just wide enough for them to pass through sideways one at a time.

They moved into the hallway then to the staircase.

Brand looked upstairs around the handrail banister. He saw nothing above in the darkness. He rounded the ornate banister rail and climbed the stairs. He listened for movement above and before him. He heard no footfalls besides their muffled steps on the carpet at the center of the stairs.

He motioned for Madison to walk near the edge of the stairs. He hoped walking atop the stringers supporting the steps might limit the creaking of the wooden treads under their feet.

They reached the third-floor landing. Brand looked both ways down the hallway. He gave his attention to the side of the house above their room. The sounds he heard had been above directly above them.

Ahead was a long hallway, similar to the one outside of their room on the floor below. Although dark, ambient light from a window at the end of the hallway provided a dim illumination. The hall was empty ahead of them.

Brand led the way along the hallway until they came to a wide arched entrance on the left side. The room beyond aligned directly above their room.

Rather than a bedroom, this space was an open anteroom sporting a full-sized grand piano. Old chairs provided seating along the walls. Near the rear exterior wall covered by floor to ceiling windows, sat an ornate desk. Cabinets and shelving lined the walls on either side of the desk area. A broad, framed archway, similar to the one at the hallway, separated that part of the room from the anteroom.

Brand led the way into the room, arriving at the desk. He paused to listen. He heard nothing. He was about to turn to Madison when he heard a door slam some distance away in the interior of the house. He pulled Madison back to the hallway. He looked both ways down the hallway from them.

Madison gripped his arm in fear.

Brand touched her hand, releasing his arm from her grasp. He glanced at her before sprinting left from the anteroom, down the hallway.

Madison ran after him, trying to keep contact with him.

Brand opened the first pair of large double doors he came to. Inside was a fully furnished bedroom. He entered the room and searched it thoroughly. He found no one there. He moved to the next room, again inspecting it with nothing and no one found.

He searched each room on both sides of the wide hallway with no result. The last door on the anteroom side of the hallway was a single, standard size door. He pulled it open to reveal a flight of stairs leading to the attic. Above them, the top of the stairs disappeared into darkness.

He felt the walls but found no light switch. He was reluctant to enter a dark attic without a flashlight. If it was used for storage, he might stumble or injure himself in the dark. If someone hid there, he might face a blind attack. He couldn't risk leaving Madison defenseless.

Madison laid a hand on his shoulder.

"You're not going up there, are you?" she asked in a whisper.

"Not without a flashlight," he replied. "There is no telling what might be up there."

"Ghosts?" she asked in fear.

"Sharp objects or holes I could fall into," he replied without humor.

"What do you want to do?" she asked in the same whispered tone.

Brand slammed the door hard.

Madison jumped, cursing under her breath.

"This was the door that slammed," Brand confirmed at a normal volume. The larger doors leading to the rooms he had searched would have made a different sound when slammed.

"That means whoever slammed it is up there."

"Yep."

"What can we do?"

"Let's go back to bed," he decided. "I can't investigate what I can't see."

Madison watched him dubiously. The idea of trying to get back to sleep with a stranger wandering the house was not something she could do.

"Come on," he said, and led her back down the hallway.

They were at the top of the stairs when they heard the squeak of a door opening slowly.

"Motherfucker," Brand exclaimed and sprinted back to the attic stairs door. When he arrived, the door was slightly ajar. He flung it open.

Madison arrived breathing hard as he stepped into the stairwell.

"I'm going to look around as best I can," he told her.

"Don't go up there, Carson," she warned him.

"Someone is messing with us," he concluded. "I need to check it out. Wait down here with the door open. I will talk to you as I go."

"What will that do?" she asked doubtfully.

"If I don't answer, you know to run away."

She swallowed, watching him climb the stairs towards the darkness above.

8

THEY WERE NEARLY FINISHED WITH breakfast when Beatrice and Hugh arrived. Brand had prepared a full repast of eggs, bacon and his specialty, homemade biscuits. Madison ate silently. Although she had convinced Brand to sleep in the bed with her, she hardly slept a wink after his fruitless inspection of the attic.

In bed, he answered her questions with dissatisfyingly vague replies. She didn't know whether he was holding back information because he had encountered nothing of importance, or to help her sleep by withholding something horrible.

Rain continued throughout the morning. The rapidly dropping temperature threatened a wintry mix of ice and snow.

Beatrice and Hugh returned around mid-morning, dressed as they had been when they departed for the after party. Unable to resist the aroma of bacon, and the table laid with food, they quickly dried themselves as best they could before joining Brand and Madison at the kitchen table.

Wet and shivering, Bea took a seat as Hugh moved to the coffee pot. Although he was soaked to the skin, he seemed more comfortable than Beatrice.

"It is so cold out there," Beatrice explained with a shiver.

She took a strip of bacon from the bowl, consuming it like she had been outside for days without food.

Hugh poured two cups of coffee then took a seat beside her.

"We have two cooks in the house, "Bea said brightly but with a trembling voice. "Another win for us girls."

Madison made no rejoinder.

Bea's smile faded as she considered her friend for a moment.

"What's wrong Mads?"

"I didn't get much sleep last night."

"You crazy kids," Bea teased her, sneaking a biscuit from under the dish towel covering a basket. "That Carson made good on his promise, did he?"

Madison glanced at Brand with a serious look.

He nodded to her.

"Someone was walking around on the third floor and slamming doors," she said gravely.

"Did someone sleep over after the party?" Beatrice asked in a reasonable tone.

"Carson searched everywhere, including that creepy attic, and he found nothing."

"Maybe you just heard the old house settling, or maybe the storm moved things around."

Madison straightened in her chair.

"We saw a door open on its own after Carson closed it."

Hugh sipped his coffee as he processed what he was hearing.

"So, you think the old place is haunted?" he asked finally.

"Don't be silly," Bea chided him. "No one believes that stuff."

Brand looked at Hugh with a curious light in his eye.

"What do you think Carson?" Hugh asked, helping himself to a biscuit.

Brand sipped his coffee, shifting his gaze from the man.

"It was dark up there," he said dismissively. "I could have missed someone if they were hiding from me."

"You went into the attic alone?" Bea asked. "In the dark, and in the middle of the night?"

Brand shrugged. He didn't want to mention he had been armed. There would be too much to explain.

"I'll take another look after breakfast," he said.

"The weather has taken a turn for the worse," Hugh announced. "Another storm is on its way, and the temperature is supposed to drop into the sub-thirties tonight."

"It's cold now," Beatrice observed. "Is there no heat in this place?"

"There is no fuel oil in the tank," Brand explained. "The wall radiators run on fuel oil heated steam. We are almost out of propane. We have barely enough to cook with. I doubt we can find a refill for either during this storm."

"How are we going to stay warm when it drops below freezing tonight?" Beatrice asked in alarm.

"I'll split some firewood," Brand offered. "There's a pile of wood outside the kitchen door."

Madison smiled gratefully. She watched Brand with a look he couldn't place at the moment. He thought she seemed more dependent upon him since her scare.

He glanced at Hugh, thinking he might offer to help cut wood.

He instead remained silent, giving his full attention to eating a biscuit with large relishing bites.

"Well, we had a great time," Bea said by way of changing the subject. "The hot tub was wonderful as the storm raged just overhead."

"It sounds like you two should have come with," Hugh observed between bites. "It was a lot less scary than wandering around an old house in the dead of night."

Hugh finished off the biscuit and drained his coffee.

"I need to check in with the office," he said, rising from the table. He grabbed one of the hand towels and walked towards the living room.

"Phones are out, dear," Beatrice reminded him.

"I'll see if the tower is back in service," he said over his shoulder.

Madison gave Beatrice a strange look. Beatrice didn't seem to notice.

"Can we stay with the couple you saw last night?" Madison asked Beatrice. "Surely they have heat in their house."

Beatrice sipped her coffee, looking at Madison over the rim.

"They aren't on the island. They left with the others last night."

"You stayed at their place alone last night?"

"Yes."

Madison waited for Beatrice to provide more information. The other remained silent, sipping her coffee as though her answer was sufficient.

"Why don't we stay at their house then?"

Beatrice seemed perplexed for a moment. Finally, she lowered her cup to the table.

"We can't," she said slowly. "We locked the place up from the inside when we left. There is no way in now."

Brand ate silently as the girls talked. Beatrice's story seemed contrived. If they were alone and comfortable, why did they return in the teeth of the storm?

He finished up and cleaned the kitchen. He washed the dishes as the girls looked on, chatting quietly. He dried his hands and headed towards the door to the stairs and the foyer.

"Are you really going up there?" Madison asked disbelievingly.

"Yeah," Brand replied flatly. "I said I would."

"You are braver than me," Beatrice admitted with a quaver to her voice.

"I'll go with you," Madison offered with little conviction in her tone.

"You two wait here," he said. "I'll be right back."

They remained at the table, huddled together as he disappeared from sight.

"He is so brave," Beatrice said in a faraway voice. "Now that is a man."

Madison made no comment. She had lost interest in their pointless contest. If this was a prank, Beatrice had gone too far. She thought about Brand and his actions the previous night. He was either brave or careless.

When he ran towards the sound of the open door, then climbed the stairs to the attic, her instincts had been, and were still, to run away. He seemed to be insulated from fear of any kind. She told herself again he was unlike anyone she had ever met.

Brand climbed the stairs and entered his and Madison's room. He collected the Sig then made his way to the third-floor attic door. As he walked the third-floor hallway, he noticed the upper floor was not so foreboding in the light of day. He arrived at the door and turned the knob. The door resisted his efforts to open it. He pulled with both hands to no avail.

He inspected the door and the frame where the knob catch met the striker plate. He saw nothing that would jam the door closed. The odd thing was the doorknob turned easily, and he could see the catch pull free of the striker plate well.

What was holding the door closed? If the door was somehow blocked from the inside, how was it done? There was no give or slack to the door as one might expect when the knob is held or tied off with a rope or chain. It was barred from within, meaning whoever stuck the door closed did it from inside the attic stairwell.

Brand's memory of the rear exterior of the house did not include a way down from the roof. He recalled no trellis, nor gutter spout, nor corner trim, sufficient to cling to at the building's exterior. The front of the house was a steeply pitched shale roof ending two stories above the ground.

He again pulled on the door more as a ceremonial gesture than expecting to open it. He had heard no hammering, nor the sound of any other tool the previous night or this morning. He was unsure if the sound of whatever was used to jam the door would have reached the kitchen. He suspected he would have heard a hammer, even as he cooked the meal.

Brand returned to the kitchen where the girls waited in the same place he had left them.

"What did you find?" Madison asked breathlessly.

"The door is jammed shut."

"Why would someone block off the attic from us?" Madison asked. "That means someone is hiding somewhere here in the house."

"The door isn't locked or nailed closed. It is just stuck somehow. I believe it is secured shut from the inside – from the attic side."

Both girls hugged one another. Their eyes were wide in disbelief and fear. The haunted house theme for the visit was becoming uncomfortably real.

"I'm going to look for a way on or off the roof from outside the house," Brand announced. "Is there a hammer or any tools around?"

"In the workshop in the stables off to the side of the house," Bea replied as if in a trance.

"I need you two to get dressed and stay where I can see you until I work this out. I'll check the outside of the house. Meet me outside in five minutes."

They muttered their agreement and hurried to obey. The prospect of staying in the house alone was terrifying. Hugh had disappeared with no promise to return immediately. They wanted nothing more than to remain near Brand.

He left the house by the front doors, his shoulders hunched, and his head bowed against the freezing rain. He searched the outside of the house for any means by which someone might escape from the attic.

The only outside access to the attic he could see was at the rear of the house. A small triangular window was high up near the peak of the roof. He saw no way down to either the ground or the second-floor deck. He saw no means by which someone could escape from the roof without a long fall. The second-floor deck was some twenty feet below the upper eaves. The ground was more than thirty feet below the roof line.

While sloshing a trek around the house, it occurred to him he had not seen Hugh lately. If he had managed to get a call out and was on the phone, he was not in any of the common areas of the house, nor was he on a deck, or in one of the courtyards or patios.

He dismissed Hugh's absence as a cold gust struck him brutally. It had been nearly five minutes and he was beginning to suffer in the cold. His thin jacket provided no warmth and little protection from the driving rain and sleet. He looked for the girls to appear from the house. He didn't wait long. They rushed out the front door. He turned as they followed him to the side of the mansion where they entered the long narrow building.

Inside, the horse stalls were empty other than discarded or carelessly stowed old dusty tack. Interestingly, parked near the front facing double doors, covered with tarps, were two snow mobiles.

He inspected them. They were out of fuel and the engines were missing parts where someone had begun repairs but had not finished. He replaced the tarps and looked towards the rear of the garage area.

A wide array of heavy implements lay on the ground near the back wall. Brand saw no tractor that might employ the rusty tools. He wondered if they towed them with horses.

The rain and sleet hammered heavily on the old slate roof above. The open framing of the mow above was missing a few boards through which the roof rafters were clearly visible. With no visible leaks, the ancient building seemed in good repair.

They passed through double doors on the house side of the main room. Inside was a workbench complete with a pegged wall of old hand tools. The sturdy workbench spanned the entire length of the wall from the double doors, where they entered, to the back corner. Outdated bench-mounted power tools were either attached to the heavy work bench or stowed in large cubbies along the side walls and under the bench. Leaned against the opposite wall were a wheelbarrow and miscellaneous digging tools.

Brand searched the bench until he found a wooden handled hammer and a short flat pulling bar. Judging by the dust covering the tools, and when removed, the clean silhouettes left on the tabletop, neither looked as if it had been used in years.

Brand returned to the house, the girls close behind. Despite his admonishments, they followed him to the attic door. He wedged the flat bar between the door and the jamb. Before applying the strength of the tools to the door he obeyed an impulse and tried the door once more. The door opened easily.

He and the girls exchanged confused looks.

Brand handed Bea the hammer and flat bar.

"Wait here," he instructed them.

He climbed the stairs purposefully. He didn't want to seem meek or frightened. He might find someone hiding in the attic. If he did, he or she would probably not greet him cordially if he seemed unsure or less than committed to the fray.

When he gained the attic level and was out of sight of the girls, he produced the Sig. A round was chambered from the previous night.

Just the feeling of expanse made the attic seemed immense, stretching away to the left and behind him. Most of it was rough framing which faded into darkness towards the lightless edges of the house.

He stood upon a smaller finished floor about the size of one of the bedrooms below. It was constructed of dusty hardwood flooring. The finished floor region was full of stored items, many in boxes, others on open shelving.

As cluttered with strewn debris as the floor was, he was surprised that during his blind investigation the previous night, he had not stumbled into any more stacks of stuff than he had, or blundered into the open framing of the unfinished attic.

He looked around thoroughly. By the scant light passing through the little triangular window high on the far wall, he could see no farther afield than the finished attic area.

He found no one hiding. He located no doors or hidden chambers by which someone could escape.

A noise behind him caused him to spin on a heel, bringing the pistol on line with the sound. Madison and Beatrice looked at him and the gun in alarm. He oriented the pistol barrel towards the floor.

"We didn't want to wait down there alone," Madison explained unsteadily as she eyed the weapon.

"Why do you have a gun?" Beatrice asked pointedly.

Madison began to explain but Brand interrupted her.

"It's a Texas thing. I never leave home without one."

"Please don't shoot us," Bea requested sarcastically. Her tone suggested she did not approve of guns. Brand knew Bea was from

California. He had no reason to doubt his suspicions about her ideological stance on guns. He sheathed the pistol in his waistline holster.

"I'll try not to," he promised with equal rancor.

"There is no one here," Madison said softly. "Who jammed the door then opened it? Who was walking around and slamming doors last night?"

Brand shook his head. He had no answers.

They moved slowly around the attic floor, looking into boxes and on shelves.

"Bea, do you know what all of this stuff is?" Madison asked.

"I've never been up here before," Beatrice replied.

She moved to the nearest stack and gave it a brief look.

"It's really old," she said. "This is a stack of newspapers from the sixties. Here is a photo album with black and white photos."

Madison walked along one of the shelving units, peeking into the cubbies without touching anything.

"There are old knick knacks mostly. Here are some old leather-bound books: a set of encyclopedias from 1956."

Brand moved towards the back of the attic where the piles seemed more haphazardly arranged. He came upon an empty space among the piles. It looked as if the space had been cleared. In the center of the clear space was an image carved into the floor with a sharp object. He recognized a pentagram but recognized none of the other icons carved around and over it. Candles encircled the macabre looking design. They looked old, covered in a thick coating of dust. This space had been untouched for years.

A smaller circle was carved beside the markings. Inside the circle was an etched wooden box. The carvings on the outside of the box were handmade and crude.

Brand lifted the box and opened it slowly.

"Bea, come here a second," he said quietly.

Both girls came over to him.

Brand handed the old box to Bea. She accepted it with a confused look. She opened the box and looked inside. The contents were nothing more than photos. Most looked old, some older than the encyclopedias. Others were nearly brand new, in vivid color.

She looked through the color photos. They were images of she and Hugh having sex in the primary bedroom. The photos were taken from above them, maybe from the height of the ceiling.

Other photos were taken of the construction crew while they renovated the house. There were more of Beatrice, taken during one of her first visits to the house. Some were from the perspective of ceiling height, while others were at eye level from the floor but at a distance suggesting someone took the photos from a hiding place behind the walls.

Older photos featured strangers, mainly women, in rooms in the house, but taken prior to the renovation. Based upon the photo quality and the fashion of the women in the pictures, they were taken years before. She suspected the women in the photos were previous occupants. Many of the photos were of women in showers or dressing in the bedrooms. She judged by the hairstyles and the clothing, those photos were taken as early as the mid to late eighties.

"Someone is spying on me," she said in horror. "We have to find this person. I have to call the police."

"Let's wait on that," Brand advised her.

"Why?" Bea demanded loudly.

Brand pointed at the wall near the cleared space.

Written in a scrawling hand in red were the words,

You Tell You Die!

The writing seemed as old as the devilish pattern cut into the floor. If it wasn't for the recent photos of Bea and Hugh, this would seem a place abandoned for decades. The long-gathered dust within the cleared space bore only his footprints. How did the recent photos end up in the box?

"Let's go," Brand said.

Bea moved to follow, carrying the box.

"Leave the box."

Bea hesitated as she struggled with the urge to bring it along. Finally, she opened the box, removing the pictures with her likeness. She handed the box to Brand who returned it to its place within the circle. He stepped over the junk forming the perimeter barrier and followed the others to the stairs. He cast a final look around the attic. He peered into the surrounding darkness but could see nothing beyond the flooring covered area of the attic. He descended the stairs.

9

USING AN AXE HE FOUND IN THE
workshop, Brand chopped fire logs into split
halves. He loaded the billets into the
wheelbarrow for transport to the porch near
the kitchen door. The rain and sleet had
slowed for the moment to an occasionally
occurring mist or frozen flurry. The air was still
crisp, but the work warmed him, and he
relished the labor. The effort soothed his
nerves and gave his thoughts a familiar
backdrop from which to work.

He had much wood to split. The night
would be dangerously cold in the huge old
drafty house. With no central heating and no
fuel to heat the water in the wall heaters,
stoked fireplaces would be the only way to stay
warm.

Since their return, the girls' conversations
were abuzz with speculation of their attic
exploration. They were convinced there were
secret passages throughout the house. They
even bandied about the theory a ghost haunted
the old place.

Brand was reluctant to share his suspicions.
He didn't believe in ghosts like those on TV or

in *YouTube* videos. He was convinced there were things in the world he did not understand, but he did not believe the unknown or the metaphysical oddities therein posed a threat to anyone with the faith and a strength of principle to oppose it.

He believed the danger they faced was from a man. A living man was sneaking around, taking photos of them from hiding. Brand was also convinced that man had watched them from the cover of darkness amongst the attic framing beyond the finished floored area. He couldn't explain the lack of footprints in the cleared area where he found the box, but he knew there was an explanation that was not supernatural.

While they explored the attic, Brand had chosen not to draw the girls' attention to the remote areas beyond the light, nor mention his suspicions. He intended to find and confront the culprit on his own terms in a place of his choosing. If his suspicions were realized, it meant the unseen enemy watched them from the darkness and knew he was armed.

This stranger had already made a blatant threat on their lives with the writing on the wall. It was possible – no, likely – he was armed. If not with a gun, he certainly had access to crude or modern edged weapons - quiet and deadly. Either way, the enemy would prepare himself to face an armed opponent. If he lacked a firearm, Brand suspected this malevolent stranger would even the odds using his superior knowledge of the house and its hidden egress points of which he alone knew.

Clandestine attacks and the element of surprise would be a critical advantage. Even Brand could stay awake only so long. The others had no ability to defend against a prepared attack.

His thoughts again drifted to Hugh. The man was an unwelcome subject. He was decidedly unfriendly towards Brand and offered little to encourage an alliance between them. Brand maintained the belief there was more to the man than he presented to them. It was unclear whether his secrets represented a threat or nothing more than an annoyance. The unknowns around the man made him an unwelcome distraction to the danger they faced from the intruder in the house.

Brand filled the wheelbarrow with split logs. He pushed the load on squeaky wheels onto the back patio. He stacked them against the wall then returned to the wood pile. He positioned the wheelbarrow for the next load and hefted the axe. He paused, sensing he was no longer alone.

He turned to see Madison standing nearby, watching him work. He lowered the axe head to the ground.

"Are you doing alright?" he asked her.

"I think we should leave."

Brand considered her for a moment.

She stood stiffly with her arms crossed. She compressed her lips in a tight thin line. Her brow furrowed with concern.

Brand sighed before making a response to her comment.

"The driver who brought our supplies today told me the ferries have stopped running for the season and they are expecting an ice storm tonight that will close the airstrip for the next several days at least. The phones are still out and there is no one on island who knows how to repair it which means we can't call a boat to retrieve us."

"We can stay at one of the inns here."

Brand nodded, lifting the axe as he once more gave his attention to splitting logs.

"Closed for the season, too," he said with a grunt as he chopped.

"Dammit Brand," she cried. "You aren't taking this very seriously."

Brand turned to her once more. He considered her carefully.

"Come here," he said, setting the axe on the wood pile.

She hesitated stubbornly before begrudgingly approaching him. She didn't want him to console her or talk her down. She was firmly entrenched in her assessment of their situation, and she did not want it questioned.

He waited until she was in reach before he gently pulled her to him, hugging her firmly. With a shudder of surrender, she returned the embrace. Her fears replaced her resolve.

"I'm frightened," she said into his shoulder.

"I know," he agreed. "I want to tell you something I can't tell anyone else."

She stepped back to see him fully.

"Okay," she said with some return of her former strength. "Tell me."

"This is no supernatural force."

"I hear you," she said tersely. It disappointed her he offered no unique insight or unexpected solution to their dilemma.

"He is a man. He is a twisted person with a lot wrong with him, but only a man."

"Brand," she said evenly and patiently as if he were a child. "I want to agree with you. The old pictures, the old writing on the wall, the dusty shrine, how do you explain the old and unused look of everything? A man would leave tracks in the dust. A man would dislodge dust even if he tried not to."

"That's twice you've said Brand," he said with a reassuring smile. "Good. I guess we are past games and playtime."

Madison looked at the ground, grinding her toe in the dirt like a little girl. He rewarded her solicitude with childish observations about her manner of speaking.

"I am frightened," she said with an unwilling appearance of vulnerability. Her fear was too great to hide.

"I will take care of you," he assured her. "I'll track this guy down and deal with him."

"What if this mystery adversary gets to you first?"

"He won't."

"You don't know that."

Brand nodded his agreement.

"You're right," he said slowly. "I can't guarantee anything. I can only tell you what I plan to do. There are no absolutes."

Madison paused, watching him to see if what he said conjured alternative scenarios where he might fall short of his promise to her.

He returned to his wood chopping.

"What about us?" she asked.

"What about you?" he asked in return, bringing the axe down, splitting a log in two.

"We aren't killers. We aren't trained to protect ourselves against crazy people who hide in attics and create devil worship altars. What if you get killed or incapacitated? What if you aren't around?"

Brand nodded his understanding.

"I promise you nothing will happen to you. I will protect you."

Madison was growing frustrated with his circular conversation. He was stubborn.

"What about Beatrice and Hugh?"

"I'll do what I can for Beatrice. Fuck Hugh."

"Brand!"

Brand raised the axe once more. He split another log. He tossed the billets into the wheelbarrow.

"That asshole can chop wood or give a hand with a chore or two around the house. If he makes some effort, we'll revisit, but I'm not holding my breath."

By evening heavy fog rolled in from the lake, shrouding the island in a frigid blanket.

Fires crackled in the two main fireplaces downstairs.

Despite the recent delivery, the scarce provisions on the island limited their larder to a half dozen whole chickens, canned items, potatoes, bread, and a few pounds of thick cut cured bacon.

Hugh reappeared around the time the delivery arrived. He grunted and shrugged but did not provide an explanation regarding his whereabouts that afternoon.

For dinner they ate a baked chicken Brand prepared in the gas oven. He used the excess chicken grease to cook up potatoes and a bag of frozen Brussel Sprouts. His companions were accustomed to higher quality fare and wrinkled their noses at the low rent food set before them.

As he served the plates, Brand boasted a little added salt and butter made the meal a regular cowboy dinner.

They ate before the living room fireplace. The crackling logs added a merriness to the room none of them felt. Discounting the threat of an unseen enemy in the house, the setting could have easily been cozy and romantic. Instead, the meal was a quiet affair with gazes continually cast into dark corners in search of the hidden observer.

Despite their refined palettes, hunger got the better of them. Madison, Beatrice, and even Hugh cleaned their plates. Brand enjoyed the familiar tasting dinner. He washed it down with icy water from the tap.

After returning his plate to the kitchen, he poured himself a bourbon and lounged on one of the velvet settees just beyond the firelight. Madison left her plate on the low table near the fireplace and joined him, wrapping herself in a thick blanket.

"Thank you for making dinner," she said quietly.

"You're very welcome," he said graciously.

"You are in an awfully good mood," she observed with confusion.

"I guess I am," he agreed thoughtfully.

He tossed back the remaining bourbon in his glass and moved to refill it. He returned to his seat. He was silent for a moment before he adjusted his position until he was quartered towards her.

"I used to have a friend. He was my best friend. His name was Bert. We grew up together in San Antonio. We met in the military."

"Is he the friend you mentioned in San Antonio?"

"He's dead," Brand said matter of factly. "He used to say most people teetered on the edge of insanity all their lives. Anyone could snap, and it never takes as much to do it as we believe it does. That's why drugs and alcohol are so dangerous for so many. We are an animal that medicates ourselves into happiness."

He looked at her squarely.

"Did you know the average life expectancy for a doctor is around fifty years old?"

Madison shook her head.

"That's because medical training focuses on treating symptoms not treating the cause of the symptoms."

Madison examined her belief in his observation.

"School shootings are a horribly destructive way of committing suicide," he continued. "Those who threaten to carry one out on social media typically talk about suicide before they do. The shooters never have an escape plan. They just want to feel noticed in those last moments. It is akin to suicide by cop, but they gain greater notoriety, all at the cost of children's lives."

Madison listened intently. Where was he going with this?

Brand sipped his drink. He looked around him. All three of his companions watched him in rapt attention, their imaginations plugging their own life experiences and opinions into his story.

"Take this nut job who spies on this house's occupants like some kind of sexual deviant. He is probably listening to us right now. He is the most depraved of all. You will never see a video from this guy. He knows he is a freak. No one will ever find him interesting or relatable. Anyone would see immediately this guy is everything we hope we will never become. He lives in the dark because he is disgusted by who he is. He takes pictures of others at their weakest to make himself feel strong. It is laughable. He is a coward and a freak. There is no strength about him. He wants you to be afraid. It's all he has."

"You aren't afraid?" Bea asked, wide-eyed at his brazen taunting of the ghostly presence.

"What's to fear? This shithead was hiding in the dark of the attic while we went through his things. He did nothing because he is afraid. He is with us right now, listening right now, and he is powerless to do anything about it. I don't fear a weak and frail coward. He fears me. He fears you. That is why he loves it when you seem afraid of him. Imagine how strong you would feel if the lion feared you."

Brand looked around him at the walls then at the ceiling high above.

"Fuck you Dark Man," Brand said loudly, looking around him at the darkened walls and ceiling. "I will find you. I will teach you what real fear is."

Above them a crash shook the room. It sounded like a huge structural component; like the very skeleton of the house had been crushed.

Brand's manner changed immediately as he jumped to his feet and ran from the room then up the stairs. He no longer exhibited good natured thoughtfulness. He no longer taunted his prey. He was the predator, pursuing him swiftly and silently, like a cat on the hunt. His anger was up, and he yearned for blood. He stopped at the top of the stairs near the third-floor landing. He controlled his quickened breathing as he listened for his prey. After the loud crash, his quarry made no sound.

Brand imagined the other, still as death, heart pounding, all senses strung on steel wires as he listened for Brand over the sound of his own rushing blood and hammering heart.

Brand heard a small movement above him. He sprinted to the end of the hallway and the attic door. He turned the handle and the door opened easily. He moved through the door and climbed the stairs into the pitch darkness above.

He could see nothing, but instead allowed his ears to guide him. During their earlier visit he had memorized the layout of the attic space. He stepped behind the shelving where Madison had been when she found the encyclopedias. He remained stock still.

He thought he heard a soft movement just beyond the edge of the attic floor. He held his breath as he waited for confirmation of what he heard.

There! He heard it again.

He remained still as he heard, more accurately, he sensed the man passing on the opposite side of the shelves.

Brand felt his rage spin up to a level of near euphoria. The Dark Man was there with him. He craved combat with this coward who stalks in darkness.

Brand eased around the shelves, testing his footing with each step. He followed his memory of the path leading to the cleared spot among the piles of junk. He heard something a few feet in front of him. With a quick move, he took a large stride, closing the gap between him and the Dark Man.

He tripped over something in the path. There should not have been anything in that area. As he stumbled, Brand realized it was a trap, but the fall saved his life. Brand felt the wind of something big rushing towards him. The silence of the attack was surprising considering the size of what he sensed moved towards him.

Brand ducked low before launching himself towards the sound of the unseen attacker. Altering his posture was the only thing that saved him.

He heard the hiss of a blade cutting the air above him.

Brand kicked a leg forward then brought both fists up as hard as he could. The man was big. Brand felt powerful arms coiling around his chest from above.

Before the arms could lock at the fingers, Brand curled in a ball and kicked again with both legs. He caught the Dark Man in the torso. The blow had a negligible effect on the assailant.

The Dark Man moved to regain his advantage. Brand could not see him, but his movements in the dark were clear.

Brand struck the Dark Man in the face. The impact sounded brittle, like a fist on bare bones.

Surprisingly, the bigger man struck Brand squarely in the face. Through the flash of stars, Brand wondered how his foe was able to be so accurate in the blinding conditions?

Maybe he wore NVG's, Brand realized with alarm. If so, his assailant could see him clearly in the dark. But he felt no apparatus on the Dark Man's face when he struck him.

With no further hesitation, Brand moved quickly. He struck the Dark Man as many times as he could then turned to flee for the stairs.

The Dark Man swung his blade in a wide arc. With a hiss through the air, the edge sliced across Brand's back and shoulder. The pain was like a string of fire pulled across his skin.

Brand turned, throwing himself at the man, toppling him to the floor. Brand leaped away as another swish of the blade cut the air a hair's breadth from his face. He fell backwards towards the doorway to the stairs. He staggered, expecting to stumble over unseen obstacles.

He heard scratching and clawing as the Dark Man scrambled to pursue. The sound was like a dog's claws on a slick wooden floor rather than the hands and feet of a man.

Brand raised himself and rushed away from the sound, running headlong into the door jamb. He lost his balance and tumbled down the stairs into the hallway below. He struggled to rise, new injuries from the fall hampering him.

The hallway was comparatively bright to Brand's night vision. The Dark Man would have little advantage if he pursued. He reached for his Sig. It was not in its holster. He had left it in the room. With regret he realized he hadn't brought it to dinner.

Brand heard the Dark Man moving in the attic above him.

Shit.

Brand slammed the stairwell door and sprinted toward the stairs.

The door slammed open behind him, striking the wall with a house jarring impact. The big man was powerful, almost inhumanly so.

Brand cast a quick look behind him. He could make out only the silhouette of a huge man at the open door, looking at him. Brand could discern no details about the man except he was a giant, bigger than Hugh even. He seemed to be disembodied, like a shadow or a trick of the eyes. He made no move to pursue Brand.

Brand loitered no longer. He took the stairs two at a time. He entered his bedroom suite. He unzipped his go bag and pulled from it the attaché containing the MDP-9. The gun was there but it was missing its magazines and extra ammo boxes. The Sig was where he left it between the mattress and the box springs of the bed. Whoever had disabled the MDP-9 had missed the pistol. Thankfully the gun was hidden and loaded. The nine-mil ammo served both weapons. He was down to 15 rounds.

He returned to the doorway and listened for noises outside the room. He heard nothing. He squatted low and stepped from the room into the hallway. The hall was empty. Brand moved slowly towards the staircase, senses alert for movement above.

He hurried to the railing. There was no movement above him. He looked down in time to see a large shadow moving away towards the kitchen and living area of the lower floor. The Dark Man was downstairs with the others.

Brand sped to the stairs, taking them two at a time. At the bottom he sprinted towards the kitchen doorway, pistol in hand. He rushed into the kitchen where Hugh drank a cup of coffee, leaning lazily against one of the cabinets.

Hugh stood straighter and appeared alarmed at the abrupt appearance of Brand wielding the Sig Sauer.

"Carson," he began uncertainly.

"Where is he?" Brand asked hurriedly.

"Where is who?" Hugh asked with a bewildered gesture of his free hand.

"You didn't see a big man come into the kitchen?" Brand asked with a tone of suspicious accusation.

"What the hell are you talking about, man?"

Brand exhaled violently as his uncertainty was replaced with frustration. He rushed from the kitchen and entered the large living room, hiding the gun behind his back.

Madison and Beatrice sat together on one of the large, overstuffed sofas near the fire.

Brand decided not to ask them if a large knife wielding stranger had passed through. He concluded they would not be calmly sipping coffee if they had witnessed such a sight.

"Are you okay, Carson?" Bea asked apprehensively.

Brand made no reply as he hurried away to search the remainder of the main floor of the house for the Dark Man. The search turned up nothing, but more empty rooms filled with antique furnishings.

Brand returned to the living room; the pistol stowed in his belt line. He sat on the arm of the nearest settee as he waited for his breathing to slow.

Madison watched him with genuine concern.

"What's going on Brand?" she asked.

Brand considered her for a moment. The girls were acting differently than what he expected after his encounter with the Dark Man then following him downstairs.

Why didn't anyone see him? The Dark Man disappeared.

Hugh entered the room and took a seat beside the girls.

"I think you need to tell us what is going on with you, Carson," he said seriously.

Brand nodded as he collected himself despite his confusion at the nonplussed appearance of the others.

Finally, he spoke in a calm and measured tone.

"After we heard that loud crash upstairs, I ran to the attic where I found our spy…"

"What crash?" Madison asked.

"The crash we heard when I was telling you the story of my friend Bert."

"All we heard was thunder from the storm that is almost upon us," she said. "You shot out of here like a man possessed. We heard no crash, as you put it."

Brand was silenced by her recounting of the event.

"Did you think the thunder was something going on inside the house?" Hugh asked with a hint of ridicule.

Brand looked at him dangerously. He was not amused.

"Look at this," Brand said turning his back towards them. "The Dark Man cut me with a knife across the shoulders."

The three looked at the back of his shirt. True it was torn, but in a staggered pattern of small holes that might just as easily have been caused by scraping oneself on a protruding nail. There was no sliced look to the holes in the shirt. There was very little blood near the rented fabric.

"I've seen knife wounds Carson," Hugh said confidently. "That is no knife wound on your back. It looks like you snagged yourself on a nail or protruding splinter – probably when you ran blindly into the attic. Are you calling this guy you think is in the house *Dark Man*? What about scaring the shit out of me in the kitchen claiming you thought a big man had entered the kitchen with me in it?"

Brand looked helplessly at Madison and Beatrice.

Their expressions shared doubt in his story. He suspected they thought he had lost his mind.

"I noticed you were packing a pistol when you rushed in," Hugh said soberly. "I'm not sure, with your imagination working like it is, that I feel comfortable with you carrying a gun around. By the way, why are you armed?"

"He's from Texas," Bea said sarcastically. "He never leaves home without a gun."

Hugh stood and approached the silent and confused Brand.

"Give me the gun," he said soberly, extending a hand. "It's for your own good."

Brand glanced at Hugh as he collected his thoughts.

The Dark Man must have disappeared into one of those secret passageways the girls guessed were in the walls.

Hugh stepped closer and reached towards Brand's beltline to retrieve the gun.

Brand slapped his hand away as he stood and left the room.

10

THE ICE STORM REACHED A crescendo in the darkest hours of the morning. Brand lay on the bedroom settee where he had slept that first night before the Dark Man disrupted their tranquility. Madison slept in her bed wrapped in blankets and a heavy bedspread like a cocoon.

Upon Hugh's insistence she had lobbied ardently for Brand to relinquish his pistol. Brand was relieved they didn't know about the useless automatic weapon in the attaché case. If they knew about the automatic weapon, there would have been hell to pay.

Beatrice showed up at one point to back up Madison's pleas. She mounted a prolonged entreaty, begging for him to surrender the weapon to Hugh.

He resisted stubbornly until they grew weary of the fruitless enterprise.

Madison ceased her efforts to change his mind long before Bea tired of arguing with him. Madison likely drew some comfort that even fraught with imagined foes in the attic and bumps in the night, he was trained extensively, and was a more reasonable wielder of the firearm than the unknown quantity which was Hugh.

After apologizing for frightening them, and repeated assurances he was no threat, Brand convinced Beatrice her efforts would bear no fruit and asked her to leave him in peace. She finally left with a few choice observations about hardheaded men and the dangers they posed to women.

Madison ignored him before finally drifting off into a troubled sleep.

Brand was yet to sleep since retiring to the settee in the second-floor suite. His vigilance was unrewarded. The house seemed silent save for the storm raging outside.

He glanced out the window beside him where heavy rain sheeted the glass, denying him a clear view of the world outside. He saw only rare lightning flashes some distance from the house; dim silhouettes of trees swaying and shaking in the gusty and variable winds. Spattering rain and ice struck the window in multiple ellipses, driven by strong gusts rushing ashore from the tossing lake.

He turned his attention to the room. The far wall danced with shadowy specters and dancing flashes of light. An unreasonable imagination could have easily made ghostly images of much of what he saw.

He ground his teeth.

The Dark Man was no spirit. He was a man, a very big and strong man. Brand made physical contact with him. He was not of the spirit world.

Brand, like everyone, had heard of poltergeists manifesting physically by moving objects or violently attacking the living. Brand was not given to flights of fancy. He admitted many of the ghost stories shown online were not easily dismissed as caused by apparent or normal forces. Of those, he estimated nine out of ten were the products of clever video editing and persuasive narration.

He silently scolded himself for allowing his mind to go down the path of the supernatural. The old house, the storm, and the strange disappearance of the Dark Man made his imaginings difficult to resist.

He watched the shadows on the far wall for a long time as he tried to work out the mystery of the disappearance of the Dark Man.

He froze as he saw the door slowly move.

Was this a trick of the changing light and shadows?

No. The door continued to open slowly and smoothly. Surprisingly, he heard no sound of squeaky hinges or creaking door planks like he experienced when he moved the door. It opened silently and steadily.

Brand gripped the pistol and crept stealthily towards the door, hiding his approach by hugging the wall opposite the bed where Madison slept. The door continued to open as he moved forward. When he arrived, the door was ajar at a 90-degree angle from the wall. Whoever manipulated the door had a full view of Madison and the settee on the far wall.

Brand squatted on his heels in case whoever was opening the door took a swing at him when he grabbed the door.

He yanked the door open and rolled into a low standing posture, pistol in position to fire.

The doorway was empty.

He moved to the wall and peeked into the hallway.

Although dark, he was certain the hall was empty as far as he could see down it. He stepped into the hallway, listening intently for footsteps or other noises. With the door opened, the sound of the storm in the house was more noticeable. The storm's attack upon the old structure was loud and violent.

Brand tested the air in the hallway. He felt a slight movement of the air currents in the hallway, probably the wind from the storm finding its way into the house through cracks and gaps in the window or door frames. A gusty wind could have opened the door. He checked the knob and striker assembly. The knob spring seemed stiff, and the striker appeared secure.

Brand returned to the suite and closed the door. Unlike when it mysteriously opened, the door squeaked and groaned as he closed it.

He turned to see Madison sitting up in bed. To avoid more conflict, he stowed the pistol.

"Where did you go?" she asked apprehensively.

Brand decided to dodge any further appearance of insanity.

"I was just checking the hallway."

"Can you come here for a second?" she asked patting the bed.

"Sure," he agreed, making his way to the big bed.

He sat near her.

"I saw the door open on its own," she admitted calmly. "Was it the wind?"

"I think so," he replied with little conviction.

"I saw you check the hall and the door latch. Is the doorknob broken?"

"It probably wasn't closed securely, maybe when Bea left."

"I want you to be honest with me, Brand," she said firmly.

"Okay."

"What you told us earlier was frightening."

"I understand."

"Let me finish. We haven't known each other long but I got a good idea of who you were when we met. Since we got here you seem different. That worries me. I trusted you because you work for Sovereign and my dad trusts Riser to send only his best men. I need to know you are alright."

Brand pursed his lips against the words he knew she would not hear. Instead, he limited his purview to this moment and this place.

Madison leaned towards him with a concerned look.

"You are scaring me, now."

Brand was uncertain how to proceed with her. It was plain she had little confidence in him. She also did not believe what he told her about the Dark Man. He was reluctant to lie to her. He promised to be honest.

After a quick deliberation, he resorted to his habit of speaking the truth and letting the chips fall where they may.

"You asked some personal questions about me before," he said with a decisive energy. "I told you I didn't want to share personal information with you. Credibility is a fragile thing.

"I ran a business, and I learned quickly how thin the line between trusted and despised is. I have acquired the habit of maintaining an at-arm's-length policy with most people, particularly business associates. Despite our agreement to portray a fantasy relationship, ours is a business association. This is the second time I am risking telling you what I think. It didn't work out very well about Hugh. I doubt I will change your mind here."

"Is that what you need from me - to change my mind?"

Brand ignored her query.

"Something strange is going on here. I know what it looks like and I am making no claims. I am not crazy, and I don't believe in ghosts. To me, this is a security issue, nothing more."

Madison cut in with a trace of understanding and even agreement in her tone.

"You have to understand I want to believe you. I can't help thinking the footsteps and the doors slamming last night were real. I don't know what caused the sounds, but we found nothing. You even searched a creepy old attic in the dark. Nothing was there.

"Maybe all of this is getting to you. How do you know this old house, the storm, being trapped on this island, and what you think you are hearing isn't stirring up some latent PTSD issue from your past life? Can you be sure you aren't having a form of combat related flashbacks and are seeing things?"

Brand laughed suddenly, causing Madison a start.

"Sorry," he said with a shake of his head.

Madison slapped him on the arm, involuntarily smiling at his display of good humor.

"You scared me, you dick," she chided him good naturedly. "What's so funny?"

"No one has ever questioned my sanity to my face. The combat-related PTSD thing is unlikely because I was never in combat. I was a weekend warrior in the Texas Army National Guard with no combat experience."

"I thought all of the Sovereign guys were ex-SEALs."

"Most are. I am a regular guy who made the cut."

"So, you are no super trooper baddass warrior?"

He grimaced at the familiar barb.

"Afraid not."

"You are not helping your case. In fact, I am more worried than I was before. Why is Riser risking my life with an underqualified bodyguard?"

Brand frowned. He didn't like her questioning his credibility. He measured his words with difficulty.

"Another example of why I don't discuss my personal life."

Brand leaned in closer to her. His demeanor became still and serious. She could not mistake the strength of his reaction to her words.

"You are not the first one to doubt me. I heard it continually from the day I joined Sovereign until I shut them up by passing their tests and defeated the tactics they used to excise the posers and the fakers. I am here because Riser trusts me and knows I am capable.

"Madison, you don't know me. You have no clue what brought me to this place in mine and your life. I hope you never have to learn it. Until we can get off this island, I will do my job. This isn't a fucking popularity contest for me. I don't need your approval."

His manner more than his words silenced Madison. She had never before experienced this type of rough candor. To her surprise, she was less offended by his familiar and divisive comments than she was unsure how to get past her words to him. It struck her as odd she cared about hurting his feelings. She reminded herself he was a hired man. The reminder fell hollow upon the truth of her connection with him.

He seemed to recognize her inner turmoil.

"Besides," he added with unexpected humor. "Who's going to cook for you? I saw you get seconds on the chicken."

Madison smiled.

It comforted her that he made the effort to soften his words to her. He was not cruel or self-absorbed. He accepted her criticism without an overly angry response. He didn't hurl a personal insult in return for her blunt reaction to his military experience. She couldn't help liking him. He had an earthy way about him, in both his confidence in himself and his guileless sense of humor. Her father had noticed it on the plane, and she saw it now. Her doubts in his ability still plagued her, but she decided to reserve her opinion on his skill and experience for now.

"Sorry for the doubts," she said. "You are right about there being something strange going on. I hope it is not as serious as you say, but this is a spooky place, and we are trapped here for who knows how long."

Brand sensed she was attempting to placate him but let it pass. He sensed he could not convince her of anything. He committed himself to doing his job, no matter what she thought about him.

He leaned back to rise from the bed.

She put a hand on his wrist, pulling him closer to her.

He smelled her perfume and her womanhood. He would not admit to himself how badly he wanted her. Instead, he gently removed her hand from his wrist.

"Too many cameras around," he said huskily with a sweeping look around the room.

She reluctantly nodded her agreement with his observation, although her expression reflected a numb acceptance. Did he feel no attraction for her? He seemed concerned only with the dangers associated with the act. Although he once again snubbed her advances, she was impressed by his unique personality. She had never met anyone like him

11

BEATRICE AWOKE FROM A NIGHTMARE. in the dream something chased her down a dark endless hallway. She dared not look behind her for fear of slowing down or encouraging the unknown pursuer to strengthen the chase.

She was frustrated at the slow gait she was making to escape. No matter how hard she pushed, her legs would not move her to a full sprint. She could muster no more than a terrifyingly slow jog. She sensed the pursuer gaining rapidly upon her. Her body stiffened with chill bumps as she realized escape was impossible.

She felt a cold hand on her shoulder. She turned. Carson Brand gripped her shoulder in a clawed hand. His eyes were two dead black holes in his face.

She shook her head attempting to shake off the horror of the dream. She rolled over in the bed towards Hugh. She was alone, the storm raging outside the windows. The room shook with sparks of lightning and loud booms of thunder close on the heels of the flashes.

Where was Hugh?

She stood from the bed, pulling her wrap from the chair next to her. She pulled the wrap tightly around her and tied the pulls with a gesture.

A thunderclap made her jump. She didn't want to cry but she doubted she could prevent it. She was helpless in the horrible dream, the storm, the weird events of the past two days - and Hugh was missing.

Hot tears dripped onto her cold cheeks.

She moved to the bathroom. She flipped the light switch. The light did not respond.

"Shit," she cried to herself.

Add no electricity to the list.

"Hugh, are you here?"

No response.

She left the bathroom and headed for the big double doors to the hallway beyond. She hesitated with her hand on the knob as she screwed up her courage. She did not know why she was so frightened. She reasoned it was the dream. It was horrible. Anyone would feel weird after that. Add the storm and the house and the rest and she would expect nothing else from anyone.

She turned the handle and the door swung in. The hall was empty.

She made her way to the kitchen. Hugh might have gotten up for a snack or coffee. Who could sleep through this storm?

The kitchen was empty.

She moved beyond the kitchen through the entryway to the living room. The fires had burned down to glowing embers. The large room was too dark to make out anything clearly beyond the limited area where the kitchen windows allowed lightning flashes through.

She decided to wait for the next lightering flash to illuminate the living room. She leaned against the door frame as she waited. Although she knew it would come, she still started at the bright flash. The lightning bolt was one of those comprised of more than one strike. The resulting flash lasted longer than the normal instant spark of light.

She cowered against the doorframe as she saw Hugh near the opposite wall in the grasp of a huge dark shadow being. Hugh was naked and seemed to be hanging limply in the dark creature's grasp.

Bea screamed and fell to the floor in a dead faint.

Brand jumped from the settee. Madison moved slowly, sleep slow to leave her.

"Was that a scream?" she asked, her voice thick with fading slumber.

"Yeah," Brand replied as he pulled on his pants. "Get up. I don't want you out of my sight."

Madison was fully awake now and jumped from the bed as her senses gathered around her.

"Beatrice," she said as she dressed quickly.

Brand collected the Sig and moved to the door. He waited impatiently until Madison joined him before opening the door, then made his way to the lower floor. He found Beatrice on the floor near the kitchen doorway to the living room. The room was empty.

Madison shook her awake.

"Beatrice," she cried. "Wake up."

"It killed Hugh," Bea cried with a wail.

"Where is Hugh?" Brand asked tightly.

Bea looked reluctantly towards the wall where she had seen him held off the ground by the dark shape.

"He was there," she said pointing at the spot.

Brand moved to the place she indicated. He saw nothing to suggest anyone had been there.

There was nothing on the floor, no personal items around. Brand moved into the foyer. It was empty as were the stairs.

Brand ran to the lower suite. He pushed the doors open. Hugh was asleep in the bed, his back to the door. Brand moved to the bed and shook Hugh. He moved groggily at the disturbance.

"What the…?"

He recognized Brand and grew annoyed.

"What are you doing in my room?"

"Didn't you hear your girlfriend scream?"

"Bea?"

"Do you see her here?"

Hugh jumped out of bed, naked.

Brand couldn't help seeing the man was packing some firepower. He averted his gaze.

"She's in the living room. Get dressed."

Brand left him and returned to the girls.

"Hugh was in bed," he told Beatrice.

"I saw him there," she argued, pointing at the far wall. "Some dark thing held him off the ground. The thing was huge."

Brand eyed her seriously.

"What did it look like?"

"It had no real shape. I guess it was kind of like a man, but more like a shadow. It was huge. It held Hugh like a doll."

Hugh rushed to her side.

"Are you okay BB?"

Brand and Madison exchanged looks at the pet name.

"I'm fine baby. Are you hurt?"

"Why would I be hurt?"

"I saw you and…that thing looked like…I thought you were dead."

Hugh pulled Bea into his arms.

"It was a dream BB. Everything is fine. Let me take you back to bed."

He eyed Brand angrily.

"All of this ghost talk is driving us all bat shit. Some of us better cool his shit before it gets him into deeper shit."

Brand considered the man and the threat. He was near the end of his patience with him and his casual threats and smart-ass side remarks.

Madison watched the two men curiously. She was surprised Brand seemed unafraid, nor did he appear threatened by Hugh. The man was bigger, more muscular, and seemed more aggressive, but Brand registered no sign any of that concerned or intimidated him. Conversely, Brand made no protest or counter-threat to defend himself or his status as an equal male, a reaction she had witnessed frequently amongst men.

She suspected Hugh also noticed the lack of concern at his veiled threat. To her estimation Hugh seemed like a man who took it for granted other men occupied secondary roles while in his presence. Whether it was his size or his manner, he placed great stock in his power over the men in his sphere of influence. It annoyed him Brand did not react as expected.

Madison dreaded a confrontation between these two. Her primary concern was the unnecessary conflict sure to cause strife within their group. The lesser worry was the bigger Hugh might hurt Brand. He appeared the more powerful of the two. It was difficult to imagine Brand prevailing against him.

Her memory of Brand's insouciance at the party returned. Was he that confident or just oblivious of the threat Hugh represented?

Hugh led Bea back to their room.

Brand looked at Madison vacantly as he worked at his own thoughts. She watched him patiently, waiting for his conclusions about Bea's tale.

Lighting flashed and thunder rumbled. The lag between light and sound seemed to indicate the storm's path receding.

"Some nightmare," he said to her.

"No kidding. Do you think that is all it was?"

Brand grunted at the question.

He wasn't about to be tricked into admitting she was seeing the same dark figure he had seen.

"What else could it be other than a dream?" he asked.

"Her story sounds similar to what you say you saw. I thought you might see a connection."

"She heard my story, and she had a dream about it. A dark presence holding Hugh in the air is a dream. There is no other explanation worth considering."

Madison nodded. She stared at the far wall as she tried to picture what Bea said she witnessed.

"Let's get back to the room," he urged her. The electricity is off, and I don't feel like tracking down the breaker panel right now."

They climbed the stairs and returned to their room in silence.

<h1 style="text-align:center">12</h1>

BRAND CLIMBED OUT OF BED AT FIRST light. The room was freezing cold. Madison had convinced him to sleep in the bed with her. He rekindled the fire in their bedroom fireplace, throwing two more billets on the coals. He fanned the coals until thin tendrils of smoke drifted lazily from under the kindling. He dressed fully and pulled on his jacket.

He was unable to see outside through the large glass doors. His view was obscured by an ice coating on the panes. He opened the door a crack and looked upon a world of frost and ice. The early sky was gray over the lake which reflected the color of an old bruise. There wasn't a whisper of wind and the world outside was silent. He closed the door carefully and returned to the fire. He warmed himself near hungry flames growing steadily as the billets surrendered to the heat of the coals.

He turned at the sound of the rustling of bedding behind him.

Madison pulled a pillow under her head.

"It's cold in here," she complained with a yawn.

"The fire will heat up soon. Stay in bed until it warms up in here."

"The best way to warm up is mutual body heat," she advised him.

"I've heard that," he agreed. "I'll go downstairs and crank up the fires for the others. Are you hungry?"

"I am," she replied with disappointment. "I'll be down in a minute."

Brand left the room, closing the door carefully. He checked the holstered Sig in his pants before moving down the hall where he climbed the stairs to the third floor. He arrived at the attic door and tested the knob. It turned in his hand and the door opened easily.

He entered and climbed the stairs. Although higher above the living areas of the house, the attic was freezing cold. He rubbed his hands on his pants legs to maintain his circulation as he approached the cleared alter on the floor.

It seemed the Dark Man spent most of his time in the attic. The pentagram symbol and the wooden box required more scrutiny.

He searched the darkness beyond the flooring as he approached the cleared space. He saw, and more importantly, heard nothing beyond the reach of the sparse light from the window above him. There was no wind stirring outside to cover any noise made nearby.

He stopped at the edge of the stacked junk creating the perimeter. The wooden box was the first thing he noticed. It remained where Bea had returned it. However, a strange item drew his attention. A lock of hair bound with a faded blue ribbon lay in the center of the symbol. Next to it was a kitchen knife from the kitchen knife block, the tip jammed into the floor at the center of the symbol. In the dim light, the hair was the same color as Bea's.

Brand stepped into the circle and with a significant effort, pulled the knife free. It was imbedded more than an inch into the flooring. The strength necessary to sink the knife point so deep seemed impossible. There were no hammer marks on the handle to hint at the knife being driven into the wood with force. The flooring was not rotten or damaged other than where the knife had penetrated.

Brand collected the lock of hair. He left down the attic stairs and carefully closed the door. He descended the main stairs and entered the cold kitchen, where he restored the knife to the block. He stoked the fires in the living room and kitchen.

He had breakfast well underway when the others joined him.

Madison took her place beside him at the stove, watching him prepare bacon and potatoes in a cast iron skillet. She leaned against him, humming her approval as his body heat heated her chilled flesh.

"You are so warm," she said.

"My ex used to call me a biological blast furnace," he said as he turned the bacon.

He enjoyed the warmth of her body against his and leaned into her slightly. She returned the pressure.

"For warmth," she said quietly in his ear, referencing her earlier comment about body heat.

"For warmth," he agreed.

Hugh and Bea entered, staying across the kitchen from them. Both appeared to have gained little sleep.

"Coffee is about ready," Brand announced, pointing at the pot on the stove with a fork dripping bacon grease.

Madison separated from their comfortable pose and gathered coffee cups from the drying rack near the sink. She filled the cups, handing them out to each of them.

Brand sipped steaming coffee, surveying Hugh and Bea over the coffee cup rim. He indicated the countertop near the couple.

"Is that your hair?" he asked Bea.

She looked confused then spun around until she found the lock of hair wrapped in the blue ribbon.

She lifted it to eye level. When she recognized it as her hair, she dropped it onto the countertop.

"It is," she replied. "Where did you get that?"

"I found it in the attic this morning."

All three registered confusion.

"Why were you in the attic?" Hugh asked pointedly.

"Not important," Brand said. "Bea, that lock of hair wrapped in a blue ribbon and one of the butcher knives in that knife block were inside the pentagram symbol on the floor up there."

"What does that mean?" Hugh asked with heat.

"Not sure," Brand replied as if he failed to recognize Hugh's show of temper. "It is odd, though."

Brand returned his attention to the bacon and potatoes. He pulled four plates from the cupboard and filled one. He handed it to Madison before filling a plate for himself. He went to the living room where he took a place before the fire.

Madison sat beside him as he shoveled a fork full of potatoes into his mouth. He wiped his mouth with a napkin and bit into a strip of bacon.

"Why did you go into the attic?" she asked him in a faint voice.

"Just doing my job."

"Brand."

He continued eating but made no other reply to her question.

The others ate breakfast in the kitchen. Their conversation was heard as no more than faint murmurs, their words failing to reach Brand and Madison.

In the kitchen Bea's plate remained untouched before her. Hugh chewed a strip of bacon as he watched her closely.

"Why would a lock of my hair be on a satanic alter?"

Her voice was hushed but urgent.

"He said it was. How do you know he didn't make it up?"

"Why would he?"

"What do you know about him, BB? I don't trust him. He is a nutjob with a gun. He is probably a right-wing terrorist. Most of those Texas assholes are."

"When did he have the opportunity to cut off my hair?"

"He was kneeling over you when I arrived last night."

"Wasn't Madison with him?"

"She might be in on it," he said with a conspiratorial look around the kitchen.

"What are you talking about?"

"I know she is your friend and all. She brought this guy here. Who knows what kind of control he has over her?"

Bea looked at the lock of her hair with the blue ribbon. Her eyes widened in fear. How did someone cut a lock of her hair without her knowledge? She addressed his question.

"Could anyone have that kind of power over someone else?"

Hugh shrugged innocently.

"I'm just looking at the facts, Bea. It obviously wasn't some ghostly presence running around cutting hair and scaring the shit out of everyone."

The memory of her nightmare challenged his reasoning. She shook her head, refusing to mention her nightmare, or vision, or whatever it was.

"You're right, she said uncertainly. We've been here since before they arrived. None of this happened until they showed up. The only question I have is who took those pictures of me…us?"

"We have had a camera around for most of our fun," Hugh replied with playful humor. "Someone could have gotten hold of our videos somehow. We never close windows or doors. Besides, that is a different matter. This shit with cutting your hair and an asshole with a gun is not harmless fun."

"Shhh," Bea warned him with a guilty look around. "They may hear you."

"I don't care if they do. I've had about enough of that guy. I don't think he comes from money at all. I believe Madison found him on the street and brought him along to save face with you."

"She would do that," Bea agreed with a suspicious narrowing of her eyes. "She has always been jealous of me. Her father is the first in her family with money. My family is old money. The more I think about it the more I think she would stoop to anything to make herself look good."

"I advise caution," Hugh said conspiratorially. "Now that you know your competition, don't let on you have figured them out. Stay with the program and you will have the last laugh, just like we discussed. Our biggest concern is that Carson doesn't ruin everything we have planned."

Bea nodded mutely. She had already said too much.

13

RISER ANSWERED THE PHONE ON HIS desk. Outside the wall-to-wall windows of his office, downtown Bethesda basked in the coppery hue of a fading sunset. He cursed the early evenings of daylight savings time. He also cursed Carson Brand, for only he could elicit an unscheduled call from Sabastian Giles.

"Yes sir," Riser said brightly into the phone, expecting yet another of his operators was banished from service to the billionaire.

"We have a problem," Giles said without preamble. "I have lost contact with my daughter and your man. I need your help."

"I need more details. Did one of my men make off with your daughter?"

"No," Giles said. "Nothing like that. Madison's best friend, Beatrice McDermott, invited Mads to an old house on an island in northern Michigan. It is called Mackinac Island. They lost phone service, and I can't get a plane into the airport there. A bad storm is preventing all access to the island."

"Why is one of my men with her instead of securing you?"

"I talked him into it," Giles admitted with a chuckle. "I'm sure everything is just fine. I just don't like not being able to reach Mads. Can you help me?"

Of course, I would like to help, Sabastian. What would you like me to do?"

"I don't know. You are the expert here. Get in contact with your man, or maybe fly a helicopter, or sail an icebreaker there. Like I said, I doubt it is a big deal but...you heard about the ship, didn't you?"

"I heard it sunk."

"It did."

"Even a McDermott can't sink an island," Riser joked.

Giles was silent.

"I'll see what I can do," Riser assured the billionaire.

He was about to hang up when he made a request of the billionaire.

"Sebastian?"

"Dick?"

"It's a minor thing, but would you mind checking with me before reassigning one of my men?"

The phone went dead.

Riser pressed the intercom button on his desk phone.

"Yes, Mr. Riser," his executive assistant's voice came through the speaker.

"Dorothy, is Conolly on an Op?"

"No sir. He is on premises. Do you want me to get him for you?"

"Please."

Riser occupied the next few minutes familiarizing himself with the island and the threatening weather patterns. The internet was alive with 'Storm of the Century' talk for the region.

"Perfect," Riser said to himself.

He located the island on a map then contacted his pilot. A short conversation with the pilot ended with his promise to be ready to arrange the details of a tentative flight plan. Riser cautioned the pilot they might have to fly in hazardous weather. The pilot was not enthusiastic but agreed to do what he safely could.

When it came to tactical operations, Riser never left travel details to his staff. Part of his job as a leader was to plan and execute the Op. He alone knew the nuances of operational details. He alone worked those details.

Conolly walked into his office.

"What's up, Chief?" he asked, taking a seat before Riser.

"One of our men is off task. We need to intervene."

"I heard," Conolly said cynically. "I hope this wraps up your experiment with the new guy. I told you he would be an embarrassment to you and the company."

Riser had trouble hiding his surprise that the news of Brand's deviation from the mission was already public knowledge, even if only within the company.

"I don't need the narrative, Mac. I need you to pick a man. Both of you stay close so we can depart on short notice."

Conolly shook his head in disbelief at his boss' stubborn defense of the Nasty Guard Guy.

"Yes sir. I'll bring Williams. He's our best."

"Mac," Riser said wearily. "I need your mind clear on this one. No vendettas or funny business. I know about the shit you two have been pulling on the new guy."

"The weekend warrior screwed the pooch. That is not narrative. That is a situation," Conolly said, throwing a leg over the chair arm. "Besides, it's just a little rookie hazing. You don't need to play papa bear to the Weekend Warrior – unless you think you do."

Riser shook his head sadly.

"It's not his fault. Can you blame him for following that hot daughter of Sabastian Giles to a remote island in northern Michigan?"

"You didn't assign him?"

"The client did."

"I guess it's hard to argue with a billionaire."

"Tell me about it. He wants me to extract her during the storm of the century predicted to be big enough to sock us all into a winter wonderland."

"You want us on location for when the weather allows an exfill?"

"Nah. It's not combat. We don't go to DefCon One because some rich girl decides to have a winter getaway with one of our operators. You may not have a high opinion of Mr. Brand…"

"Nope."

"I get it, Mac. He'll be okay locked away with a beautiful woman for a few days. He is in deeper shit with me than he could possibly be in wherever he is now."

"Do you believe that?"

"Don't you have something better to do than bust my balls about the new guy?"

"Nope."

"Get out of my office, alert Williams, and be ready if we have to move."

"Aye, sir."

Conolly rose, leaving the room without further comment.

He was relieved Riser hadn't queried him about how he happened to know about the rookie wandering off the reservation. Conolly let it slip accidently. Of everything Riser said, one point was gospel. Conolly needed to control his hatred for the new guy. It almost got him in trouble. His orders came from a higher authority than Riser and Sovereign Services. He didn't want to risk alerting Riser or losing the giant payday for the rookie's head.

He found Williams in the ready room, eating ramen noodles from a clear bowl.

"Will," he said.

"What's up Mac."

"We are on deck to pick up the rookie and the girl."

"I thought they were handled…"

"Shut your mouth," Conolly snapped. "The walls have ears here. We have to go through the motions."

"Sorry, Mac. I was confused that the plans might have changed when you said we were going after them."

Conolly moved in close to Williams. He spoke close to his ear in a hoarse whisper.

"This is a big payday, Will. We will start our own agency with the seed money we will earn. This ends only one way for the kid and the girl."

Conolly straightened as Williams watched him, nodding his understanding.

"Clear," he said.

"Good. Organize your shit for departure. We are on stand down until Riser says so."

"Roger that."

14

BRAND SPLIT WHAT REMAINED OF THE wood pile stacked behind the house. He had no sooner arranged the logs against the house than the stillness of the previous few hours gave way to a far-off moaning in the trees. The sound emanated from the windward side of the house. With a crash of the trees on his side of the house, the storm bent the trees nearby to the ground and the violent weather front bashed into the side of the house. The freezing air roiled around the big house like churning flood waters, jerking the wheelbarrow from his hands.

In that first blast the temperature dropped what felt to Brand like a dozen degrees. The storm savaged the island as it rushed south from the northern reaches of Canada like an out-of-control freight train.

Brand shuttled as much of the firewood onto the kitchen floor as he could. Wind gusts punished him for his temerity in defying it's might. With most of the billets inside, he fled the cutting wind and shouldered the door closed against the violent conditions outside.

He rubbed his limbs, warming them against the sudden temperature drop. Leaves, branches, and debris struck the house in eddies and waves. The multiple impacts popped against the windows like a crackling string of firecrackers on new year's eve.

Madison entered the kitchen from the living room.

"It's getting bad?" she asked.

"Yeah," he replied. "We are going nowhere soon. This is all that's left of the firewood. I suggest we all camp out in one room to conserve our fuel."

"I'm not sure that will go over," she said.

"Why not?"

"Beatrice is acting weird towards me. I guess that lock of hair got to her."

From the kitchen floor, Brand collected as much wood as he could, carrying it into the living room. When he returned for the next load Madison stopped him. She leaned close so he could hear her whisper.

"Something is wrong. Both of them are being short with me. Beatrice has ignored me since breakfast. Hugh won't look at me or talk to me."

"Let me get this wood moved and we'll talk about it."

Brand carried the remainder of the billets into the living room, stacking it before the main fireplace. He brushed off his clothes, taking a seat on the settee.

Madison joined him, her legs folded under her.

"The fun has been completely sucked out of this place, Brand. They are acting like we are the enemy. You are of particular interest to them. The gun is a huge bone of contention. I think I should come clean about your being a bodyguard."

"Maybe," he replied.

"You disagree?"

"With the timing. Hugh is an unknown quantity here. I am convinced there is more to him than he is admitting."

Madison shook her head at the prospect of another conspiracy theory from Brand.

He recognized her skepticism.

"Do you want to talk about it, or do you want me to keep my thoughts to myself?"

She shrugged helplessly.

"He seems pretty knowledgeable about knife wounds. He disappears for hours on end with no explanation. None of the weirdness going on here seems to be scaring him at all. I already told you about his actions at the party and how he carries himself. There is too much here to poo poo off as shadows in the dark."

Madison looked him in the eyes.

"Do you still believe his motivation is my...my family's money?"

"I do."

"Okay. Let's talk about the depth of this plot against me."

Brand leaned back in his seat.

Madison shook her head, frustrated with Brand. Her back straightened as she broke down her response to his fantasy laden theories.

"According to your theory, Hugh plotted to get me onto a remote island in Michigan. He assembled a ruse complete with ghosts, dire warnings, failed cell towers, and the storm of the century. What is the rest of the plan? Am I to be held for ransom until the storm clears? How will he transmit his demands? How will he collect the money and get off the island?"

Brand listened without interrupting her. She was oversimplifying it, but it helped his understanding to hear her ideas aired openly. Maybe he could glean an inkling of the true plot in the process.

"I don't think he arranged the storm," Brand said carefully, so she would understand he was working with her towards an answer, not belittling her. "But I am certain he picked a time when the island was for all intents, empty. If anything, the downed cell tower works in our favor. This Dark Man is a mystery. Is he part of the plan or a part of the house's past?"

"I thought you didn't believe in ghosts."

"I don't. If he is a ghost, he is also a Peeping Tom. That's what isn't adding up. If the Dark Man is part of the plot, the photos and the lock of hair seem like unnecessary complications."

Madison nodded with his reasoning.

Brand grinned at her.

"I see why Beatrice is so enamored with Hugh. The man is hung like a mule."

"What are you talking about?"

"He was naked when I woke him up last night. Maybe he figured out the key to Beatrice's heart and used it to gain her trust."

"It's a big key, you say."

"Oh yeah."

"Impressively so?"

"Terrifyingly so."

"It scares you?"

"It makes me want to cross my legs when he is around."

Madison hit Brand playfully on the shoulder.

"Enough talk about another man's cock."

"You sure?"

"Shut up."

"We are making jokes, but if any of what we suspect is true, we could be in some trouble. What about their change in attitude towards us? You mentioned that, not me."

"I'm certain of the change in them," she confirmed. "Let's keep our eyes opened. With some proof, I might be persuaded to believe some of what you say."

Brand was silent for a moment.

Finally he said, "I need you to stay close. I hope you are right, and this is just some Halloween prank. If it isn't, this could be bigger than we think."

15

RISER CALLED GILES WITH THE NEWS. An early Canadian Arctic Storm had struck the island. The saturated ground and foliage would freeze. The gale force winds will make a boat or air extraction impossible for the next several days. The storm was huge, threatening to affect the weather even hundreds of miles away on the east coast. There was no way to reach Madison and Brand until the storm passed.

Giles stubbornly rejected the forecast. It was difficult to imagine a blizzard while sitting on sunny Malibu Beach with temperatures in the mid-eighties. Finally, after several back and forths with his security contractor, Giles accepted Riser's news under a bitter surrender.

Riser ended the call with the promise to send help to the island as soon as it was possible to do so.

Giles hung up on him again.

Riser's Lear rocketed off the runway, the reds, and golds of the rising Sun falling away behind. Ahead of the jet, a roiling mass of tortuous weather paralyzed much of the upper

Midwest in its frozen grip. Following the pre-flight briefing, Riser, Conolly, and Williams travelled in silence, the aircraft buffeted by unpredictable gusts ahead of the storm mass.

Per the pilot's cautious recommendation, they were bound for Gaylord Regional Airport. It was as close to the towering storm front as they dared fly.

The first plan was to hold tight until the weather cleared enough to fly rotor wing to Pellston, the closest airport south of the island. The extended forecast revealed the storm would not reach its peak in Gaylord for another day or more. Riser reasoned by the time they were cleared to fly from Gaylord to Pellston, they may as well have flown directly to Mackinac Island. That meant losing as much as a full day.

Instead, Riser leased a car and they drove the few hours through severe weather to Pellston. The small regional airport would clear soon after the storm passed beyond the island, saving them several hours, or as much as a day.

They arrived at Pellston as the brunt of the storm struck the small town with the force of a bomb. Radar showed a giant storm footprint. Giles predicted it would last days, not hours as the weather experts were predicting. They would have a long wait before they were cleared to fly to the island.

After settling into one of the few hotels in town, Giles bought dinner for he and his men at a locally popular eatery. Locals filled the small café. They cast curious glances at the three hard-looking men at the table near one of the large windows. They weren't unaccustomed to strangers, just to strangers so late in the season.

The waitress took their order with a sprinkling of poorly concealed casual questions about their business there. Her undisguised curiosity yielded no satisfying results.

"We are going to be here a while," Conolly said in a low voice. "This place is too Podunk to provide any distraction while we wait."

Williams looked around the café. He was certain there weren't many blacks in town, based upon the interest he was creating. He said nothing, but he made it clear he wasn't a fan of the townspeople either.

Riser patted Conolly's shoulder gently.

"This is a job, Mac. Remember that."

"An unnecessary job with little upside," Conolly said. "Giles will ultimately remember this as an S.S. failure, not his error."

Riser gave his full attention to his coffee. For months Conolly had become increasingly critical of him and how he ran his organization. Mac was the first man hired and had seen much the others had not. As with any new business, growing pains and adaptation to an industry, can be awkward. Mac had seen it all, good and bad. The company was past its growing pains, but it seemed in Conolly's estimation, some of Riser's credibility had also passed. Mac considered himself a peer, not a subordinate.

'Familiarity breeds contempt,' Riser mused ruefully.

Williams watched Riser's reaction to Conolly's observations.

With pathos he added, "That snot nosed leg needs to go, sir. There is no other solution."

The waitress approached carrying three plates piled high with steaming food.

In turn, Riser eyed both of his men with a dangerous look.

"I suggest we drop it and eat."

The waitress set the plates before the men.

"Can I get you boys anything else?"

"No thanks," Riser replied with a professional smile.

16

SNOW FELL HEAVILY. Despite Brand's advice, Hugh and Beatrice refused to stay in the living room with them. Brand carried the remainder of the wood from outside into the living room, where he arranged a sleeping palette near the fireplace.

Initially, Brand had refused to share the chopped wood with the other two, but Madison insisted. Under threat of nameless reprisals from her, he allowed them to take no more than two armfuls to their room.

As a moaning wind moved low hanging clouds over heavy snowfall, darkness fell earlier than usual. Neither of them was accustomed to the conditions they faced.

For Madison, New York could yield harsh weather, but the lights and bustle never waned, lessening the noticeable ferocity of winter storms. Brand's home in Texas rarely saw forbidding winter weather. Snow was a novelty. Most winters required no more than a warm hoody and an extra pair of socks.

If not for the strange noises the house made as it groaned and creaked against the relentless storm, and the awkward actions of their sullen companions, Brand would have enjoyed the unfamiliar experience the storm provided. He perceived no real danger. They had food and fuel for the fire.

He glanced at Madison who studied the flames dancing in the fireplace. He had to admit trapped in a storm with a beautiful woman was a bonus no matter the conditions.

The threat of the Dark Man was all but forgotten in the face of the preeminent hazard the weather represented. The storm pummeled the house with a din they could not ignore or relegate to background noise. The storm was loud, occupying most of their attention.

From their snug bed before the large fireplace, he could easily watch all sides of the room and detect anyone descending the staircase beyond. He kept the Sig close but out of sight. Their position was tactically advantageous. He saw only one drawback. There were no doors he could close to limit access to the large room. He would have to remain alert, getting little sleep so long as the storm lasted. He planned to maintain a night watch, sleeping during the day as he could.

He crawled under the layers of blankets and bedspreads that covered the bottom pad making up their sleep palette. Madison snuggled against him, warming her cold hands against his chest under his shirt. She rubbed her hands against him for a time before finally falling asleep.

For a long while Brand tried to ignore his need for her. After failing to master his desire, he moved slowly from under the covers. He took a seat before the fire, poking the embers to get as much heat from them as he could before adding more fuel.

Madison was difficult to resist. He was confident she wanted him too. The urge to join her under the covers, to give into his deepest longings, tortured him. His imagination provided him endless pleasures with her. He stood, moving away from the fire's warmth. Maybe time in the cold darkness would calm his urges.

Beatrice gasped. Although she could hardly catch her breath, she felt a warm comfort spreading throughout her body. In a flood of passion, her fears and doubts fled from her.

Hugh rolled off of her, panting with his exertion. He rested for a moment before standing from the bed and moving towards the roaring fireplace.

Beatrice admired his naked backside as he moved. He lifted another log.

"Shouldn't we conserve those?" she asked breathlessly.

"I'm a little cold. Once I get to sleep, I don't mind the chill."

She let her head sag, resting upon her pillow.

Hugh knew what was best. He was her rock, her security, her hero. She was safe with him, no matter what.

With a shower of sparks, he dropped the log into the blaze then returned to bed. He rolled himself in covers and settled in with his back to her. She crossed the space between them and pressed her breasts against his back. She coiled her right arm around him, feeling his muscular chest. She felt him relax as he drifted off to sleep.

Beatrice opened her eyes. The fire had burned down to a steady flame, licking at the blackened saddle backed logs atop a soft hot bed of ashes. Beatrice watched the fire with a contented smile. The storm raged outside, but she was cozy in her protected lair. The glow of the flames danced on the walls. The crackle of burning wood comforted her. She moved upward towards the towering ornate headboard, supporting her head on a folded pillow.

She looked aside where Hugh slept. He was still and she heard none of his typical light snoring. She concluded he was deeply asleep.

She dragged a finger across his round shoulder and down his arm. His skin was cold. No wonder he wanted a large fire. He was very cold natured. She rolled towards him, pressing her body against him. His entire body was cold. He lay stiffly against her.

She sat up in bed, pulling him towards her.

He flopped onto his back. His eyes were black holes in his face, staring unseeingly into the unknown. She screamed and leaped to her feet. A powerful force pressed her back onto the bed, jamming her face into the bedding. She felt a heavy weight atop her, forcing her roughly into the mattress and the rough bedding.

She turned her head to see who or what was atop her. She felt a hard blow across her cheek. The brief glimpse revealed a huge dark presence. She knew instinctively it was the dark presence she had seen in the living room, clutching Hugh like a rag doll. Now it had her.

She felt her legs pulled apart. She screamed, but the mattress muffled her cries. She struggled but the dark force was powerful. She managed to turn her head to the side. She screamed again, louder this time.

Brand was beside the waning fire, his passions at bay. He was about to return to the palette when he heard Beatrice scream. He jerked his head towards the sound. Leaping to his feet, he sprinted through the kitchen into the foyer. He turned down the hallway and arrived at the closed doors to Bea and Hugh's suite. He turned the handle, but the door would not open. It was locked from the inside.

He heard more muffled screams inside the room. He tested the doors with a shoulder. They moved but did not open. He backed to the far wall then charged the doors. He hit them with his shoulder at the center point where the doors met. They broke with a splintering of the door panel near the knob.

The doors sagged but clung to one another by the latch and knob catch. Through the narrow space between the damaged doors, he could see nothing inside, but he heard a struggle. He backed once more to the wall and rushed the door again. This time the door buckled. The Dark Man was on the bed, Beatrice naked under him.

The Dark Man turned his head, looking at Brand with black eyes. Brand rushed him, launching himself at the huge figure. He struck the Dark Man with all his weight. The impetus of Brand's charge knocked him off of Beatrice. She screamed and pressed herself against the headboard, her eyes red, streaming with tears as she watched the struggle.

The Dark Man struck Brand solidly in the face. Brand staggered from the blow. He felt a familiar rage warm his belly. A euphoria of blood lust gave him a lightheaded thrill.

He rushed the Dark Man with an angry sound in his throat. He struck the Dark Man hard in the face.

The giant recoiled.

Brand struck him three more times hard in the face. The Dark Man seemed confused at the punishment he was taking from the smaller man. He shoved Brand from him, knocking him to the floor. He turned and ran towards the tall glass doors leading to the outside patio. He hit the doors at full speed. The doors buckled under the force. The Dark Man faded into the darkness and the storm. Brand followed him, stopping in the broken doorway.

He was dressed only in boxers and a tee shirt. The cold and the storm prevented him from giving chase. He returned to the bed.

Madison had arrived after Brand. She held Beatrice, both crying as they watched him with terrified eyes.

Brand looked at Hugh. The man was dead. His eyes were black holes where they had been gouged from his skull.

"Get her dressed," Brand ordered. "And take her to the living room."

He waited with them as Madison helped Beatrice with her clothes. After replacing the broken door in the damaged frame as well as he could, Brand returned to the living room where Madison helped her friend into a chair near their palette.

"What can I do for you?" Madison asked Beatrice.

Beatrice shuddered as she cried uncontrollably. She managed to force herself to speak.

"Is Hugh dead?" she asked.

Brand nodded.

She shuddered as grief overcame her once more.

"Did he hurt you?" Madison asked gently.

"Hugh?" she blubbered

"No. The other one."

Beatrice looked at Madison then at Brand.

"I thought he was going to rape me," she said with a strange depth to her voice. "He didn't. He went through the motions, but it was like he couldn't – like he didn't have the right parts."

Brand looked at Madison.

She returned his look.

They had all seen him. It was difficult to believe what they saw was a man.

"What do you remember?" Brand asked Beatrice.

"I woke up and Hugh was ice cold. I turned him over and his eyes were…"

Madison hugged her tightly.

"You're safe," she assured Bea. "I've got you now."

Brand moved from them. He made a security check of the immediate area around the living room and kitchen. He checked the locks on the doors and windows. He returned to the living room and fueled the fire.

There was no sleep after that. They sat next to the fire all night, listening to the storm rage outside, trying not to think of Hugh, dead in a nearby room. Brand spent his time making coffee and stoking the fire when it waned.

Beatrice cried off and on as her thoughts wandered in and out of the horrors she saw.

Madison held her, casting frequent looks at Brand who sat stoically watching for another attack. He kept the Sig close to hand but out of sight. He didn't want to risk panicking Beatrice in her weakened state.

Night dragged on mercilessly. They yearned for daybreak, if for nothing else than at least to put another day between them and the tragedy and horror. When dawn finally lightened the frozen windows, it provided little joy, nor the relief of the cleansing light of a new day.

Brand opened the kitchen door. He looked out upon a frozen landscape ending at a hard edge against languid steely waters and a lowered sky. The chill was the type that soaked into the house and inside of one's bones. There was no fire hot enough, nor layered clothing warm enough to dispel its grip. Brand closed the door, convinced they faced hours, possibly days, of the same dismal conditions.

The girls suffered more than he under the absence of communication with the world. Despite having no cell service for days, they kept their cell phones with them. Brand likened it to a fondness for an old photo album or a useless childhood toy for which new batteries can never reanimate.

Like the girls, his idle moments returned him to thoughts of the dead man in the bedroom. He had a mental image of what might be the condition of the bedroom. He had closed the doors to the hallway, but after the Dark Man's escape, the broken exterior doors remained ajar. He had no doubt the room was a frozen crypt. His mind's eye conjured the image of an abandoned house during an apocalypse, covered in white, the corpse lying still on the bed, frozen in place.

He knew he would have to deal with the dead man sooner than later. He reasoned, if his imagination nettled him with macabre scenes, what must be in the minds of Madison and Beatrice, whose experiences with the dead were few.

He returned to the living room where Madison and Beatrice huddled together under a layered blanket nest, speaking quietly amongst themselves.

Their conversation stopped as he entered.

He stirred the fire, waiting for them to make conversation, if that was indeed their intention. He didn't wait long.

"What are we going to do about Hugh?" Beatrice asked with what seemed almost a challenge.

"I'm sorry Brand," Madison added. "We were just talking about how wrong it seemed for him just to lay in there. We need to do something. We can't just leave him there in the bed…Don't you agree?"

Brand rested on the arm of the settee. The idea of dealing with Hugh's naked frozen body seemed daunting in concept and in practice.

"Brand?" Madison urged.

Brand stood from his seat.

"I'll handle it," he said with a less than resolute tone.

He left the living room and made his way to the doors of the master suite. The doors held wearily to their frames. His assault upon them had ruined the frame and hardware for good. The space between the doors was wider at the top than at the bottom. A steady flow of cold air escaped the frigid room, freshening the hallway near the doors with an arctic chill.

Hoping for a preview to soften the shock of seeing the dead man as he imagined, Brand peered between the doors. A covering of ice obscured his view. He resigned himself to the assured morbid surprise he would have to endure when he opened the door.

With a mighty push, the doors sagged into the room, the bottom of each digging into an inch or more of ice covering the floor. Missing exterior doors exposed the room to the full force of the storm as it raged off of the lake and onto the island. Snow and ice eddied in its violation of the room. Brand moved towards the bed. He stopped short of the big wooden frame.

The bed was empty. No Hugh, and no blankets lay atop the bare mattress. The mattress was rent with a huge "X" cut into its surface. White stuffing bulged from the cuts like damaged tissue from a wound. Through the wide-open doors he had a clear view of the lower patio and the lake shore. He moved to the patio doors and surveyed the area nearby. He saw no footprints in the ice and snow. It was likely the continual snowfall could quickly blot out any trace of movement in or out of the room.

He returned to the bed, pulling a lamp loose from the wall outlet. He tugged several times on the lamp's electrical cord before it came free of the lamp.

He moved to the hallway doors and pulled them closed as best he could. Once reasonably replaced in the closed position, he looped the cord around the door handles, tying the ends tightly. He hoped the doors would hold against the elements or maybe an intruder.

He returned to the living room where the girls waited in wide-eyed dread. Their imaginations worked feverishly from their memories of the grisly scene and the horrible task he faced in the frozen room.

Brand took his place on the arm of the settee. He offered no comment. He had no reasonable explanation for what he found in the room. Likewise, he had no desire to weather the frenzy of panicked speculation sure to come from the news Hugh's body was missing. The respite would be short, but he appreciated the moment to collect his thoughts.

"What did you do with him?" Beatrice asked breathlessly. "You were so quick. Did you leave him there?"

Brand took a deep cleansing breath.

"He wasn't in the room," he said.

Beatrice screamed behind her hand.

Madison jumped at her unexpected reaction.

"He wasn't in the room?" Bea cried. "He wasn't in the room?"

The repeated words were for her own benefit, as if the admission could help her make sense of it all.

"The blankets, sheets, pillows, and the body were gone. Someone cut a big 'X' in the mattress. I found no tracks in or out of the room. The hallway doors were as I left them. No one has passed through them since we left."

"I have to see the room," Beatrice said.

"I tied the doors shut. If you want to go outside and enter the room from the patio, you can do that."

Madison remained silent during the conversation, but her face was a study of inner turmoil. Brand watched her from the corner of his eye, giving most of his attention to Beatrice.

Madison stood, moving closer to the fire. She took a seat on the hearth, watching the flames dance around and under the billets.

Brand watched her back for a moment. He looked at Beatrice, who was crying once more. Her sobs caused her shoulders to shudder, but she made no sound.

He stood. Returning to the kitchen, he put a pot of coffee on to boil. He was baffled by nearly everything he had witnessed since arriving at the old house. Nothing made sense from any experience he could conjure. Cryptic figures roving an old house, attacking with physical results; murder committed within reach of a sleeping girl; the victim disappears; and the unrelenting storm; why was this happening? Who was behind it all? Was he wrong about the supernatural?

To this last point he shook his head stubbornly. He refused to resort to superstition and voodoo theology as an explanation. He fought this "creature." It had mass. It was real. He had affected it with his attack. It could be wounded or killed, as far as Brand was concerned. He planned to do either or both when he had the opportunity.

He attended the coffee pot until the brew was ready. He returned to the girls with three fresh cups. He sat the cups on the small table near the fire. Taking his cup to his usual place, he sipped gingerly at the scalding liquid.

The girls collected their coffee and returned to their wrapped blankets.

Their desire to talk about Hugh's disappearance was plain. They seemed to struggle with a manner of broaching the subject with him. Brand offered no help. He was not willing to chat aimlessly about something he could not explain no matter his efforts. Pointless and speculative musings were not in his makeup. He needed quiet and solitude to digest his considerations. He feared muddying what he knew with fearful fillers and unsubstantiated guesses.

In the void of conversation, the storm worked its way around them, its might ebbing and flowing much like a frustrated beast, desperate to get at the cowering three within the house. Brand considered the house an adversary, in league with the forces arrayed against them.

His admiration of the deft hands which had constructed it moved him no longer. Lost upon him was the majesty of the lofty ceilings and intricate finishes within. One might as easily admire the curve and grace of the claws of a mythical beast as it descended upon them with disastrous intent.

Brand's opposition to the horrors targeting them lay within the limited means he possessed as a trained fighter, a 9mm pistol with only fifteen rounds remaining, and their ability to hold out with limited food and scant fuel to heat the house. None of them possessed winter clothes. Their phones were no more useful than the broken snowmobiles in the barn. The town was some two to three miles away. If they left the mansion the storm would finish the work started by the Dark Man.

Madison cleared her throat, drawing Brand's attention.

"I think we should try to sleep. It seems like the creature only attacks at night. Do you have a plan for tonight? Is there something we can do to protect ourselves?"

Beatrice looked at Madison curiously. She knew Brand had courage based upon his attacking the creature when it was upon her, but she didn't understand why Madison would defer to him for their safety.

Madison divined her doubts.

"Bea," she began. "Brand is one of my dad's bodyguards. He works for Sovereign. I convinced him to go along with us in our little game. That's why he has a gun."

"You think this is a little game?"

"Not now," Madison explained. "I'm talking about our boyfriend game, not this."

"Well, my boyfriend is dead, and some ghoulish creature stole his body and carried it away. I can't imagine what horrible atrocities are being done to Hugh's body. I don't appreciate the lies, Madison. We are in deeper trouble than some bodyguard can solve."

"Lies?" Madison repeated with a flaring temper. "Every time you invite me to one of these stupid outings, it ends in a catastrophe. I don't mean someone breaks a nail or wears linen after Labor Day, I'm talking about inviting me to a ship and it sinks. I'm talking about inviting me to some old, haunted house in B.F.E. where we are attacked and one of our number is murdered and carried away in the night.

"Don't even get me started about your shitty timing in bringing us to a resort island at a time when every other reasonable person has left it for the season, and we are stranded by the storm of the century. Don't lecture me about the deception I caused by telling you a cute guy is my boyfriend and it turns out he isn't."

Brand smiled despite their situation. He liked this girl.

As Madison excoriated her, Beatrice watched Brand. His grin pressed her to anger.

"Fuck you bodyguard," she said to him. "You are the hired help. You are not one of us. Do your job and keep your mouth shut."

Brand's grin evaporated. He expected some gratitude for saving her life. He believed his presence was a comfort to her. This blatant attack represented an insult he couldn't have imagined. His eyes darkened as he assessed his role.

She was right. He was the hired help, and he was not one of them. What allegiance did he have to them? What right did they have to expect his help? His responsibilities were to the father. He was not beholding to his daughter or her spoiled and overindulged friends.

Madison's anger faded as she saw Brand's sobering transformation. She guessed at what he thought. She stood and moved to him. She sat beside him, taking one of his hands in hers.

He fought the urge to shake off her grip. Instead, he watched her with a steady gaze, devoid of emotion or caring.

"Brand," she said seriously. "Don't listen to her. She is freaking out. I'm with you here. I need you now. I have gotten to know you. You are not the hired help. You are not just a bodyguard. Not to me. We are friends. That will never change. I see in you what I will never find in those who call me their friend. You care. You care about me. I see it. I care about you. I can't help it. Stay with me Carson. Stay with me Brand. Please."

Brand was surprised by her heartfelt entreaty. He didn't expect to be moved by the depth of her heartfelt admission. Her eyes conveyed warmth and genuine feeling. He believed every word she said.

His anger faded as quickly as it appeared.

"I made you a promise," he said with the difficulty of waning wounded pride. "I won't break it."

Madison nodded her gratitude.

"What about Beatrice?" she asked, knowing his answer.

Brand grinned once more.

"Fuck her. It wouldn't kill her to help out around here. If she makes some effort, we'll revisit, but I'm not holding my breath."

Madison laughed despite the gravity of their predicament.

Beatrice reacted with derision that a hired man would speak to or about her that way.

"He's kidding, Bea," she explained, her anger fading. "Inside joke. I'm sorry for the crack about the shipwreck and this place. I'm as freaked out as you are. We need to stick together."

Bea and Madison stood. They met halfway and hugged warmly.

Brand watched them from his seat. He was glad they were no longer at odds. Seeing them make up, he resolved to avoid further emotional outbursts. His duty to them was more than his job. It was a matter of honor. He wouldn't have shirked his responsibilities. The consideration of abandoning them was a satisfying fantasy he would never act upon.

As their emotions receded, Madison and Beatrice returned to their blankets.

Madison asked Brand, "Will you watch over us while we sleep for a little while?"

"No problem," he replied simply. "You are safe. Don't worry."

They snuggled under the covers, together in one another's embrace. Soon they were asleep, exhausted from fear and spent emotions.

Brand watched over them until late in the afternoon.

17

RISER, CONOLLY, AND WILLIAMS MET in
the lobby of the hotel in downtown Pellston.
The storm was severe. The snowfall was heavy
as snowplows cleared the streets. The local
radio station urged residents to stay indoors.

The pilot hired for the flight to the island
was pessimistic about a reasonable timeline for
departure. The pilot waited out the storm in
his home/office in the airport hangar where he
stored the chopper.

According to the national weather service,
the storm was an historically significant
weather event and would last at least another
48 to 72 hours before it weakened enough for
them to cross to the island.

The pilot said he was monitoring the
weather conditions and would notify Riser and
his team when they were cleared for departure.
Only then would they cross to the island and
collect Giles' daughter and Sovereign's Carson
Brand.

There was still no cell service on the island.
The few land lines connecting with permanent
residents proved fruitless in soliciting local
assistance in contacting those in the old house

at the opposite side of the island. Those few residents they contacted refused to help with casual comments about the safety of the guests in the old house. They told of party guests last seen arriving at the harbor by horse and wagon to board a chartered ferry boat for the mainland.

Much detail was provided claiming the vessel had been lucky to leave the island harbor due to the deceptively rapid speed of the storm and the high winds ahead of the front.

The idea of a party tended to dispel any concern Riser might have about a threat of danger to the castaways other than from the natural fury of the storm.

For the girls marooned there, the absence of cell service would probably be the most worrisome and frightening aspect of their stay at the house. Riser's bill for mustering his forces for an obvious fool's errand would be ponderous, even for his billionaire client.

He sat at a table in the small breakfast area of the lobby, sipping hot coffee when Conolly and Williams arrived. They helped themselves to microwave oatmeal and packaged Danishes. They made small talk, but their manner clearly demonstrated frustration at the waiting and the mission itself.

Despite his misgivings about the two, these men were his finest. They were cut from a pattern reserved for a scant few. Both were blooded warriors, tested in combat. Riser believed if he offered them the opportunity, and if it wasn't for Brand, each of them would volunteer to swim to the island, even under these forbidding conditions.

"Listen up for a second," Riser announced. "We are on stand down until this storm weakens sufficiently for our chopper to cross to the island. That means we are stuck in BFE for a couple more days. I trust you will conduct yourselves as soldiers. Leave the local men intact and the local women pure of virtue. We stay together, we eat together, and we watch each other's backs until wheels up. I don't want any trouble with a local *Barney Fife* cop who might see hassling a group of tough guys in a bar as a challenge. Am I clear?"

Conolly gave Riser an irritated look. Williams grinned at the warning. He would be lucky if he wasn't hung from a cross in the front yard of the hotel.

Finishing his second bowl of oatmeal, Conolly leaned back, locking his fingers behind his head.

"Has anyone discovered what the weekend warrior was thinking when he agreed to go off mission?"

Riser arranged his empty plate and utensils for clearing.

"The client made a last-minute change without following procedure."

"You told me that at the office, Chief," Conolly pressed. "Every man in the company knows to get approval from HQ before altering a protection contract. Your new man knew the protocol as well as any of us."

Riser watched his second in command wearily. He had already considered everything Conolly was relating. The breach of protocol was blatant and strictly prohibited. He was also aware Conolly was far from Brand's biggest fan.

"Noted, Mac. Don't take any of this personally. The job is the job. That's why I am warning you both about taking your emotions out on the locals."

"Their funeral," Williams muttered under his breath.

Asking his men not to engage a hostile local was like forbidding a hungry dog from eating raw meat on the bone. Like a pack of dogs, Riser knew his men were more likely to find trouble as a group than they might individually. That aspect of their nature was another reason Riser was there personally. He couldn't risk any more trouble in connection with the Giles account; the other reason was the obvious danger these two represented to Brand.

Although Conolly was the lone dissenting voice brave enough to face Riser on the matter, he was certain that Williams and the others, even Lansch, Brand's newest fan, held a dim view of the break in process.

"We'll talk again at dinner at 1700 hrs.," Riser said finally. "Mac, can I have a word?"

Conolly watched Riser silently as Williams left the lobby to return to his room.

"I can't have you continually challenging me in front of the men."

"It's only Williams, and I'm not challenging you, Dick. You seem to have lost focus on what we built here; what makes it work; the mistakes we made along the way."

"I'm not forgetting anything, Mac. I am not going to make the same mistakes."

"No, Dick. You are working on a whole bunch of new ones."

Riser controlled his temper with difficulty.

"Forget meeting this evening," Riser spat angrily. "We'll talk tomorrow. I'm not sure I will be able to take much more of your free and easy criticism without doing something about it."

"I'm here, Dick," Conolly said calmly. "Don't strain yourself too much. We can work this out anytime you want and in any way you want."

"Get the fuck out of my sight, Mac, before I test your resolve."

Conolly's jaw jutted forward stubbornly. He was spoiling for a fight. He resented the authority Riser believed he held over him. By Conolly's estimation, their conflict was long overdue. The prospect of the huge payday at the end of this mission assuaged his need for recompense. He felt a satisfying happiness in the knowledge that Riser thought he was calling the shots, when Conolly and Williams were using him to achieve their own separate goals. Riser was only as useful as his continued participation advanced the wishes of their new employer. After that, Conolly would deal with him.

Conolly rose and stalked from the lobby.

Riser decided to stay busy, keeping to himself until the following morning. With his growing issues with Conolly, it was going to be a trying day and a long night.

18

MADISON AWOKE WITH A START. She thought she had dreamt it, the yelling. Sleepy cobwebs slowed her reason. As they cleared, she realized the shouting was no dream. The living room was immersed in darkness, illuminated only by the low flame of the crackling fire in the fireplace, and two lamps creating small islands of light in the far corners of the large room.

She peered into the darkness towards the foyer. She identified the voice as Beatrice's, screaming frantically. Her words were almost incoherent.

"I don't care…you asshole…he'll kill us all…you can't save me!"

She heard Brand's voice only as a murmur, muffled by the wall between the foyer and the living room. To Madison his tone indicated he was trying to reason with the shrieking girl.

Madison heard a loud crash then the squeak of the large hinges on the front doors. A rush of wind and weather penetrated the warmth of the old house. She struggled to disentangle herself from the blankets coiled around her.

Finally, she was able to stand, rushing clumsily to where Brand stood at the open door.

"Beatrice," he called over the roar of the storm. "Get back here. You are safe here."

"What happened?" Madison asked, clutching herself against the cold.

"She woke up and headed towards the bathroom, or so I thought. She went into the kitchen. I followed her thinking she might do something crazy. I tried to talk to her, but she wasn't having any of it. She ran from me as I tried to comfort her. She shouted she was going to die and there was nothing I could do to save her. Then she ran into the storm."

"You have to bring her back."

"I know I do. I need you to wait here for me. Keep the door closed and locked. Don't open it until you are sure it is me, okay?"

"Fine. Just find her and bring her back, Brand. She will freeze to death."

Brand nodded, then ran into the night in the direction he had seen Beatrice flee.

Madison slammed the door against the gusting wind, ice stinging her face and arms.

Brand sprinted into the dark. He saw no sign of Beatrice. He ran as far as the top end of the drive. She was not down the driveway towards the road. He guessed she could have made her way towards the stables building. Perhaps she planned to try one of the derelict snowmobiles.

The cold chilled his wet skin as he arrived at the large sliding doors. They were securely latched. He moved towards the side door at the workshop. The door was ajar. He pulled the Sig from his beltline. There was no way to be sure the Dark Man was not hiding there.

Inside, the lofty ceilings and thin plank walls offered no protection from the cold. The thin construction blocked only rain and snow from entering. Before him, the large room was black as pitch.

Although reluctant to trap himself within the darkness, he closed the door to prevent the icy gusts of wind from chilling the room further. He listened for movement within the noisy building. Roof panels rattled and loose boards slapped noisily against the buildings framing. If Beatrice moved within the building, it was impossible to hear her over the storm's attack upon the structure.

He heard the grind of metal-on-metal to his right. He located the sound as coming from the end of the workbench, opposite the door leading to the garage area. Keeping himself close to the bench table, he crept towards the noise, his outstretched hands feeling for obstacles. He progressed nearly to the end of the bench when he again heard the metal-on-metal noise. It came from below the bench table.

He squatted low, his eyes trying to pierce the darkness for some view of what made the noise. He saw a small square of darkness within the darkness under the workbench. It was about three feet square. To his diminished view, it appeared to be an opened door. He reached a hand towards the dark square. Indeed, the dark square was an opening. He hadn't seen the door during his previous visits when he obtained tools and the wheelbarrow. Committing to search beyond the secret door was a huge gamble. Brand wasn't convinced Beatrice had entered the building nor summoned the nerve to enter a hidden doorway beneath the table. The metal sound could have been a result of the storm. Time was critical. Beatrice would not survive long in the cold dark clutches of the storm. He was chilled to his core. He was concerned how much she suffered in the cold. Did he dare commit precious time to a long chance?

He was inclined to resume his search outside. A frantic girl could just as easily have wandered into the woods. If she did, her chances for survival were much lower than they were here. If he failed to locate her after a thorough search of the grounds outside, he could always return to explore the hidden doorway.

A feminine grunt drew his attention back to the doorway. It sounded like someone tripped or stumbled in the darkness. Without further deliberation Brand stowed the pistol, then dropped to his hands and knees, climbing through the doorway. Beyond the small doorway, he entered a narrow chamber. He could tell it was narrow because when he stood, he could touch the walls on either side. Ahead, his hearing detected a region dead of acoustics, like the void near a tunnel or a hole in the ground.

He pulled the Sig from his beltline, moving forward carefully. He extended a hand before him as he shuffled forward, carefully searching the ground for terrain features. Below his feet was hard-packed earth. He moved a short distance before his leading foot lost contact with the ground. He took a knee and felt before him with an outstretched hand, locating a drop to the top of the first of a flight of stone stairs. He eased himself onto the stairs, descending slowly.

He was a half dozen steps along when a light flicked on below him. By the new light he could see the remainder of the stairs dropping away some fifteen or so feet to the dirt floor of a stone walled cellar.

The light moved away from the stairs and his way became darker, though still visible. The light came from a flashlight, held by someone ahead, searching the cellar as he or she moved. The feminine grunt he heard was Beatrice. She owned the house. It was possible she had previously explored the place, finding the hidden door and the cellar below.

Brand stowed the pistol again, wanting to avoid another hysterical display, in case he startled Beatrice. He reached the bottom of the stairs. The cellar smelled old and musty. It reminded him of the Cartel dungeon he had escaped, minus the smell of death.

He saw by the receding light the cellar contained old wooden boxes and all manner of discarded bric-a-brac from years of disuse. The dancing glow of the flashlight emanated from beyond a rough wooden doorway at the end of the cellar chamber. Brand moved forward silently. He passed through the doorway into a smaller room. He saw Beatrice leaning against the wall, watching him calmly. He was surprised at her demeanor after her impassioned display in the house.

"Beatrice," he said. "You can't stay down here. Come back to the house."

"Sorry Carson," she said with genuine regret.

From the darkness to his right and behind him, a weight struck him, tackling him to the ground. He struggled but he was stunned by repeated blows to his head and face.

Moments later he recovered from his hazy stupor. He tried to move, but his hands and feet were bound securely.

Before him stood Beatrice with the flashlight. Beside her, a Hugh and a giant black man watched him warily. All three wore heavy jackets, gloves, and wool hats.

"Some security man you are," Hugh scoffed.

Dark shades of a black coating framed his eyes. Brand guessed he had not fully cleaned whatever substance he had applied to make his eyes appear gouged from his head.

The large black man was formidable looking. His eyes conveyed a rage he scarcely contained as he surveyed Brand.

"The Dark Man," Brand said appreciatively.

"Is that what you call him?" Hugh laughed. "That may stick, Vittorio. I like it."

"Call me that if you want to die for it," Vittorio said with a thick Jamaican accent. "I will kill him now."

"No murder," Hugh warned him. "That carries a life sentence. We don't need to raise the stakes."

Vittorio gripped the air in rage.

Hugh put a hand on his huge shoulder.

"The cold will kill him long before anyone finds him here. Stay focused on the task at hand, my friend."

Brand watched them silently. Beatrice seemed unaffected by the discovery of Hugh's being alive, indicating she was a part of whatever they planned to do. Brand ground his teeth. He had once again ignored his instincts. To him this looked like a kidnapping plot.

"Kidnapping, Hugh?" he asked with contempt. "Why didn't you have more patience and work the Beatrice angle?"

"Beatrice angle?" Hugh replied with a chuckle. "Clever. What do you think about that Bea?"

"I think there is too much talk going on here," she replied with an unfamiliar edge to her voice.

Brand began to suspect she was more than the love-struck innocent dupe in this plot.

"I'd have to marry her to get the money," Hugh said carelessly, squatting before Brand. "Neither of us wants that."

Hugh took Brand's gun with a gesture.

Brand watched Beatrice. She looked displeased with Hugh's answer.

"You're kind of a bitch, Hugh," Brand said calmly. "She has everything to lose, and you tell her you don't want her while you set her up for twenty years behind bars."

"Shut up," Hugh spat though set teeth, kicking Brand hard.

"What's he talking about?" Beatrice asked, the confidence leaving her voice.

"Don't listen to him, BB. He is trying to work you, that's all."

"You said this was a great plan. What do I have to lose, Hugh? You said nothing could happen to me because I wasn't doing anything but inviting her."

"Have you ever heard the term accessory, Bea?" Brand said through a groan of pain.

Hugh cocked the hammer on the Sig. He pressed the gun to Brand's temple.

"Shut your mouth," Hugh growled through bared teeth.

Brand glared at Hugh but remained silent.

"What does he mean by that, Hugh? You said I was safe. You said I wasn't involved with the kidnapping…"

"Godammit Bea," Hugh snarled as he stared at Brand. "He is trying to scare you. The plan hasn't changed. Go to the house. Madison will let you in. I'm sure Carson told her to lock herself in and only open the door for him. Tell Madison our hero here found you and told you to return to the house. He said he wanted to take another look around for the Dark Man."

Hugh laughed at the name, regaining some of his composure.

Beatrice hesitated as images of police and prison dominated her thoughts.

"I don't appreciate you scaring the shit out of me with the ghost act. I really thought you were killed. The photos and the lock of hair. What was that supposed to do?"

"I couldn't count on your acting skills if you knew. Your reaction had to be real if this was supposed to work."

"You never told me about this giant Jamaican. He tried to rape me in the room."

"It's not too late for that," Vittorio warned her.

Beatrice frowned. She was unsure of everything now.

Hugh looked at her imploringly.

"Come on Bea. Get going before we run out of time."

"The boat," she said testily. "I know. The boat can't wait for long. I got it."

"Shut your mouth," the big Jamaican said roughly. "Stop talking about the plan in front of him."

The big man turned a violent gaze upon Hugh.

"Control that bitch and her mouth, or I will."

"Be cool Vittorio," Hugh said soothingly. "Carson isn't leaving this room alive. He can't tell anything to anyone."

"I don't like that part or it either," Vittorio said with a scowl at Brand. "The cold may not kill him. I want to guarantee he is not a problem."

"Murder is a life sentence," Hugh insisted. It's well below freezing here. He is in jeans and a tee shirt. Have faith."

Brand glanced from the big angry Vittorio to Beatrice. She glared at the Jamaican with narrowed eyes and set lips. She was not happy with this stranger's participation in their plan. She certainly wasn't happy with his threats. She was in charge. She was the only reason they were able to get close to Madison.

Hugh looked at her.

"Please BB, do your part. We'll be there as soon as you get inside. It's almost over."

"I've been doing my part all along, Hugh. This is bullshit!"

Beatrice turned from them, her nose high in the air. She stomped from the cellar chamber, the flashlight lighting her way, leaving them in darkness.

Brand was blind once more. He turned to locate his captors. He felt the impact and saw an explosion of stars from a heavy blow from Vittorio's fist. As he faded into dark oblivion, he knew it was not Hugh who landed the punch because of the size and weight of the fist. His head swam and he slumped, his face falling to the cold dirt floor.

Brand opened his eyes with a groan of pain. His head ached and he felt blood caked dirt sticking to his face where Vittorio's blow had split his skin.

He listened for the others. He determined he was alone. He struggled to sit upright. He had no way of knowing how long he had been unconscious, but he feared it had been too long. He tested his bonds. To him they felt like plastic pull ties. He would have to find a way to cut them.

Searching his memory of the room, he recalled nothing he could use to free himself. Scant hope struck him as he remembered the Sovereign Twenty card. Did they take his wallet? He rocked in place. He felt his wallet in his back pocket.

He rolled onto his side and, with a painful effort, retrieved his wallet from the pocket. He managed to work the card out of his wallet. Dropping his wallet on the ground, he felt around the card, trying to identify a knife blade, or the saw blade he had noticed when Riser gave it to him. He was unable to single out the tool he wanted. Instead, he twisted and pulled each implement one at a time. He found the knife blade when it sliced his left middle finger. It was surprisingly sharp, causing him to bleed.

With a muttered curse he applied the blade to the tie on his wrists. The angle was awkward, and the short blade made the cutting tedious. After several minutes of effort, he felt the plastic tie separate. His hands were free. He collected his wallet and scooped the loose card implements, stowing them in his pockets.

He cut the ties on his ankles, standing uncertainly as his circulation resumed, and feeling returned to his extremities.

He made his way to the stairs. At the top step the secret door was closed. He felt around the frame until he found a hidden catch. He opened the door, crawled through the doorway, and moved to the double doors leading to the back yard of the mansion. He pushed them open a crack, the wind resisting him. He cast a cautious look around. He saw no one outside. He left the workshop and ran to the kitchen door. He saw no sign of anyone inside the house. He listened but heard nothing other than the storm. Testing the door, he found it locked.

He felt carefully inside his pockets where he had stowed the card and its loose components, he was able to recover from the dirt floor. He found the knife blade and used it to jimmy the knob on the door. Like all doors, it was spring loaded and was easy to defeat. If the deadbolt had been thrown, the task would have been more difficult.

The kitchen door opened soundlessly. He stepped inside, closing the door against the brisk wind. He was chilled to the core. He rubbed his arms and legs while he listened for any sound of those who might be inside the house. Again, he heard nothing other than the familiar sounds of the storm's assault upon the house. He entered the living room. He found no one there.

Hugh and company had made good on their plan to kidnap Madison. He knew they had taken her to an awaiting boat somewhere on the island. But where?

Brand stopped short. He thought he heard a voice. It was faint but unmistakable. He listened intently; his nerves stung tightly. It sounded like a female voice. Could it be Madison?

There. He heard it again. This time he located the direction. The voice came from outside, behind the house. Brand decided he should prepare for a prolonged duration in the cold. He sprinted to the stairs, taking them two at a time. He entered the second-floor suite he and Madison shared. Her bag was gone, her things too. He donned his coat and changed into his *Durashock* tactical boots. They were warmer than his sneakers and light socks. The *Gore-Tex* light jacket was scarcely adequate for the conditions.

He wanted to excoriate himself for being unprepared for the current weather conditions and danger levels. He packed for balmy California weather and the standard hazards of corporate security. Despite the change of plans mid mission, he vowed to update his go bag with a permanent inventory of beyond mission critical supplies. A flashlight would have been handy as would have been a knife or multi-tool. It was too late to worry about it now, but he disliked being unprepared no matter the excuse.

He gathered his belongings, including the MDP-9 and his attaché case. He stuffed his bag full and slung it on his back by the shoulder straps then left the room.

Arriving at the head of the stairs he took them two at a time. He reached the bottom floor, then the kitchen. He stepped outside, into the storm. He moved away from the house, senses on edge as he waited to hear a cry like he had inside. He didn't wait long before he heard another muted cry. The swirling wind and precipitation convoluted his efforts to pinpoint the direction from which the sound came. He was able to isolate it to the woods on the opposite side of the house from the garage and workshop structure.

He pushed through the dense brush constituting the ground clutter within the trees.

"Who's out there?" he called over the wind and sleet.

He heard an immediate but indiscernible reply. With the wind reduced within the copse of trees, he was able to locate from where the voice came. He pressed a rough path through the brush. He advanced only a dozen yards or so before he arrived at a clearing.

Stripped to her underwear, Beatrice was bound to a tree by daisy chained pull ties, similar to those with which he had been bound.

He pulled the blade from his pocket and cut the plastic bindings. He lifted her in his arms. She was cold. Her flesh appeared pale blue even in the dim light filtering through the trees.

He placed her on the ground, dropped his go bag, and pulled off his coat. He shouldered the bag then wrapped her in his coat. He picked her up, carrying her from the grove.

The underbrush pulled at them, scratching her bare legs and feet. He passed through the brambles, returning to the lawn surrounding the house. He carried her through the kitchen and into the living room where he sat her in the blankets before the waning fire in the fireplace. He wrapped her in the blankets and rubbed her extremities to get her blood flowing.

Her teeth rattled and she shuddered. Her lips were blue and her eyes glassy. He threw two billets on the fire. The dry tinder caught quickly, and the air warmed uncomfortably for Brand, who was not suffering from exposure.

He sat close to the freezing girl, rubbing color into her cheeks. He needed information from her. His mind was on Madison and the two men spiriting her to regions unknown.

"Beatrice," he said urgently but with as much compassion as he could muster under those grave conditions. "Where did they take Madison?"

Bea simply looked at him as if she failed to understand the question. She shook her head helplessly, violent shivers shaking her entire body.

"You're safe, Bea," he assured her. "You're going to be okay. We have to help Madison now. Do you understand?"

Tears welled in her eyes.

"They left me to die. Vittorio hit me. I woke up in the woods and the storm. I would have died…"

She looked at Brand with sudden understanding.

"Madison," she said as though her plight was a sudden revelation. "Hugh told me I was a liability…because I listened to you. After that…Vittorio hit me, and…I woke up…"

"I understand," Brand urged her. "Where did they take Madison?"

"British Landing. A boat is waiting in the shallow…alcove on the beach. There is a hiking trail that leads…to the road, then to…British Landing."

"Which way is that?"

Beatrice struggled to compose a meaningful reply. Finally, she shook her head. She pointed an unsteady finger towards her room.

"I have a map in my bag…in our room."

Brand left her.

At the broken entrance to her suite, he cursed as he fought the lamp cord knot. He finally untied the knot, then pulled one of the doors completely from the frame as he tugged it open. It crashed to the floor with a loud bang.

Snowflakes and ice chips blew into the hallway as he pressed forward into the cold of the room. He searched quickly, finding an expensive leather bag beside the dresser. He opened the stiff frozen bag. It contained women's items. He dug through it until he found a folded yellow sheet of paper. He opened it to find a primitively scrawled map with labels. Additional notes in a woman's handwriting appeared below the strip map. He was unable to make out the writing in the dark.

He returned to the living room where he examined the details of the map and notes. He quickly learned the details of the kidnapping.

A childlike drawing of a house represented the mansion. Below it was the word "house." A twisting and turning line was labelled "woods trail." The writing beneath another scrawled line read "Scott Shore Road." It wound in a semi-circle, ending at a crude sketch of a boat with the text, "British Landing." An arrow indicated a northwesterly direction, across the lake, to a drawing of a lighthouse. Beyond that was an "x" labeled "Airstrip."

Brand turned to Beatrice who watched him with a fearful gaze. She had recovered remarkably since placed before the fire.

"How long have they been gone?"

"Are you going to turn me into the police?"

"That's not important right now. What kind of head start do they have on me?"

"I don't know," she said distractedly. "I don't want to go to jail, Carson."

Brand's tolerance for Beatrice and her self-centered concern had reached its end.

"Beatrice," he growled dangerously. "Your only chance of getting out of this thing alive, much less out of jail, is to tell me exactly what I need to know so I can stop them from carrying out this plan. If you give half a shit about your best friend, you have to tell me everything you know. That pissed off Jamaican will not allow her to live once they get their money. He is an animal."

Beatrice sobbed.

"Hugh told me," she blubbered through her tears of self-pity. "It would take about fifteen minutes to walk the trail, and half an hour to get to the boat. I don't know how long ago they left me out there to die. It had to be at least a half hour."

"When did he tell you the travel times?"

"When he came up with the plan before you and Madison arrived."

"So, he didn't take the storm into consideration in his time estimate," Brand said mostly to himself. "How far is it to the boat in miles?"

Beatrice shook her head.

"This whole island is only a couple miles wide and maybe three and a half long. It's close. The way is rough on the trail and hilly on the road. That's why it takes so long. They haven't walked it before. They may take longer because it's at night and the storm."

She grabbed his arm.

"I've told you what you wanted. You have to help me, Carson."

Brand shook off her hand as he stood.

"What do you expect me to do?" he asked. "I'm just the hired help."

He left the room, pulling on his coat.

19

HUGH LED THE WAY ALONG THE DIM trail. Snow and ice flurries stung his face as he pressed through the dense undergrowth beneath the swaying trees. Much of the trail was rocky and slick with ice. It took additional time to navigate the treacherous ups and downs where ice had built up on the exposed stone surfaces.

He heard Vittorio following, dragging Madison behind him in the irresistibly strong grip of his huge hands. He sounded like a giant beast, breaking limbs and muttering his complaints about the hard going.

Madison was silent in her surrender to the frightening strength and constant rage of her captor. She wondered what they had done to Brand.

At the house Beatrice returned with the story that Brand intended to stay out in the storm to look for the Dark Man. She had grown immediately suspicious. He would not leave her alone. Beatrice appeared wearing a heavy parka, but that detail didn't occur to her until they moved to the living room where they sat before the fire.

Beatrice left the warmth of the fire and went to the kitchen, returning with Hugh, surprisingly alive. With him came the giant Brand called the Dark Man. It was then Madison recognized the depth of the plot against her. Brand's absence assured her he would not return to save her. She could easily imagine him perishing at the hands of the giant. He seemed indomitable. He was most certainly a savage beast.

Beatrice gathered her things from the second-floor room then returned to the men who waited to lead them outside. They had no more closed the back door than the giant struck Beatrice in the face, knocking her out cold. The Dark Man carried Beatrice's limp body into the woods beyond the house. He returned without Beatrice, carrying her Parka. He tossed the coat to her, and she put it on.

Hugh moved out first and they began their trek.

Despite the warmth of the coat, her thin shoes and thinner pants did little to insulate her from the cold. As they moved deeper into the woods, her hands and feet grew numb.

The Dark Man dragged her along with no concern for her discomfort. He gave no attention to the difficulty she experienced trying to keep her feet below her on the rough trail. In his painfully strong grip she had trouble keeping her balance on the icy trail. She slipped often. She barked her shins and dinged her knees repeatedly, yet he never slowed or looked to her safety. It was like being chained to an all-terrain vehicle, dragging her carelessly at high speed. When she fell, he continued to drag her, forcing her to regain her feet by desperate effort or luck.

The strain of fear and her exertion to keep up with the kidnappers exhausted her. She groaned her relief when they left the rough trail and stepped onto a narrow, paved road. They moved more quickly on the pavement, but the discomfort of brambles and sharp rocks was replaced by a lifted pace and no freedom to adjust her body to a fully erect posture. The giant's grip upon her arm limited her stance to a slouched posture, making the effort to move monumentally uncomfortable and doubly as difficult.

The road topped a rise before beginning a long descent. Snow and sleet pelted them relentlessly. Strong gusts of wind, formerly blocked by the trees and brambles, attacked her unfettered. The cold plucked at her flesh like icy fingers, even beneath her coat.

They walked for a long distance, the dull shine of the lake drawing nearer in the stormy night. They stepped from the road onto a stony beach. She saw a white open boat held ashore by a man in dark clothing. As they approached, he raised his arms in frustration.

"What the hell took you so long?" he asked loudly. "The wind is picking up. It's going to be rough as hell out on the water."

"Shut up," Vittorio snarled at the boatman.

The boatman was about to retort, but one look at the Dark Man made him bite his tongue.

Madison saw Hugh cast a wary glance at his large companion, turning towards the boat without a word. The Dark Man was obviously a danger even to them. Fear gripped her as her future grew more doubtful. She watched him strike Beatrice and drag her into the woods, returning without her. Madison held little hope her former best friend was still alive, not that she cared as much after her betrayal. Beatrice's fate provided her a likely portent of her fate in his hands. Fear caused her to pull violently away from the Dark Man. He strengthened his grip and favored her with a terrifying glare.

She resisted no more as he lifted her into the open boat as though she were a rag doll. He placed her in the bow of the boat, facing the stern of the little craft. The others took the remaining seats facing her. The boatman pulled the starter cord and the little outboard motor popped and gurgled to life. They left the shore for the tossing waves of the stormy lake.

Madison watched the shore recede slowly into the dark. With a start, a movement on shore caused her to catch her breath. She saw someone appear from the road and run onto the shore. She could not be certain, but she thought the man was Carson Brand. She noticed Hugh watching her and averted her gaze to a study of the bottom of the boat to avoid drawing attention to the shoreline behind him.

20

BRAND LEANED ON HIS KNEES, sucking frigid air as the storm and the distance swallowed the glow of the boat's white sides. He was too late, although he was unsure what he could have done to stop them. They had his gun, and all he had was an all-purpose business card tool kit. He needed a boat. He was unfamiliar with the island other than what he had seen on the carriage ride to the house and his late-night trek to this spot. He knew the airstrip and the town were south of his position. He had no other option than to try to get to town and find a boat.

He headed south along the shore road, running as quickly as he was able. According to Beatrice, the island was no more than three miles long. His search for an available boat to commandeer was a long shot at best. Even with his quarry in an open boat, in rough waters, he would have trouble overtaking the kidnappers if he did find one.

Fatigue and bitter cold forced him to moderate his pace. He experienced some relief that the wind was more at his back than before. It aided his progress and reduced the discomfort of the blowing snow and ice particles.

He hadn't gone far before houses appeared on the island side of the winding road. These were large homes, none of them showing interior lights. Brand suspected the homes were vacant for the off season. Few showed telltale signs of recent occupancy. There were no toys or tools in the yards. Most had outdoor security lighting, but that was no indication of current occupancy.

He understood that nine out of ten homes were used only seasonally. Of those few residents who remained on island during the off-season, most were of the working class, filling those positions required to keep the island operational year-round. These expensive estates didn't seem like permanent homes of the working class. These were remarkably opulent homes on sprawling grounds.

He continued south. The road quartered inland away from the shoreline. He soon learned why. Houses appeared on the lake side of the road. He gave these homes closer attention. If he were to find a small boat, these were more likely to have one he could manage to get onto the lake.

With no cars on the island, he doubted the existence of trailered boats. This left only those in the marina, or smaller vessels aground, near the water's edge. His only hope was to find a small boat that lay aground near the shore. He held little hope the many expensive houses he saw would yield a dingy or small open fishing boat. The local demographic trended more towards yachts and sailboats than it did the trot line and bobber crowd.

The first house offered no opportunity. Behind the second, a smaller frame house, he spied an open wooden boat with a small outboard motor. It was covered with a stained tarpaulin, caved in from the weight of the snow.

Warily, Brand scanned the house and property from the street. It looked as empty as the others he passed. Desperation and the urgency of time passing moved him. He left the roadway, vaulting over a small wooden fence. He moved to the back of the house, alert for movement behind the closed and curtained windows.

He made it to the boat, resting several yards from the water's edge. It lay tilted at an angle, aground on its "V" shaped hull. He pulled on the tarp. The motor was relatively new. He looked to the two red gas tanks in the stern. He lifted the nearest tank by the handle. It felt empty. He placed it on the ground beside the boat. He hefted the other tank. It felt a little over half full. He returned the tank to the boat and examined the motor. It was a low powered pull start outboard.

Locking the motor in the up position, he pulled the bow of the boat around, facing the lake. He dragged the boat towards the water, the ground covering of snow and ice aiding his efforts.

A light flicked on inside the house He ducked behind the bow of the boat. The back door opened, and a man approached the boat. He wore a jacket and insulated hat with lifted earmuffs. He carried a long gun, probably a shotgun.

"Shit," Brand hissed under his breath.

He didn't want to deal with an armed encounter. He certainly did not want to harm an innocent homeowner – ironically, he didn't even want to steal the man's boat.

"Step away from my boat," the man said. "I may be old, but I can see well enough in the dark to hit a full-grown man."

Brand stood with his hands raised.

"Howdy friend," he said to the older man.

"Howdy yourself. What are you doing out here in the middle of the night, in foul weather, trying to steal another man's boat? Is this a drug thing?"

Despite his frustration at the delay, Brand laughed aloud. The man's simple, straightforward manner reminded him of the people back home who raised him. The old man's matter-of-fact approach to a thief in the night was refreshing.

"I'm sorry for stealing your boat. I can pay for the boat or rent it."

"It's too late for that. You could have knocked on my door with an offer. The boat's not for sale or let."

Brand lowered his hands as his impatience grew. His internal clock was ticking.

"Keep 'em up, son."

Brand raised his hands once more.

"You goin' fishin' or what?"

"No sir," Brand said with a shake of his head. "This is a matter of life or death."

"Sure it is. I deal with a life-or-death situation every day. I wake up every morning thinking it may be my last. That doesn't warrant being a thief."

Brand nodded. He wasn't agreeing, he was accepting the situation in which he found himself.

"I am pursuing a couple of kidnappers who are taking a rich girl off the island. They took a boat from a place called British Landing and they are on their way to a lighthouse across the lake, then they are going to fly her out of some nearby airfield. I'm not a thief. I didn't think anybody was home, and I didn't have time to tell the story if they were. If you won't loan me your boat, I need to move on until I can buy, steal, or rent one."

"I'll let the police work this out. Why didn't you call them in on this?"

"I haven't had cell service since I got here, and I wasn't aware there were any cops on the island. Sir, I don't have much time. They are getting away while we talk. Can I move on now?"

The old man raised the gun to discourage Brand from trying anything.

"Answer one question and I'll tell you my decision."

"Alright," Brand said.

"Where are you from?"

"Texas, sir."

"I thought so. I am too. I recognized the slight drawl. I know the lighthouse and I know the airstrip. This boat is a little light for these conditions, but I'll drive you. I've been on the island for twenty years now. I'm used to the weather and rough water on the lake."

"Thank you, sir," Brand said with heartfelt gratitude. "What's your name?"

Brand grabbed the bow rope and pulled the boat to the water's edge.

"Edgar Crouch. What's yours?"

"Carson Brand. Are you related to the Crouch who used to live in Luckenbach?"

"Distant cousin," Crouch chuckled, setting the shotgun in the boat. "But you just confirmed you are from Texas. Not many could put those two things together. Get in son. They're getting away."

The old man demonstrated his piloting skill as he plied the tossing waters. The little open boat made way slowly, Crouch stubbornly pressing the craft into the very teeth of the storm. With the strong headwind, Brand was hardly able to detect them making headway.

"Are we moving?" he asked over the howling wind and the crashing of the bow slamming against opposing waves.

"We'll get there," Crouch assured him in a surprisingly collected tone considering the weather conditions and the dangerously choppy water.

"Why do you want to go to the lighthouse when I can drop you nearly at the airport terminal – or at least at the end of the runway?"

"I don't know much about where we are going. Everything I know is on the kidnappers' written notes I found earlier."

"They must not know the area very well. Maybe they have a car at the marina."

"That's how it seems." Brand replied.

"I don't see how anyone can fly a light plane in this weather. Are you sure they are going to the airport?"

"They made the plan before the storm. I don't have any updates on a contingency plan. I have to go on what I know."

"Makes sense."

"You only have a half a tank of gas. Can you make it back if we get there?"

"You worry about you, and I'll take care of me, son. That girl is our only concern right now."

Brand's heart swelled with gratitude. He treasured the singular generosity and concern of the man, a total stranger who put another before himself.

Brand promised himself to be more like Crouch in the future. His misdeeds and violent actions flooded up in a rush of tortured memories until he reminded himself the normalcy of his old life was behind him. He would have to find another way to improve himself.

He gripped the edges of the tossing boat, searching the snowy darkness for lights on the shore ahead.

21

MADISON HELD HERSELF ALOFT ABOVE the tossing bow seat. Waves pounded the open boat, soaking her through her thin pants and canvas shoes. Ice formed on the seat and on her clothing. She was horribly cold. Guarded glances at her captors provided no clue as to their discomfort or mood. They were dressed well for the weather. Their faces were set in hard lines, focused upon their foul deed. She noticed the boat pilot checking his compass then making slight corrections to their heading.

If it was Brand she had seen rushing onto the beach, what help could he provide? Her heart swelled with relief that he lived but she doubted he could help her. He needed to find a boat and pilot it over these rough waters. He didn't know where they headed. He had nothing to go on other than a guess based upon the direction he saw them taking.

She couldn't tell if they followed the same heading or if they even followed a legitimate heading. To her reasoning, even with the compass, the light duty open boat, tossing waves, and shifting winds made navigation impossible.

She assumed their destination was the mainland. What other option did they have? But where were they taking her? She knew this was a kidnapping. If the prearranged rendezvous with the boat and boat pilot was any indication, there could be more players than these three in the plot.

She again conjured dark thoughts of Beatrice. Her best friend – ha, that was a joke. What did she hope to gain from this? It was apparent she had run into the storm to draw Brand out of the house so Hugh and the giant could capture him.

The memory of his appearance at the beach gave her heart a lift. Her joy helped her ignore some of her discomfort. She wondered why she cared so about a bodyguard. She had to admit since they met he had acted as more than a body guard. He was uncomfortable with the game in which she asked him to participate, but he never betrayed her confidence, even when it would have benefitted him.

Who was Hugh? How had he and Beatrice met? It appeared Brand was correct in his summary of the kidnapper. It was convenient he had friends on the island. What was he doing when he disappeared for hours at a time? What was the story with him and the giant Jamaican?

The thought of the cruel giant overwhelmed her with a helpless foreboding. She doubted he would allow her to live, no matter the ransom. She watched him bludgeon Beatrice, dragging her into the woods and killing her without a second thought or hesitation.

A particularly large swell crashed into the boat breaking her reverie, nearly tossing her from her seat. Hugh grabbed her thick jacket, hauling her roughly back into her seat.

Tears welled up behind her eyes. She didn't want to cry. She scolded herself. She was stronger than this. She would not feel sorry for herself. She could find a way out of this if she maintained control over her thoughts, feelings, and emotions. She steeled herself, focusing upon the harsh conditions. Unable to resist the urge, she stole a glance at the Dark Man. He watched her steadily, as if he read her thoughts.

She averted her gaze, fear contributing chill bumps to her goose flesh caused by the frigid air and her soaked clothing.

The pelting of snow and freezing rain slackened, and she caught a glimpse of scattered lights ahead. They were drawing near the mainland. The storm fell behind them like a willful creature, concentrating its fury on the island. To Madison it seemed the farther away they moved from the island, the weaker the storm's ferocity.

The snowfall lessened until it fell as smaller flakes, drifting and eddying in the wind. She saw a lighthouse ahead. The boat pilot adjusted his course until they were on a direct line with its scanning beam, reaching infinitely outward from a tall white tower.

It was several minutes before they neared the squat building with the slender light tower above. They passed the lighthouse and entered a protected marina.

The marina was deserted. Boats rocked in the wind, chains and mast rigging rattled, but no one stirred either on the docks or aboard the boats.

They moored the open boat to the nearest peer jutting out from the main wharf. The men deposited her unceremoniously upon the snow dusted wooden dock. She collected her bag as the Dark Man grabbed her arm. He led her to the parking lot in front of the frame buildings constituting the marina's offices. The marina headquarters and the surrounding tourist shops were dark. The big Jamaican pushed her into the back seat of a snow-covered car.

The boatman got behind the wheel and cranked the engine, allowing it to warm up for a moment before he drove towards the street. Turning right, he drove slowly along darkened empty streets, at one point passing near the lighted lanes of an interstate highway.

There were no cars on the roads. The snowfall intensified as they travelled. Minutes later the paved road ended, and they continued along a rough dirt road. Soon they entered an open area which she recognized as a small airfield.

With effort she mastered a rising panic. They planned to fly her away. How could anyone track her if they flew from here?

The few buildings bordering the airstrip were dark. From the dull orange glow of the sodium vapor streetlights, she saw no terminal or control tower. No one would know they had departed. The boat pilot turned off the dirt road onto a narrower road, pulling in amongst a group of metal airplane hangars.

He stopped the car before wide double doors. He stepped from the car, allowing a flurry of snow dust inside of the warm car. He slammed the car door then crossed to one of the hangars, entering a standard sized door. After a few minutes the large double hangar doors opened, pushed by the driver and another man in a leather bomber jacket.

Two long fluorescent lights illuminated a twin engine airplane berthed within the hangar. The giant opened the car door and dragged her out of the back seat onto the paved drive. He led her towards the hangar as she clung desperately to her bag. The chill air was doubly cruel after her brief time in the warm car. Her wet clothing quickly transmitted the cold onto her moist skin.

Hugh shook hands with the man in the bomber jacket.

"Damn glad to see you Brett," he said to the man.

"You too Steven," Brett said.

As she approached under the irresistible force of the big man, Madison heard the exchange between the two.

The man called Brett watched her and Vittorio them as they drew nearer. It made sense to her that Hugh had not used his real name with them.

"Good god that's a big man," Brett cried with a grin as Vittorio approached, Madison in tow. "Is he going with us?"

"I am," Vittorio said in a low growl.

"Take it easy big man," Brett said soothingly. "I'm glad I brought the twin engine."

The jest did nothing to lighten the Dark Man's bearing. To Madison he seemed continually dangerous and cross.

"Help me push the aircraft out of the hangar," Brett said as he moved to pull the wheel chocks.

Brett entered the cockpit, manipulating the yoke as Steven and the boatman pushed the plane out of the hanger.

As if to demonstrate he would not help with the menial labor, Vittorio waited with Madison outside the hanger, his jaw set defiantly.

Once the plane faced towards the taxiway, the others moved to the hangar doors to push them closed. Vittorio led Madison to the plane. He opened the door and pushed her inside. He stepped in after, the aircraft listing alarmingly under his weight.

After securing the hangar doors, the boatman returned to the car and started the engine. He backed up, then drove away in the direction from which they had come.

Steven, formerly Hugh, took a seat in the co-pilot chair. He donned a second pair of headphones as the pilot started the engines. The plane shuddered as each engine started and the propellors spun up to speed.

After a few final checks, Brett released the brakes and the plane moved smoothly forward. As the aircraft cleared the protected hangar area, the wind turned its fury upon it. Without the buildings to block the gusts, the little plane's wings dipped and shook. They taxied a short distance to the runway. Brett oriented the aircraft into the wind, decreasing the wind's effects on the wings. Brett powered up the engines and the plane eased forward.

"What the fuck is that?" Brett called over the noise of engines and weather.

"Shit," Steven yelled as a muffled explosion sounded outside the plane. The aircraft shuddered as if from an impact. Another muffled blast sounded. Madison looked out her window to see Brand wielding a shotgun. He fired two more times into the starboard engine. The motor belched smoke and flame as it sputtered to a halt.

Hugh unlatched his safety belt and climbed out of the door, freezing air chilling the cabin. Vittorio flung open the back door and squeezed out into the chilly night.

Steven pulled Brand's Sig from his pants.

Brand shot him dead center.

The pistol clattered onto the tarmac as Hugh fell on his face, his head striking the pavement with a sound like a hurled melon.

Vittorio charged Brand, his hands at his sides, curled into claws. Brand pumped the shotgun and pulled the trigger. The mechanism clicked hollowly. He was empty.

Vittorio was upon him, grabbing his arm. He pulled back a giant fist and punched at Brand's head.

Brand ducked the blow, bumping into the bigger man, pulling him over his lowered shoulder.

Vittorio grunted as he struck the ground with his full weight. Brand kicked him in the head. A second kick ended in one of Vittorio's big hands. He twisted Brand's leg, forcing him to the ground rather than suffering an injury from the powerful wrenching.

The big Jamaican rose to his feet, clinging to Brand's foot.

Brand slammed the heel of his free foot onto the man's big fingers.

Vittorio's grip weakened sufficiently for Brand to free himself with a violent tug.

Brand rushed the bigger man, surprising him with the move. He brought a knee up into

Vittorio's groin. An elbow followed to the face causing a stream of blood to leak from Vittorio's nose.

With the power of a huge pneumatic hammer, the bigger man swung an arching punch at Brand.

Brand stepped inside the path of the punch, striking him twice in the face. A left to the throat constricted his airway and Vittorio clutched his neck as he struggled to breathe.

Brand moved to Hugh's body. He collected his Sig, checking it for a round in the chamber. He pulled the magazine clip. It was full. He turned as Vittorio who clutched his injured throat with one hand, using the other to crawl on his knees towards Brand. His face was a contorted mask of hatred and fury.

Brand shot him three times in the head.

Vittorio sagged to the tarmac.

Brand turned his attention to the plane. As he approached the plane, the pilot shut off the remaining functioning engine. Brett stepped from the plane, his hands aloft.

"I'm just a pilot," he explained. "Don't shoot me."

"Help the girl out of the plane and I'll consider it."

"Yes sir," he agreed, hastily moving to the rear door of the plane.

Brand collected the discarded shotgun and moved to the aircraft.

Brett helped Madison out of the plane, retrieving and handing down her bag.

"Do you have a car here?" Brand demanded as the pilot latched the door.

"Behind the hangar."

"Lead the way."

The pilot moved away.

Brand took Madison's hand.

"You're freezing. Are you okay?"

"I am now," she said weakly. "How did you get here?"

"Come on," he said, ignoring her question. "Let's get you to safety."

Madison looked at the bodies of Steven, formerly Hugh, and the Dark Man. She then looked at Brand. He had just engaged in a deadly fight with a giant beast of a man. He had known Hugh personally. He killed both men, yet he seemed to have left that behind him without any further consideration. As he passed, he didn't' even glance at the dead he left lying on the frozen ground.

She recalled her doubts of his strength and even his courage. To the untrained eye Hugh would have seemed the better of the two. Brand never doubted himself while discounting the man. At the mansion he attacked the Dark Man without hesitation, without a pause for fear. He fought him three times, the last time fatally for the big Jamaican.

Her reason demanded she fear this strange man who dealt death as a matter of course. Her instincts, honed by her personal relationship with him over the past few days, craved his company. She was fascinated by him, his innate strength, his courage, and most remarkably, his ability to come to her aid despite the odds against him. Once more she wondered how he happened to arrive at the airport when he did.

The pilot led them behind the closed hangar where the plane was stored. He stopped before a late model sedan, covered in snow. Brand opened the driver side rear door and helped Madison inside. He kept his pistol on Brett as he closed the door.

"You drive," he ordered as he moved to the passenger side.

"You don't have to do this," the pilot protested. "I don't want to get any more deeply involved."

"Get in and drive."

Brett sat behind the wheel as Brand took his seat.

He glanced at Madison as Brett cranked the cold motor.

Madison watched Brand with a serious set to her face. She nodded towards Brett.

He watched her with a raised brow and a barely noticeable nod of curiosity.

"What?" he mouthed silently.

She lifted a dark windbreaker just high enough for Brand to make out the FBI logo on the back.

Brand's face froze in an expressionless mask. He faced forward.

Madison returned the jacket to the seat beside her, watching the back of the pilot's head.

"Get onto the interstate," Brand directed as he saw a sign notifying them of an approaching on ramp.

"You are making a mistake," the driver warned him with growing alarm and frustration.

"Don't think because you are FBI, I won't hesitate to shoot you."

Brett gripped the wheel tightly. His jaw worked nervously.

"You killed one agent already. I don't think I doubt you will do it again. How many times can you be executed, right?"

"Hugh was FBI?"

"His name is Steven, and yeah, he is - was FBI."

"Why is the FBI kidnapping daughters of billionaires. Did you guys miss out on a budget increase this year?"

Brett cast a sidelong glance at Brand. He was annoyed by his trite humor.

"I've got nothing to say to you. You killed one agent and kidnapped another. I might as well be talking to a dead man. You are fucked."

Brand leaned towards Brett, grabbed the wheel with his left hand, and struck the agent hard in the face with his pistol. Blood spurted across the seat, Brett's lap, and onto the driver side door upholstery. If Brand hadn't taken control of the wheel, the car would have careened off the road.

"What the fuck?" Brett cried through clenched teeth and dripping blood.

He pinched his bleeding nose with his left hand.

"You smart ass me again and I'll put one through your knee cap. What is the FBI doing kidnapping this girl?"

Brett made no reply as his bloody nose occupied much of his attention.

Brand suspected the agent was stalling for enough time to manufacture a lie.

"Think about your next words," Brand warned, cocking the hammer. He placed the muzzle of the pistol against the agent's knee.

Madison watched silently, fascinated by the transformation of the man with whom she had spent the last several fearful nights. He was hard as steel, formidable, indomitable. His casual manner of dealing out death and injury was breathtaking in its immediacy and finality. He allowed few opportunities for his victims to plead or negotiate.

Brett eyed the gun fearfully, his fingers maintaining pressure on his busted nose. He began to speak slowly, in a nasally tone.

"Her father, Sabastian Giles, purchased the largest social media platform in the world. He has threatened to remove the filters and information dams the previous ownership placed upon the platform. Few people understand the danger social media poses to society and our country. If left unchecked, the unmanaged flow of erroneous information and disinformation would lead to a national security crisis of unimaginable proportions."

"Your plan was to kidnap his daughter to pressure him to comply with your wishes?"

"That is putting it simply, but yeah."

"You admit you planned to kidnap me?" Madison cried from the back seat.

She scooted forward in her seat as anger filled her with the desire to strike out at the agent.

"Madison," Brand said calmly. "Don't get too close to him. If you want to bloody him up, I'll help you do it. Agents are well trained and tricky. I don't want to kill him here because he acts on some ill-advised plan to use your emotions as a diversion."

Brett placed his other hand on the wheel to demonstrate his helplessness. He was certain Brand would carry through with his threat if provoked.

"What is the story with the big Jamaican?" Brand asked.

"Steven recruited him on the island. He was hiding in the house and Steven caught him there. He offered him something in return for his help. I don't know what that was. I suspect it might have been her when we got what we wanted from her father."

Madison struck Brett in the back of the head, causing Brand to grab the wheel again.

"I'm being honest with you," Brett complained loudly, grabbing the back of his head. "I don't like the plan any better than you do. I follow orders. I do what I am told. Steven was the primary on this Op. I was to fly the plane only."

"Where were you taking her?"

Brett hesitated.

Brand's eyes narrowed at his resistance.

"Chicago," Brett admitted. "We were taking her to a secret location in Chicago. Only Steven knew the exact location."

Brand considered what he was hearing, keeping watch on the agent with a half attentive eye. His mind compared the agent's claims to his previous experiences with the bureau.

He was beginning to believe federal law enforcement was more similar to a crime syndicate than a policing organization. The Justice Department targeted him before. He narrowly escaped that one with his life. Now he was in the middle of a federally sponsored kidnapping plot involving the daughter of one of the richest men in the world.

Brand determined to return Madison to her father. He could do no more than that. The FBI agent provided valuable insight as to his fate if the authorities captured him. If the kidnapping had been successful, Madison would not have lived through the ordeal. She would certainly have perished by the Dark Man's hand, or the FBI would have killed her to conceal their part in the plot.

Brand leaned back in his seat. He needed to come up with a plan to save Madison and himself. He had no allies here. He was unsure where Dick Riser would land in this, but he doubted it would end with Riser on his side.

22

SEBASTIAN GIILES THREW HIS favorite desk lamp across the room. It was a gift from the man who brought him into the firm he now owned. The billionaire gave no thought to the lamp as he listened to the FBI agent calling him with the worse news he could hear. The very man charged with protecting his daughter kidnapped her.

"How did this happen, Agent Taylor?" Giles asked through an iron bitterness in his throat.

"I spoke with Richard Riser at Sovereign Services. He said the man was one of his newest and brightest rising stars. He seemed genuinely shocked and confused when I called him."

Giles stood with a hand on his hip, the other clutching the phone to his ear.

"I have been in touch with him continually since I lost contact with Madison and her party. What do we know right now?"

The agent's voice was muffled as he covered the phone, speaking to someone nearby. His hand came away from the telephone as he returned his attention to the call.

"We are still piecing it together, Mr. Giles. We were unable to reach the island until this morning, after that huge storm weakened enough to cross. Our agents found your daughter's friend, Beatrice McDermott, suffering from exposure after being tied to a tree outside. She said this Carson Brand kidnapped Madison with the help of a large Jamaican. The Jamaican appears to be a seasonal worker employed at one time by a large event services company on the mainland. He quit a couple of years ago and has been unaccounted for since. We don't have much on him other than what the girl was able to tell us."

"What is the Jamaica angle on this?" Giles asked confused.

"No angle," Taylor replied. "Most of the hired help on the island are Jamaican immigrants. It is one of the many peculiarities we have found."

"Was Beatrice able to shed any light on a motive…anything unusual she may have noticed?"

"She claimed another man, someone named Hugh – her boyfriend, disappeared around the same time Carson Brand took your daughter. We were able to trace the kidnappers to a small airstrip north of the island on the mainland. Brand killed his accomplice, the Jamaican, and the boyfriend on the tarmac. The airplane they were using to get your daughter out of the area was shot up, possibly by the boyfriend.

It is our theory Brand killed the boyfriend as he tried to rescue your daughter. They stole a car parked at the airfield and they are at large now. We were able to identify the make and model of the car, but we have nothing more specific."

"Good god," Giles exclaimed. "How could I have exposed my daughter to this killer?"

"Mr. Giles, these security types come from a violent, and often a troubled background. The men who work for Sovereign have a penchant for showing up in our databases as troublemakers and often end up behind bars."

Giles had no response to Taylor's observations. His thoughts were filled with images of his daughter in the line of fire as a madman gunned down other human beings around her.

'She must be beside herself with fear and doubt,' he thought.

Taylor cleared his throat, indicating his intent to continue his report.

"The surveillance camera that recorded the car had a decent angle, and we were able to confirm there were three people inside, including your daughter who was in the back seat. We haven't identified the other man in the car."

"This seems remarkably well planned," Giles said thoughtfully. "I only assigned Mr. Brand to my daughter on the plane as we took off from New York. How could he have planned this thing so quickly? He was scheduled to fly with me to Los Angeles. He didn't know she was joining us on the flight. He didn't strike me as a tactical genius who could anticipate any of this."

Mr. Giles," Taylor said uncertainly. "Do you think he might have had help from someone who could be a careful planner?"

"What are you saying?" Giles asked roughly. After a pause he continued. "Are you suggesting Riser and his organization had something to do with this?"

"I'm covering every base, sir. We are leaving nothing to chance. We are in the first mile. The FBI doesn't overlook any detail. You are making a particularly good point and I am considering alternatives."

Giles grew silent.

Taylor continued his report. "State Police have set up roadblocks and we have an All Points on Carson Brand and your daughter."

Now that Riser was a possible suspect, Giles' manner was more guarded.

"Did Riser and his team make it to the island while your men were investigating?"

"He did. He arrived by helicopter. My lead investigator on the scene threatened to arrest him and his team to keep them on the sidelines until we could process the crime scene. Riser appeared very aggravated. If he is not involved in the abduction, we may not get a chance to apprehend the suspect if he gets there first."

"Good," Giles said softly.

Despite his misgivings, the idea Riser was on the trail gave him some comfort and hope.

"Mr. Giles," Agent Taylor continued. "The kidnappers will try to contact you sooner than later to make their ransom demands. I need you to remain in place and allow my team of negotiators and the Abduction Task Force to monitor all communications between you and them."

"Of course," Giles agreed. "I am here at my Malibu house. I'll text the address and gate codes."

"We know where you are, sir. My team is en route now. Thank you for your cooperation."

23

THE ROADBLOCK WAS EASILY SEEN under the low hanging storm clouds of a premature dusk. Red flares and brake lights from the long line of waiting autos, reflected on the snow like signal fires, providing Brand ample warning. Helicopters circled overhead prepared to aid in a pursuit if necessary.

Brand directed Brett to stop the car well short of the string of waiting motorists. The agent's reluctance to evade the roadblock was apparent. His mind worked at a plan to notify the authorities without risking his own life.

Brand had Brett pull into a gated drive. The gate was not the type used to guard the primary driveway to a house. It was a corrugated ranch gate sporting a *no trespassing* sign. He stepped out, opening the gate. He motioned Brett to drive through, keeping the pistol trained on him. He hoped Bett wouldn't make a break. The resulting gunshots would give them away. Once through the gate, Brand motioned Brett out of the car. The agent obeyed, fear obvious in his expression and slow gait.

Brand noticed fallen branches under a nearby grove of trees.

"Gather a couple of those branches and bring them here," he ordered.

Brett obeyed.

Brand took one branch from him.

"Through the gate," he directed the agent.

They returned to the drive beside the road. Brand brushed the snowy ground with the branches, clearing tire tracks and footprints from the snow at the gate entrance.

Brett numbly followed suit.

Brand suspected the agent was counting on leaving signs of their detour. Brand sent Brett to the rear of the car as he put the finishing touches on the cleanup job. He tossed the branches into the trees and pulled the gate closed. They returned to the car.

Madison remained in the back seat, watching them silently.

Back in the car, Brand instructed him to drive with the headlights turned off. The snow covering naturally intensified the scarce ambient light. Before long, their eyes adjusted, and they followed the road easily in the gloom of the forest. The primitive dirt road meandered through dense woods. The trees provided good cover from the street, and overhead concealment from the choppers. They travelled slowly, careful to follow the frequently fading then reappearing trail. The darkness and the undergrowth made the road difficult to follow at times, but they managed to maintain a decent pace.

After a time, Madison broke her long silence.

"Do you know where we are, Brand, or are you planning on us travelling aimlessly, sleeping in the woods until this all blows over?"

"I'm still working on that," he replied seriously. "The roadblock was a surprise. I can't figure out how they located us so quickly. The plane and the bodies should have led to a slow investigation including a search for motive. That kind of thing takes time, not minutes: sometimes days. We need time to make a viable plan. That may involve staying outside tonight. Can you handle that?"

Madison made no reply and Brand did not risk a look into the backseat to gauge her mood.

"It's not going to work," Brett said wearily. "If roadblocks have been set, that means the police have identified the car and they know our probable range. We are in a net. The net will be closed off until they find us. We can't hide from their search."

Brand considered what Brett was saying as they travelled slowly along the dim double tracked road.

Brand turned to Madison.

"Do you want to check your phone for signal?"

"I had phone signal when we got in the car at the airport," She replied hesitantly. "I lost it just before we hit the roadblock. I have no bars now."

Brand's expression registered alarm at the admission.

"I know why they got on our trail so quickly," she said with the manner of someone about to share a secret. "My dad has been blowing up my phone for hours. Don't worry, I haven't texted him yet."

"Why not?" Brand asked curiously.

"One of his texts claimed you kidnapped me, and he wanted to know where you were taking me."

"I kidnapped you?" Brand blurted. "Why would he think that?"

No one spoke for a few minutes.

"Shit," Brand said finally. "Beatrice probably told the FBI I was behind the kidnapping. I saved her life back there. She would have died of exposure if I hadn't brought her to the house and warmed her up. No good deed…"

"Bea's alive?" Madison asked brightly. "Thank god."

"Yeah," Brand repeated sardonically. "Thank god."

"That big black man dragged her into the woods and returned with her clothes and this coat. I was certain he had killed her and left her out in the woods."

"She was in her skivvies tied to a tree when I found her. She gave me the details of their plan. I convinced a local to get me across on his fishing boat. That shotgun is his."

"She may not be behind this," Madison said. "Maybe the FBI coerced her into making up the story, or they came up with the story and made her go along to cover their part in it."

Brand shook his head as the memory of her conversation with Hugh and the Dark Man in the underground chamber replayed in his mind.

"When they captured me and tied me up, she spoke to Hugh and the Dark Man with a lot of authority. If she's talking to the FBI, she's covering her own ass. The FBI is more likely providing her cover in this thing."

Brett slowed the car to a stop as the road ended at another dim dirt road crossing their route. Brand looked both ways. The new road looked more primitive than the one they travelled. A left would return them from where they came, back into the net to which Brett alluded earlier.

"Turn right," Brand decided.

"There is no telling where these roads lead," Brett complained. "It's hard enough to see. What if this one ends at a cliff or something?"

"Shut up and drive."

Brett turned the car to the right, heading north along the new road.

"You are a true friend," Brand observed. "Beatrice has a key role in kidnapping you, and you are still trying to find the good in her."

"I guess I don't understand what your goal is here," Madison said crossly. "Why didn't you turn me in to the state police at the roadblock? The longer we hide, the guiltier you will look."

"The FBI kidnapped you. This asshole is one of them. How can I be certain if I deliver you to the state cops, they won't immediately turn you over to the feds so they can finish their work?"

Madison shook her head defiantly.

"That would be a very public kidnapping. I don't believe this conspiracy goes to the state police level, do you?"

"I have seen official government agencies take bigger chances than that," Brand replied, his memory fresh with his own betrayal by government officials.

Madison crossed her arms over her chest, giving her attention to the dark wilderness around them.

Brand glanced at Brett. The FBI agent was preoccupied with his own thoughts Brand presumed were focused upon escape.

Good luck with that, Brand thought.

He was yet to decide what he would do with the agent. He didn't need another dead Fed to add to his growing reputation, and he also didn't want to damn himself further in Madison's eyes.

Although he hadn't killed any of those credited to him other than Hugh, or Steven, or whatever his name was, the agency believed he killed some three other federal agents since his life became what it now was.

His contact inside the Bureau was his friend, Special Agent Dennis Moore, with whom he had trained at a facility near Houston.

After Brand rescued Moore from a hit squad, he arranged for Brand's employment with Sovereign Services, vouching for him with Riser. He also swept the unsolved deaths of the agents under a rug of mysterious circumstances where Brand acted on behalf of the DEA against compromised operatives placed within agencies inside the DOJ.

Brand was doubtful sweeping the matter under the rug would last. At best he was a liability to many in power. This latest frame up by the FBI was familiar ground, a recurring theme, repeating more often than he was comfortable with.

A glimmer of light flickered through the trees ahead and to the left of their direction of travel. Brand focused upon it, placing a hand on Brett's shoulder.

Brett stopped the car, also noticing the light.

They waited silently. The light was a mystery so deep in the woods. Brand was certain its portent was more likely negative than beneficial to their plight.

24

DRIVING A USED CROSSOVER SUV HE purchased from a car lot in town, Riser listened to the portable police band radio. His men rode in silence. Conolly occupied the passenger seat and Williams sat in the back. They travelled north. There were no police alerts reporting Brand and company had been spotted.

He doubted a roadblock would snare Brand. He was highly trained in escape and evasion techniques. He would change vehicles or go on foot. There were no reported stolen cars, so he was either off grid, on foot, or hiding out. Hiding was not a good plan either. If Brand made that error, Riser would find him.

He knew in his heart Brand was not behind the kidnapping. The girl at the mansion was lying. The FBI's theory about Brand's kidnapping plan was too unbelievable. Why were they supporting it? Riser tried to get the girl alone for a quick but persuasive question and answer session. The FBI watched her closely, taking her with them when they left.

He was forced to take up the manhunt no matter his belief in his man, no matter his theories. The reputation of his company and his credibility amongst his men required he act upon the facts as they were presented. The FBI and state authorities pursued Brand as a fugitive from justice, the prime suspect in a kidnapping case. He had no choice but to treat the matter as a real case. He had to treat Brand as a real suspect in the crime.

Giles called him regularly. His questions and his tone set Riser ill at ease. Of late the man seemed curiously guarded and stand-offish. It was apparent he believed Brand guilty, but that was not why he was keeping a wary posture with Riser. Did he think Sovereign was involved in the abduction? Ridiculous!

The police radio crackled with state police chit chat and procedural communications – nothing helpful.

They rounded a turn. Ahead they saw a roadblock with a lengthy line of motorists waiting to be cleared.

Riser scanned the area for side roads. There was nothing other than the occasional motorized gate protecting a driveway, and a few roadside farm gates. He saw no tire tracks or footprints to indicate recent use.

The chances this was the road Brand had taken to affect his escape were remote. As they halted at the end of the line of waiting cars, Riser surveyed the area around them, searching for an alternate escape route.

"This is a goat fuck," Conolly said in a low rumbling voice. "Leave it to us and we'll come up with the kid in half a day."

"Is that right?" Riser retorted angrily. "You want to take over this operation, Mister?"

Conolly locked his jaws, the muscles in his face rippling as he controlled his anger.

"That fucking door opens out too. All you have to do is open it, Mac."

Conolly stiffened at the insulting tone and the finality of the offer. He made no response but sat tight. He stifled his anger with the knowledge he would have the last word and riches beyond imagining.

Williams shifted uncomfortably in the back seat. He was uncertain where he stood in the rapidly changing environment between the men in the front seats. Conolly included him in his plans, but addressed him roughly, with little respect. Shouldn't a partnership bring an end to addressing him as an underling? His position with Sovereign was a good one, allowing him an income he had never imagined. He doubted he could replace it in the private sector. If Conolly could betray Riser, his longtime friend and former SEAL teammate, why wouldn't he betray him?

Riser was past the point of patience with his second in command. Since leaving the island mansion, the man had grown increasingly dour and negative. He gave unquestioning credence to the FBI's theory and vehemently conjured additional insight and motives into Brand's part in the crime. Despite Riser's doubts, clearly detailed, Conolly discarded any denial of Brand's guilt as falsely sympathetic and transparently self-serving.

After waiting in the slow-moving line for nearly fifteen minutes, they arrived at the state police check point. A trooper in a round hat leaned towards the driver side window, looking over the men inside.

"Where are you folks coming from?" the trooper asked.

"St. Ignace," Riser replied. "My men and I are working with the FBI on the manhunt for Carson Brand."

"Is that right? And who are you, sir?"

"I'm Richard Riser with Sovereign Services. These men are my team."

"So, this guy is one of your boys, eh?"

Conolly grunted and faced the passenger side window.

"Afraid so."

"Why aren't you helping with the search inside the operational area? You giving up so soon?"

"I doubt your roadblock will stop him. We're following a hunch."

"Got it all figured out do you."

"I trained him. Your cordon wouldn't get me. So yeah, I got it figured out."

The trooper considered Riser for a long moment, his face a mask of frustration as he controlled his temper. He was working late at this roadblock and wouldn't make it to his ex's house in time to pick up his boy, and this grinning asshole was telling him he's wasting his time.

"Thanks a lot."

"You're welcome."

The trooper frowned then waved them through.

"Williams," Riser called to the man behind him. "The rookie will have to change cars. Where is the nearest city, but look at least ten miles outside of the cordoned area?"

Williams looked to Conolly as if for approval to follow the request before pulling and examining the map Riser purchased at a convenience store.

"Trout Lake to the west; Kinross due north; and not much between here and Canada to the east. I don't see anything with much to attract someone who knows what to do."

"Let's find a place to bed down," Riser decided. "We'll monitor the radio. When he sets a course, he will leave sign for us to follow, minor disturbances or dead bodies."

"Yes sir," William replied.

25

BRETT FOLLOWED THE ROAD FOR several more yards until the light shone solidly beyond the screening forest. The path narrowed to a trail hardly wide enough to allow the car passage. Fortunately, the snow had not fallen heavily enough to create drifts or deep falls in hidden depressions. Unkempt foliage barred the way. The trees overgrew the narrow road on both sides. Branches scratched along the sides and top of the car like evil claws, reaching for its trespassing occupants.

As they slowed to a stop, the passenger side mirror snapped off on a thick stob, flinging it into the darkness. In their keen focus on the strange light in the middle of nowhere, the noise startled them.

Brand told Brett to stop the car.

The FBI agent seemed reluctant to follow the order. He turned the ignition key off with compressed lips and a furrowed brow. He was growing weary of his prolonged confinement.

Brand opened the passenger side door, directing him to get out of the car with him. There was no place for the agent to go, but Brand didn't want to risk an escape attempt.

Even in so secluded a place, Brand recognized the hazardous possibilities of the agent at large.

Madison opened the rear door, stepping from the car.

"I need you to stay here," Brand warned her.

"I have to pee," She said seriously.

Brand nodded.

"We'll wait here until you're finished. Then I want you to lock yourself in the car until we get back."

They turned their backs as she answered nature's call. When she finished, she closed the car door and joined them.

"I'm not staying here by myself," she assured them. "Not in this car – in the dark."

Brand was accustomed to her resistance and nodded in resignation. She was willful, though he suspected he would do the same in her place. Even to him, the dark chill of the night and confining gloom of the forest was ominous and strange.

"Stay close," he said as he pushed Brett ahead through a dense cluster of clawing foliage.

They moved with difficulty, twisted branches tugging at their clothes like petrified but willful creatures. With a significant effort, they emerged from the undergrowth and entered a broad clearing where stood a small ramshackle cabin. The light which caught their attention shone from a lone window on the facing side of the house.

The structure was a roughly constructed affair of twisted siding boards and a shake roof. It was no bigger than a storage shed, though it was tall, with a metal smokestack pipe poking out the top near the roof peak.

The starkness of the crooked little building in the unnatural brightness of the snow-covered ground gave the scene an eerie surreal look. As they moved closer, they saw that the light emanated from a kerosene lantern sitting on a windowsill inside the shack.

Brand stopped Brett with a tug on his sleeve. They listened for noises from within the little building. Brand heard nothing other than soft wind rustling high above amongst the tree limbs.

Against the starless sky Brand could just make out a tendril of smoke drifting lazily from the smokestack. Someone was inside.

Brand drew Brett's attention and motioned for him to give the shack a wide berth. Brand was wary there might be makeshift defenses built, or possibly noise maker traps set near the shack. If he lived there, he would have placed them.

They moved stealthily towards the cover of two trees set closely together. Brand grabbed Brett's arm, stopping him cold. Between the trees in a taut, thread thin line, just above the level of the fresh snow, was strung a trip wire. Brand traced the wire to where it terminated at the trigger of a claymore mine. The mine was attached to the right side of the tree in textbook military fashion.

The shack's occupant was more than some backwoods hillbilly with tin cans strung together to scare off wolves or a bear. This trap was a deadly piece of area denial ordinance, created to defend against the approach of men.

Brand gripped the Sig firmly. They were in real danger here.

He pulled Madison closer behind him. He was certain they were walking into more than they might be able to escape. They needed to return to the car immediately before they were detected. It would be a grave mistake to go further.

Carefully scanning the area around them, Brand guided the others back to the car. The going was slow until they left the open area. Despite scratches and pinches of the resistant trees and bushes, they returned to the car with decent speed. When they arrived, a voice froze them in place.

"Where do you all think you are going? Unlimber that pea shooter son."

In the comparative darkness of the grove Brand could just make out a dim figure leaning against the hood of the sedan. He held a long gun, pointed casually in their direction. Brand guessed if he made a sudden evasive move the gunman would shoot, possibly hitting Madison. He couldn't risk it. He hesitated as he decided what to do.

Brett made the decision for them.

"Put the gun down. I'm a federal agent."

"Is that right?" the stranger asked with grim amusement.

With a gesture, he lifted the gun and shot Brett.

Madison screamed at the rifle report and the unprovoked murder. She began to cry as the agent fell to the snowy ground, a dark pool spreading beneath him as he died.

Brand reacted spontaneously. Too many feds were dying around him these days.

"Goddam mister," he complained with an out of place tone of casual annoyance. "You are making my life harder than it needs to be."

"Sorry to inconvenience you. I told you to drop the pistol. Unless you want to end up like your partner there, I suggest you comply."

The man pointed the rifle directly at Brand.

Brand placed the Sig on the snow with a slow and measured motion.

"You got a shovel in the car?" asked the killer.

"I don't think so," Brand replied.

"Too bad. I have one at the house, though. We'll go get it so you can bury your friend."

At gunpoint, the gunman coaxed them away from the car, collecting the Sig from the ground. They returned to the clearing and the shack. They were nearly at the house when the gunman cleared his throat dramatically.

"I wouldn't step there," the stranger warned Brand with what sounded like genuine amusement. "I got booby traps everywhere. Turn right and make a beeline towards the corner of the house."

To Madison he said, "Keep your distance from your boyfriend miss. If he blows up, I want to keep you in one piece."

Without a thought, Madison slowed, allowing Brand to move further ahead.

They located a shovel near the front door of the shack, then returned to the car. The stranger watched as Brand dug a hole beside the car. Cautiously, he directed Madison to remain near Brand until he finished.

Brand shoveled the last of the fill atop the agent's grave.

"It's good you're strong," the man noted. "It's starting to get cold out. Come on. Back to the house we go."

Madison hesitated to obey the strange man. Brand nudged her gently ahead. He didn't want to annoy the stranger for fear of ending up filling a hole beside the FBI agent.

Brand took stock of the killer. The man gunned the agent down casually with no remorse and no regret.

Touching her gently, Brand felt Madison stiffen. She shuddered at his touch. He was unsure if her trembling was from the cold, or the violence and killings she had witnessed during the last two days. He doubted she had ever seen anything like it outside of the movies. Despite the darkness, the whites of her eyes shone in her pale face, casting her in a ghostly pallor. He feared she was in shock or very nearly so. He hoped she wouldn't panic and do something to draw the ire of their captor.

Brand led the way, careful to follow his previous tracks. With tersely delivered directions, their captor guided them until they entered the door of the small shack. An economical fire burned in a rusty wood stove. The lantern sat in the window, the flame dancing merrily to the small drafts seeping through thin fissures around the glass panes.

"Sit," the man ordered, indicating two frame chairs pressed against the far wall.

They obeyed and he quickly used thin cotton ropes to bind their hands and feet to the chairs.

Madison wept silently, tears ploughing lines down her dirty cheeks.

Brand finally got his first clear look at the man who tied them to the chairs.

He was in his fifties, whipcord lean, unshaven but not bearded, with stained teeth appearing regularly due to his habit of smiling and chuckling as he worked. Once Brand was securely bound, the captor straightened with a grunt. He surveyed his handiwork with a satisfied pursing of his pale lips.

He shifted his attention to Madison. He inspected her for a long moment, taking in every detail.

"The darkness did you an injustice, girl. You are absolutely beautiful. What are you doing with him?"

He laughed loudly, a mocking facsimile of genuine mirth.

Madison made no reply. She avoided his eye, preferring to study the rough planks of the floorboards.

"My name is Jed," he said. "Jed Clampett."

Brand nodded blandly as though he failed to recognize the reference.

"What's next Jed?" he asked with affected casual interest, as if he was not tied to a chair in the middle of the woods at the mercy of a psychopathic murderer.

"I've given that some thought son. I guess I'll have to kill you both. I can't let you go after I killed your FBI buddy."

"No offense," he said to Madison. "It won't be easy with you girl. I might have to keep you around for a while after I do your boyfriend. You might even like it."

Madison's jaw muscles worked as she writhed under the images his words conjured, and her efforts as she pulled on the ropes with all of her strength.

"I tie a real good knot, honey. Might as well relax. Ole Clayton Williams said it best when he was running for governor against that ole gal from Texas, 'You can't do anything about it, so you might as well lay back and enjoy it.'"

"You from Texas?" Brand asked him, remembering his luck with the owner of the boat.

"Hell no. You?"

"San Antonio," Brand replied lightly.

"Mexican town, I hear. 'course, there ain't nothing but steers and queers in Texas. Boy, you ain't got any horns."

He laughed loudly at his jest.

"Good one, old timer," Brand said without humor. "What's your excuse?"

The old man's face lost its smile, and a snarl escaped him. He rushed over to Brand. Grabbing his hair, he pulled his head back roughly until he looked into his eyes. A thin line of drool streamed from his maw onto Brand's chin.

Brand leaned as low in the seat as he could, pulling on the ropes as far as they would slide on the chair arms.

The old man's voice rumbled from him like a growl.

"Don't humor me, motherfucker," the old man spat. "I won't tolerate any smart ass from you. I'll kill you deader than hell without a thought."

Brand watched him dispassionately. No fear showed in his face.

"You're a hard case, aren't you?" the old man said in a low husky voice. Then with a strangely contrasting dismissive tone he said, "I used to be like you."

He released Brand's hair. Turning his back on him, he moved to the dying fire. He threw another stick on the flame and watched it for a moment.

Brand said nothing for a long moment. He struggled with the ropes, watching the old man carefully.

"You are nothing like me," Brand said finally. "Don't flatter yourself."

Madison looked at Brand with panic clearly etched on her face. She had no doubt how far he could push the old murderer. Not far!

She froze, her mouth opened in amazement. Brand was no longer tied to the chair. The ropes lay on the floor below the chair, though Brand held his hands in place where they had been when he was bound.

The old man turned to face Brand. He didn't notice the ropes lying below the chair. Madison reasoned he was looking his victim in the face, focusing on nothing else but his anger at him.

"I'm gonna gut you like a fish, then I'm gonna have my way with your pretty girlfriend."

He pulled an evil looking hunting knife from a scabbard slung from his belt. He stepped towards Brand with a grim set to his jaw.

Madison wanted to scream at Brand to stand up and fight. Why was he waiting? The old man was nearly upon him.

Brand stood; his feet still bound to the chair.

In that moment Madison understood why he waited. If he reacted too soon, the old man could retreat out of range and Brand would be unable to close on him.

The old man stopped short and recoiled from Brand. His face registered surprise at the sight of Brand's free hands, but he wasn't frightened. With confidence in his training and experience, the old man was certain he would be more than enough for a snot nosed city boy.

The old man stepped slightly to his right to put weight on the knife hand side of his body. With a quick thrust from the waist, the blade shot forward towards Brand.

Brand twisted left, the blade narrowly missing him. He gripped the knife hand with his left hand and punched the old man in the throat with his right fist.

His airway crushed, the old man reacted instinctively, grabbing his throat. The knife clattered to the scarred floorboards.

Brand scooped up the knife, and with a gesture, cut the ropes binding his legs to the chair. The knife was terrifyingly sharp. The ropes parted like pasta noodles in hot water.

He grimaced at the injuries he might have sustained if the conflict had gone against him.

Brand stepped forward, kicking the prostrate man in the ribs as hard as he was able. He thought he felt a rib break under the blow.

The old man grunted loudly. He doubled up and groaned, cursing as he was able through his slowly opening airway.

Brand stepped to Madison and freed her from the chair.

She stood, hugging Brand desperately.

Brand returned the hug quickly then separated himself from her embrace. His focus was on his anger and the old man.

He moved to the table where the Sig lay next to the leaning AR style weapon. Collecting the pistol, he crossed to the narrow bed, pulling a filthy pillowcase off the only pillow.

He chambered a round in the pistol and returned to the old man. He tugged him to his feet, the injured old killer complaining and begging.

"Come on, son," he said grimly. "I was only kidding. I was just trying to get a rise out of you."

"You succeeded," Brand said with no detectable anger in his voice. He spoke with a certainty, knowing how his interaction with the man would end. "Step outside."

The man obeyed with an uneasy step. He was enduring terrible pain.

"What you gonna do, son?"

Brand stepped behind the old man, shoving him towards the edge of the clearing. He stopped him near the twin trees where he had found the claymore mine earlier. He pulled the pillowcase over the man's head, covering his eyes. He used a length of the cotton rope to tie off the pillowcase at his neck. He spun him around and around several times. Finally, he stopped him where he was facing the house.

"Walk," Brand commanded.

"Fuck you," the old man screamed. He recognized his fate. "I ain't moving from this spot."

Brand stuck him in the ass with the point of the knife.

The old man squealed and jumped forward.

Madison remained behind Brand, watching the bizarre scene in silent terror. The old man claimed to have booby traps everywhere. She was not certain what Brand had found between the trees, but she was sure it was bad. Brand didn't seem like someone who frightened easily.

"You murdered a man without a thought. You were about to do the same thing to me. The worst part is what you promised to do to my girlfriend. Walk."

The old man shook his head, the pillowcase remained tightly drawn against his face. His head drooped in surrender, and he took a careful step forward.

Brand touched a finger to his lips for Madison's sake as he searched the ground near them. Finding a path he trusted, he led Madison along until they found their tracks from before. They moved without a sound as the old man wandered behind them. At a distance, they watched the sightless old man walk in small semicircles, his hands outstretched before him.

"Where are you boy?" he called with as congenial a tone as he could muster through his fear. "You got the last laugh on the old man. Say something, son!"

Brand made a "shh" gesture to Madison then led her carefully back along the path by which they had arrived. They entered the edge of the surrounding trees when the concussion of a powerful explosion buffeted them.

Madison ducked, moving closer to Brand.

He lifted his pace and soon they arrived at the car.

He helped her into the front seat, then took his place behind the wheel. He started the car and put it in gear. He drove forward, the car breaking through the tight foliage. Fortune favored them and the dense grove gave way once more to a more open pathway. The early morning sky to their left was dark. It was still a few hours before dawn.

Brand decided to put miles between them and the old shack before looking for a place rest. He felt a nagging hunger, though he was certain Madison was worse off.

"How did you get free?" She asked.

He leaned against the driver side door, reaching into his right pocket. He withdrew a small sliver of metal.

"This thing has been a godsend," he said with a sardonic grin. "I'll never look at promotional products the same again."

Madison had no idea what the shard was, nor what he was talking about. Her relief at their escape dulled her curiosity. She moved closer to him and leaned her head on his shoulder.

He leaned into her a fraction to let her know he was okay with the intimacy.

"Oh well," he thought. "Riser would have to deal with it."

26

RISER OCCUPIED ONE OF THE EIGHT
cabins. Conolly and Williams had the second at
the lakeside resort deep in the Michigan
backwoods. So late in the season, they had no
problem booking the rooms. The proprietor, a
friendly older man, with cottony tufts of hair
over his large ears, and a heavy northern
Michigan accent, was pleased with the
unusually late seasonal business.

Riser lamented the slow Wi-Fi, but it
worked. He had cell service as long as he
stepped outside the little red wooden planked
cabin. The portable police band radio provided
no information he could use. Brand had not
been seen. At this point, Riser presumed he
had evaded the net cast around him.

He stepped outside the cabin.

The lake was still enough to walk across.
The murky sky and the penetrating cold gave
the air a heaviness that threatened to stunt his
breathing. Dawn lightened a cloudy but less
threatening sky.

He was alone outside his cabin. He
presumed the others were asleep in their racks.
Riser had not slept for two days but he felt as

sharp as ever. He trusted only in himself during taxing conditions. It troubled him Conolly was so moody and antagonistic. He hoped sleep might dull some of his edge.

He pulled his phone from a jacket pocket. It took only a minute for the network to update his texts and call log. He had several missed calls from Giles. The accompanying texts were frustrated efforts to cajole him into returning the calls.

He pressed Giles' number.

"Riser, I've been calling you all night. I think Brand got away."

"Agreed. What is the FBI saying?"

"That's what I wanted to talk to you about. They are spinning a pretty unbelievable story. If he was able to do what they say he did, this man of yours is a modern-day *Scipio Africanus*."

"What do you mean?"

Africanus was the Roman general who defeated Hannibal..."

"I get the reference, Mr. Giles. What is the FBI claiming Brand did?"

"Somehow, he was able to plan this thing, literally on the fly – meaning we were in the air on my plane when I changed plans and decided to send him with Madison. They believe he was clever enough to know she would be on the plane and secretly communicate with his confederates to get in position. He arranged for the abduction by arranging for a boat and an airplane, complete with boat driver and pilot. Being greedy, he killed his partners to keep the ransom for himself. He has not called with demands and Madison has not returned my calls or texts. They tracked her phone until it lost signal somewhere in the backwoods country of Michigan."

"Then who do you think is behind this?" Riser asked, relieved the billionaire was coming to his senses.

"You're not going to believe me, Dick."

"It's the feds," Riser said simply.

"How did you guess?"

"I have gone through the whole thing over and over and it seems to be the only reasonable conclusion."

"Do you think your man is working with the FBI?"

"No, I don't. I think he thwarted their plot and is on the run – protecting Madison."

"What are we going to do about it?"

"Wherever your daughter is, she is safer with my man than she is with the cops, or even with you. We need to figure out why the FBI tried to kidnap your daughter. We need to learn what they hoped to gain.”

“It’s not money,” Giles said in a musing voice. “They can print all they want. He’s your man again, is he?”

“Never stopped being my man.”

“I’m glad you agree there is something fishy going on here.”

“As I learn more, I’ll keep you informed. Look into why the FBI might want to target you. This is not about your daughter, as I am sure you have already guessed.”

“Kidnapping never is about the victim. It is always about something else.”

“The FBI has taught you well, sir.”

“Don’t be a wise guy, Dick. Thanks for the talk. I was starting to doubt myself.”

“That’s my job, sir.”

The call went dead.

Riser pocketed the phone. He watched the floating steam of his breath in the still air as he worked out what he heard from Giles.

Brand was in the center of a well-planned conspiracy. The kidnapping was about Giles and something in which he was involved. No one anticipated one of his Sovereign men would be involved.

Brand was green, but he was capable, as he had demonstrated thus far. Dead men on the tarmac, disabled aircraft, roadblocks defeated, all of this demonstrated ability on his man's part.

His and his small team's original mission was to neutralize a rogue operative. Now it appeared Brand was at war with the federal government.

At present, Riser's role in the matter was neutral. But if he intervened on Brand's behalf, he crossed a line he could not uncross. He was about to put his reputation and his company's future on the line - for what?

Back home he watched the news and kept up with the political climate as a part of running a business where many of his clients are politically involved or dependent upon the politics of one party or another. Lately, the news was rife with tales of DOJ misdeeds. Until now, Riser discounted the stories as political manipulation of the electorate. Now he found himself in the middle of one of those unbelievable stories. The idea that the FBI would participate in a kidnapping was hard to believe. Kidnapping the daughter of a tech oligarch was the stuff of espionage fantasies, yet this whole mess left no reasonable alternative.

It was time to brief his men. He could not ask them to move forward without full disclosure. Their actions over the next twenty-four hours could change their lives dramatically or end them in shame.

Riser turned from his brown study, absently looking towards the lake. Behind him, Conolly sat before his cabin, on the bench of a dilapidated wooden picnic table. The man watched him with a steady gaze, his fingers knitted, his arms resting atop the plank tabletop.

"Boss," Conolly said with a steady thoughtful voice. "Can we have an honest back and forth here?"

With a dubious look, Riser approached the picnic table. He pocketed his phone and sat opposite his second in command.

"Sure," he replied. "Why not? What's on your mind Mac?"

"From the sound of it," Mac said without moving from his supported posture. "You believe the kid is innocent of all charges, which means our mission is no longer a search and destroy, but rather a search and rescue. Am I reading that right?"

"You can hear," Riser replied curtly. "Do you disagree with the reasoning?"

"It's not up to me to disagree. The job is the job."

"So, we're done here?"

"Not quite," Conolly said, leaning back from the table. "I'm curious why this snot nosed punk is getting cover from you? You claim you don't show favoritism – because the job is the job – yet, if the kid is innocent of kidnapping, as you say, he still violated the most critical of our rules and you are giving him a pass. Why? What is causing this breach of the most fundamental values in our world?"

For a few moments Riser thought about his answer, surveying Conolly carefully. Finally, he leaned forward, speaking in a measured tone so, in case he was eavesdropping, Williams could not hear their conversation.

"Your unprovoked hatred of Mr. Brand is clouding your judgement. Despite yours and your little club's efforts to wash him out, the kid, as you call him, succeeded where no one with his background has."

Conolly inhaled in preparation to retort.

"Let me finish Mac. You and your men are among the best we have, if not absolutely the best, yet you have not broken him. You have not been able to defeat him."

Conolly leaned forward towards Riser with a dangerous look in his eyes.

"Wait one, Mac," Riser urged with a boss' authority. "I brought on the kid as a favor to a friend to whom I owe everything. I warned Brand he gained entry as a favor to someone I respect. I warned him he would have to earn the right to stay. The kid has proven himself to be better than everyone else in my employ, including you.

"He represents the new model of the Sovereign Services Operator in a peacetime future. You and the others are relics. Your battlefield success is precisely what holds you back in this evolving environment in the civilian world.

"Hell, Mac, even the role of the armed services has evolved beyond you and your type. It used to be the military's role to kill people and break things. Its new job is to police and peace keep. That doesn't make you a bad guy, Mac. It just makes you irrelevant. And your inability to see it confirms I am right."

Conolly glared at Riser with a dangerous intent. He was plainly furious.

"What has changed about me, Dick," he snarled, with an unmistakable deadliness.

"That you now believe you can talk right up to me like this?"

"You wanted an honest back and forth. Are you saying I should lie to you?"

"I'd say you might remember what you owe me, Dick."

Riser nodded his reluctant agreement.

"You have been invaluable in my building the organization into what it is today. My reputation would not be what it is today if you hadn't joined us."

Conolly eased back a fraction although he regarded Riser with unabated anger and not a small amount of suspicion.

"Those days have led to a new way," Riser continued. "I am making a business decision that will determine the way forward for me and Sovereign and you are not in it, Mac. I'm sorry. I'll always give you credit for everything you have done."

"It sounds like I'm already gone."

Riser shrugged his heavily muscled shoulders.

"I guess I have nothing to lose," Conolly snarled as he rose from the bench.

Riser stood in a motion, his eyes blazing with an eagerness for combat.

"You forget yourself Mac," he said between his white teeth. "Don't make the mistake of reading your own press and thinking you alone are enough to handle me. Sit down or move out. Staying here will be the end of you."

Williams emerged cautiously from his cabin, drawn by the elevated volume and the dangerous sounds of the conversation between the leaders. He approached to within a safe range, in case the posturing became combat.

Conolly's eyes were riveted to Riser. His lean jaw worked as the fury driving him sought escape.

Riser waited for the other's move, carefully balanced on the balls of his feet. He knew this was the end, and he was prepared to resort to any measure necessary.

Finally, Conolly stepped back from the zone of imminent conflict. He spit on the ground at his feet. He glanced at Riser then at Williams before, with a muttered oath, he returned to his cabin.

Riser moved to return to his cabin.

Williams approached with a steady look.

"Chief, can we have a word?"

Riser halted and gave him a long look. To Williams, there was no mistaking he was angry.

"Can it wait?"

"You will want to hear me out," Williams said in a faint voice.

"Come inside," Riser said finally. "It's cold out here."

Williams followed Riser into his cabin, closing the door behind him.

Riser began packing his bag, stuffing the police band radio inside.

"What's on your mind, Will?"

"Mac is off mission."

"I can see that," Riser said curtly.

"Chief, you don't know the half of it. I don't have much time. Listen up."

There was something in the man's tone that set off Riser's alarm bells. He paused his packing and turned fully towards Williams.

Williams took a step closer and continued in a voice barely audible despite their close proximity.

"Conolly is working for someone else. He offered me a piece of the fee. He has been hired to kill the girl and the rookie."

"Who hired him?"

"He didn't tell me who, only how much. They are paying him five-hundred grand for the girl and the same for Carson Brand."

"Who pays that kind of money for a sanction?"

"Like I said, I don't know."

"That explains the attitude."

"Boss, this isn't attitude. Mac plans to take over Sovereign Services or start his own shop."

"He told you this?"

"Not in so many words, but yeah."

Riser grabbed his bag, zipping the top flap. He gave Williams a dangerous look.

"I appreciate the heads up, Will. Pack your gear and meet me at the car."

Williams nodded then left the cabin. He crossed the few yards to his own cabin and entered. Conolly sat on his bed, his bag packed, on the floor at his feet.

"Where have you been?" Mac asked him.

"I had a word with the Chief."

"About what?"

"About you, Mac. I told him everything. I'm sorry brother. I can't be in the middle of this thing. You two have been spoiling for a row for a while now. This has nothing to do with me."

Conolly's lips stretched into a tight straight line and his eyes narrowed.

"You told him everything? He knows about the contract?"

"Like I said," Williams replied as he turned to pack his own bag. "I told him everything."

Behind Williams, Conolly made no further comment. The other's silence troubled Williams. He zipped his bag, turning quickly towards his mentor, a pistol in his hand.

Conolly was on his feet, a pistol with a silencer in his hand, He shot Williams between the eyes. The black man's mouth sagged open as his knees buckled under him. The pistol wilted in his senseless hand, and he fell on his face.

Conolly picked up his bag and moved to the door of the cabin. He opened the door, checking carefully before stepping outside. He hurried to Riser's cabin and knocked on the door.

The door opened. Conolly trained his pistol on Riser who was fully dressed, wearing his heavy coat and gloves. He held his bag in his right hand.

"Step back inside," Conolly ordered in a dangerous voice.

Riser obeyed.

"Have a seat, Dick," Conolly said, nodding at the bed.

Riser sat on the bed, dropping his bag to the floor.

"What are you doing Mac?" he asked innocently.

"Williams told me he let you in on my little secret. He shouldn't have done that."

The finality of Conolly's words confirmed to Riser Williams was dead.

"The man worshipped you, Mac. What have you done?"

"Shut up," Conolly snapped with remorse. "You already said all I need to hear from you."

Riser nodded, accepting his fate.

"Who would pay a million dollars for a hit? At least tell me what else they offered you that was worth killing your closest friend."

Conolly's eyes glistened with his emotion.

"They are called the Lexicon, Dick. Like I told you, they have a lot more money than you do. They want me to work exclusively for them."

"You killed one of your brothers for money, Mac?"

"Shut up, Dick."

Conolly shot Riser center mass.

Riser fell back on the bed, gasping for air.

Conolly collected Riser's bag and left the room, closing the door behind him.

He tossed both bags into the back seat of the SUV and got in behind the wheel.

His eyes shone with tears as he started the car and drove from the silent lake resort.

GILES ENTERED THE SUN-BRIGHTENED living room of his Malibu beach home. FBI agents spoke quietly in tight groups, and monitored equipment stacked on every available table and desk. Agent Fay, the lead agent on the Abduction Task Force greeted Giles with a barely recognizable nod as he crossed the distance between them.

He was a middle-aged man with a caterpillar mustache and hairy arms and knuckles. His brow furrowed, conveying his serious intent. as he took his position before the billionaire.

"We have nothing so far. The kidnappers thus far have eluded the State Police roadblocks. Either they managed to get though their cordon, or they are in hiding. Have you had any updates from Riser and his team?"

"He just told me the same thing you are saying, Agent Fay," Giles replied crossly. "How can someone so easily elude the efforts of the federal government and all of its tools and power?"

"This is a temporary situation, Mr. Giles," Fay assured him with eyes narrowed persuasively. "We miss very little in cases like this. The perpetrators sometimes find a temporary blind spot. Generally, the false confidence they gain from the perceived victory results in a larger error, and we get our man. Be patient, sir."

"Alright," Giles agreed. "I'll be patient. I wonder if in exchange you might recount how you think this kidnapping plot went down."

Agent Fay pursed his lips. He reminded himself he was talking to one of the richest men in the world. His daughter's kidnaping could easily create greater difficulties than the crime itself. His superiors were clear about what he should and should not discuss with Giles.

For a long moment Fay crafted his response. Finally, he nodded.

"Our analysts have worked tirelessly on a likely scenario profile for the case. Most of what we have shared with you is unchanged but other facts have recently come to light. Most of those facts have been confirmed.

"I will include a few of the facts we have been able to confirm peripheral to the kidnapping plot, but this is what we know so far.

"The man we suspected was the leader in the kidnapping plot, Carson Brand, was only recently employed by Sovereign Services. He has a past filled with clandestine dealings with underworld figures including members of the Mexican Cartels. He has remained under the radar of law enforcement, but he has surfaced continually on the scope of many of our intelligence resources.

"He was hired as a clandestine contractor for the DEA. His handler, and another DEA agent, were killed under mysterious circumstances. It was never proven Brand was the killer, but it is our belief he was involved. He traveled back and forth across the border, making frequent contact with the Cartels, flagging him as a person of interest by two of our human trafficking task forces. Again, we don't have enough evidence to bring him in, but his involvement is irrefutable.

"He was involved with a political campaign tied to middle eastern dissidents. Again, he was a person of interest in a plot to infiltrate the federal government with terrorist cell organizers, but we don't have enough evidence to indict him yet.

"We believe he is now working with an international arm of an Eastern Bloc crime organization called *Solntsevskaya Bratva*. He was not the planner as we at first guessed. He is a

Gopnik - a foot soldier. We believe they recruited him and planned this entire plot. He is acting on their orders. I know you believe sending him with your daughter was a spontaneous decision. If you think carefully, didn't your daughter suggest the idea?"

"Yes but…"

"We believe she was acting upon a suggestion by her friend Beatrice McDermott, who we have concluded was compromised by the same organization. Other members of Sovereign Services have accompanied your daughter on Ms. McDermott's outings. The S.G. found out about it and arranged to get Carson Brand into Sovereign Service's ranks and on that flight. The rest was a calculated risk with a reasonable chance of success."

Giles tapped his toe and nodded his head. It was obvious he was not agreeing with the agent's summary, but instead he was confirming something he was thinking.

"Agent Fay," he said patiently. "After committing the entire might and will of the Federal Bureau of Investigation to my daughter's kidnapping; and after exhaustive investigation and following up leads, you have concluded the Russians did it?"

Agent Fay shrugged.

"They have been highly active in our country. All you have to do is watch the news."

Giles raised his voice so everyone in the room could hear his next words.

"I have watched the news, Agent Fay. The Russians are the new boogeyman when you guys can't or won't come up with the real culprit. This is the most preposterous explanation I have ever heard. I don't believe any of it. When word of this latest Russian hoax makes it onto my new social media platform you people will be a laughingstock for every American and the world to see."

With a look of self-righteous authority, Giles surveyed the men and women around him.

The FBI agents watched him closely. They remained where they were, unmoving. They did not smile or shift their weight uncomfortably, as one might expect after so foolish a conclusion as they were proposing. Instead, they considered him in silent judgement.

Despite his demonstrably triumphant and superior observations, he felt manifestly exposed and vulnerable. He looked once more at Agent Fay. The man frowned at him with a stormy brow.

"Mr. Giles," he said formally, no longer exuding professional good will and patience. "That kind of talk is not helpful."

"I don't care if you think it is helpful..."

"That's enough from you sir, unless you feel we need to bring you into headquarters to answer a few more questions for you."

Giles bit his tongue.

His keen instincts, which had guided him during his considerable successes at the negotiating table, warned him to say no more.

He paused for affect. Finally, he shook his head, feigning compliance.

"I'm just a little stressed out by this whole affair," he explained with an easily construed regret. "Keep up the good work, Special Agent Fay. Again, I apologize for my outburst."

Giles and Fay locked eyes, each gauging the other's trustworthiness and tolerance.

Finally, Fay smiled behind his bushy mustache.

"I understand completely, Mr. Giles. Sometimes our findings are not what we expect either. However, as they say, we always get our man."

Giles swallowed and nodded.

"Let's hope so in this case too."

"Indeed," the agent affirmed with a significant look at the billionaire.

At that moment Giles felt more like a perpetrator than the victim. The reason the FBI targeted him was no longer a mystery. Control of his new social media platform was their goal. His ads leading up to the purchase touted the promise of "free speech no matter what."

Prior to the purchase, his advisors warned him the deal would not be without its dissenters. Now he knew the Department of Justice and the FBI were among those who took exception. He was working alongside those who had kidnapped his little girl. What else would they do to get what they wanted? He had never felt so threatened as he did now.

28

MADISON AWOKE WITH A START. She looked at the drooping headliner above her with confusion until she remembered where she was. Even that recognition was confusing. She didn't truly know where she was. Save for the knowledge she lay in the backseat of a dead FBI agent's car, she knew only she was somewhere in the backwoods of northern Michigan.

She sat upright in the seat.

Brand slept in the front, his breathing soft and measured. She looked around her as the early morning light brightened the encumbering forest. Thankfully, the trees were no longer the forbidding sentinels guarding fearful secrets of the creatures who endured their dreadful nights amongst them. The light of day cast a balm abating their stationary bitterness beneath a bright screen of innocuous apathy.

Her overtaxed mind conjured a dark poetic description of the trees. The involuntary soliloquy issued from her fears and the suffering she had experienced during a night amongst them. She experienced their brittle fingers, scratching at her clothing, and tearing at her flesh. Were these giants envious of those nomadic souls, unbound to the earth, capable of leaving their midst, if only for a moment?

Her bizarre contemplation relegated this imagined jealousy as selfishness. To her mind it was a fair trade. The trees remained in place, abiding for centuries, while mobile creatures occupied the earth for only an instant, their remains interred to feed those same trees. After the terrors of the previous night, she found it difficult to relegate them once more to the typically overlooked background of her life. For eternity they bear silent witness to the deeds evil men visit upon one another. They watch in judgmental silence, assured of their existence beyond the brief time men spend amongst them.

Her scanning gaze fell once more upon Brand who slept soundly, despite being curled in contorted defiance of the cramped width of the car, and the prodding of the steering wheel.

About her feelings for him she teetered from one extreme to another. Since rescuing her from the kidnappers at the air strip, she had suffered doubts and misgivings about him. In other quiet moments, when she had nothing to do other than lament her current dilemma, she found herself in an unbelievable tale where Carson Brand was the central figure.

She rejected her baser instincts she knew attracted her to him. She recognized innately the attraction issued from the most fundamental of all human instincts, her will to survive. In her vulnerable state, he represented an all-in-one desideratum. Although her intellect discarded such a concept, her needs persisted, drawing him closer to her.

He was a bodyguard. His job was to protect and preserve her. Still, she couldn't reason away her need for him. She believed at their core all humans were animal in nature. That odious belief meant, to a degree, she acted upon that nature. A lifetime in upper class polite society, with developed life and social skills, and years of schooling including higher learning, could not subvert her baser instincts.

She once more focused upon the here and now. She had never before slept overnight in a car in the middle of nowhere. She had never been exposed to the brutality and evil actions of others. She had never doubted the future and what it held for her - if she could truly count on a future.

Although she was experiencing all of those things, she realized she had never felt more protected; more cared for than she did now. With a gesture, her previous life had been stripped away. The wealth and the cushion of distance evaporated like a mist, leaving her exposed and vulnerable. She recognized with a surety she could not dispel, there was no returning to the oblivious safety of her old life. As if blinders had been removed from her eyes, she recognized she had always been vulnerable. Gone was her fantasy belief that hierarchical distance and social class were palpable barriers ensuring her safety. She was a fool. This final indictment shoved a dagger through her world view.

She feared falling into a paranoia, a Howard Hughes worthy reaction to her fears. Money could buy only seclusion, a prison of the most luxurious making, but still a prison. She concluded risk was a part of life. She was only now realizing this.

She watched Brand as he stirred, sleep gradually falling from him. She knew Carson Brand recognized this component of life. He accepted it as a reality and conducted himself accordingly. He was probably unaware he confirmed the ill-founded obliviousness of those around him with his altruistic role in their lives.

She had borne witness as he directly or indirectly took the lives of three men. Presenting it in that way necessarily caused her distress. Society holds a narrow view of the killing of another, no matter the reason, no matter the necessity.

She questioned withholding judgment against him for his violence. Her ability to overlook his sins were akin to her view of a soldier's actions on the battlefield.

Although she avoided trite absolutions like kill or be killed, he had no other choice. She knew she was not abducted, dead, or worse because of his intervention.

She glanced at Brand. With a short inhalation, his breathing paused. Although he hadn't moved, she knew he was instantly awake, taking stock of the world around him. He sat up with a groan of aching muscles and cramped tendons. After a brief scan of the woods outside, he stretched then turned to her.

"You're awake," he said warmly. "How are you feeling this morning?"

She ignored the discomfort in her stomach.

"I'm fine. Do you know where we are?"

He again looked around him.

"I think we are beyond the state police cordon. We need to eat and get a new car."

"Carson," she said hesitantly. "What are your plans for me?"

He looked at her with mild curiosity. His expression exhibited a measure of confusion.

It occurred to her she sounded like a victim negotiating with her kidnapper.

"What I mean to say is, we can't run forever. If I have the chance to explain all of this to my father, maybe to the press, you will be in the clear."

Brand nodded.

He had entertained the same thoughts. He had also rejected them because of what Madison did not know about him. She was unaware of his history with federal law enforcement. They were framing him for the kidnapping. There was no scenario he could imagine where they assumed culpability for the crime and let him walk.

Madison was in more danger than she suspected. She knew the truth about who was responsible for the plot against her and her father. They had to silence her: another body on the pile they created to hide the truth of their misdeeds and secret plans.

He would not risk her life to save his own. If what Beatrice said was the truth, then Madison's father was in as much danger as she was. Delivering her to him, or arranging to meet with him, would be the same as giving her to the FBI.

He thought about Riser and Sovereign. He doubted they were on his side. The FBI would turn Riser against him. As Madison and he sat there in the woods in a dead FBI agent's car, the owner of Sovereign surely led *The Ten* in pursuit. Like the FBI, if The Ten caught up with them, there would be no capture then jail time. He would join Brett, the FBI agent, in a hole in the ground deep in the Michigan wilderness.

After her liberation by The Ten, Madison would find herself in the hands of those who sought to silence her.

"Are you listening to me?" she asked.

"Every word," he replied immediately. "If you need to pee, now is the time. We have a long day ahead."

Madison looked at him as though he were oblivious to their plight. His focus was on her basic bodily functions? This wasn't a weekend camping trip. This was no pleasant outing to the backwoods. The stakes were as high as they could get.

She struggled to keep her own emotions under control. How could he understand the dangers and still waste his valuable attention on unimportant details?

Brand seemed to sense her misgivings.

"I mention it because I need to go. Wait here if you don't. I'll be right back."

Brand exited the car and moved to the tree line.

Madison opened the door and stood next to the car. The idea she and Brand might be separated, even by the steel and glass of the car door, moved her to eliminate any barrier between them.

Her thoughts returned to the overly dramatized impression she held of the trees and the dangers they concealed. For a moment she experienced a rising panic, overwhelming her with former fantastical whims. She feared Brand might not return from his visit amongst the trees.

To her relief, he emerged from their clutches, nonplussed, walking with a casual stride.

She entered the passenger seat of the sedan. He took the driver seat and cranked the engine.

"How are we on gas?" she asked in an attempt to insert practical topics into the demanding urges of her out of control imagination.

Brand canted his head to see the dash gauges around the steering wheel.

"I think we have at least a hundred miles of fuel left. We should be able to make a car change before then."

"Do you know where to go from here?"

"I don't," he admitted with unnerving candor. "We don't have a map and I have never been to Michigan before."

Her eyes widened with fear.

"We could wander around in this wilderness for another hundred miles," she said. "We might be here overnight again, but this time on foot. I'm concerned."

"I understand," he said hesitantly. "I am out of ideas other than to keep going west until we find a way out of this. We escaped a dragnet, but I expect the perimeter to expand as time passes. I'll listen to any ideas you have. What should we do?"

"I don't know," she cried in frustration. "I'm not trying to be critical here."

Brand put the car in gear and drove forward. He waited for her to add to her comment.

She maintained her silence for a long time.

Brand cleared his throat, unwilling to antagonize her further.

She spoke quickly to head off any defensiveness from him.

"I can't spend another night out here, Carson!"

He glanced at her with concern.

Was she losing it? He hoped not. Primarily, he had enough to worry about without adding her retreating sanity to the list. Secondly, he didn't want to lose respect for her strength and courage. He valued those things he believed about her. It would be a huge disappointment if he had overestimated her.

"You won't have to," he said with as much confidence as he could muster.

She stared at him, the forest moving slowly by beyond the driver side window, as though waiting for her fears to become reality.

He did not turn his face from the route before them.

29

BRAND PULLED THE SEDAN ONTO THE snowy gravel apron beside the pavement. He searched the area around the sixties-style filling station. It was built in a large clearing amongst the dense forest along the highway. There were no patrons save for a man at one of the two pumps, standing outside his running car, filling it with gas. Most significantly, he detected no police presence at the station nor in the vicinity. An older model pickup truck sat near the roadside with a red and black "for sale" sign in the windshield.

He shifted the car into gear and pulled into the station lot, parking the sedan beside the old pickup. He stepped from the car and began a quick inspection of the truck. It seemed soundly maintained and well taken care of. Even the upholstery seemed gently used.

A gray headed man in heavy boots, and a Mackinaw Jacket, covering worn overalls appeared from the front door of the station, approaching while wiping his hands on a red shop rag.

He spoke when he was in range.

"Good morning," he said. "You interested in buying Fred?"

"His name is Fred?" Brand asked with an appreciative smile.

"Yep, named after my dad's best friend."

Brand nodded, continuing his survey of the truck. The name "Fred" was stenciled on the rear of the truck bed.

"How much?"

The overalled man frowned as he conjured his best sales skills.

"I can't give it away son," he said carefully. "I rebuilt the motor myself. It's hardly been driven since Dad passed two years ago."

"Sorry for your loss," Brand said with the sincerity only another who had lost their dad could feel.

Overalls nodded appreciatively.

"How does $2,000.00 sound to you?"

"It sounds fair," Brand replied.

He pulled his wallet from his pants. He counted out several hundred-dollar bills.

"Here's $2,300.00," he said, handing over the cash.

"$2,000.00 is the price, son. I won't take a dime more. Follow me. I've got the title inside."

"I'll be right there," Brand said, moving to the open window at the sedan's passenger door. To Madison he said in a low voice. "Can you drive the car into town and park it off the main road?"

"Yes," she replied uncertainly. "Where do you want me to take it?"

"Find a grocery store or somewhere else with a crowded parking lot. Pull into the first place you see. I'll pick you up there."

Madison moved to the driver seat. She started the car and put it into gear.

Brand watched the car enter the street and drive away before he turned to the gas station office. Inside. He signed the title transfer paperwork and purchased a Michigan state road map.

He located Madison and the gray sedan in the parking lot of a strip center about a mile away. She sat in the driver seat waiting for him when he parked the truck in a space beside her.

He got out of the truck, looking around the parking lot.

Madison stepped out of the sedan, joining him beside the truck.

"Is this okay," she asked.

"I think so," he replied. "Gather your stuff and let's get going."

"Do you ever eat?" she asked.

Brand gave her an embarrassed look.

"Sorry, about that," he replied. "I forget to eat sometimes. We'll get something at the next place we see."

The next place was a small truck stop along the narrow road they followed headed west. Brand parked in a space to the side of the store.

"Probably there is an all points on us," he explained. "We can't risk being seen together, and we can't stay in one place for long."

He pointed at the two doors on the side of the building. Depicted on the doors, one had the silhouette of a man and the other a woman.

"You can freshen up in the bathroom while I get us something to eat."

"I'll wait here for you," she said, holding his arm.

"You're safe for now, Madison," he assured her placing a hand on her hand. "I'll be right back."

She said nothing as she decided.

He looked her over. Her face was dirty from their time in the woods. Tears had left streaks on her cheeks. She looked much different than the confident billionairess he remembered stepping from her limousine outside her father's plane so long ago.

"You will feel better if you splash some water on your face and clean up a little. I'll meet you back here in five."

She released him.

He stepped out of the car, and she watched him until he disappeared into the store. She pulled down the passenger side visor. The little mirror revealed to her a view of her which was vastly different than her self-image. She quickly made her way to the bathroom doors.

Madison was in the bathroom when Brand returned, a burgeoning plastic bag in his hand. He took his seat placing the bag in the middle. He opened the map and quickly located their position. He estimated they were some one-hundred miles from the Wisconsin border. He suspected the state line would be heavily guarded. Lake Superior and Canada were to the north. If he were able to cross the lake, entering an international border sounded even more risky.

The women's bathroom door opened. Madison emerged, her appearance much changed. Her face was clean and bright once more. She was able to clean most of the dirt spots from her clothing. She took her seat beside Brand, attacking the plastic bag without a word.

"The white paper bag has some warmed up kolaches and sausage wraps," Brand explained as he surveyed the map.

Madison found the paper bag, withdrawing a warm kolache. She took an unladylike huge bite, chewing with a full-mouthed smile.

"You look better," he said, selecting his own kolache. "This map tells me where we are but not how to get somewhere safe."

Madison wiped her mouth on a napkin and drank orange juice from a bottle. She again wiped her mouth as she swallowed.

She held out a hand for the map.

Brand passed it to her.

After a brief review of the map, she handed it back to Brand.

"I need a phone," she said finally.

30

CONOLLY PULLED INTO A GAS STATION, parking beside one of the two gas pumps out front. He stepped out of the car and made his way to the store to pay for gas. He looked around him, surveying his surroundings carefully. How he handled himself over the next few hours would determine the course of his life. He could afford no further foul ups after sharing too much with Williams, resulting in him having to close the loop on his former friend, and his former boss.

Inside the small store was an older man. He stood behind the old-fashioned cash register with an expectant smile.

"Can I help you?"

"I need to fill it up."

Conolly handed over a hundred-dollar bill.

The old man opened the cash register to deposit the bill. He lifted the divided cash drawer. Beneath the tray, notes filled the drawer.

"Busy day?" Conolly asked indicating the full drawer.

"Not so much," the clerk assured him. "Just sold my old truck to a young guy. I hated to lose that truck, but I needed the money. With your hundred, I guess I'll have to stop at the bank today."

"A young guy you say? Was he with a pretty blonde?"

"Yeah. In a hurry – a beautiful young girl with him."

"How long ago was that?"

"I don't know," the old man replied guardedly. "Friend of yours?"

"Just curious."

Conolly's look gave the old man pause. It was unclear why the man gave him the willies. He decided to provide the stranger no reason to be unfriendly.

"I guess they passed by less than two hours ago, headed west. If you hurry, you can catch them. That old truck is sound but not fast."

"Describe the truck."

"1996 blue Ford half-ton with "Fred" stenciled on the bed."

"Thanks."

Conolly returned to the SUV and gassed it. He was able to get to eighty-six dollars before the tank was full and the pump stopped. He didn't bother to collect his change as he got back on the road.

BRAND SAT IN THE TRUCK, sipping a root beer as he watched Madison, talking on one of the two payphones at the front of an old grocery store. She gave him the thumbs up sign as she hung up the phone and returned to the truck.

She took her seat and closed the door, beaming at Brand.

"We need to get to a town called Crystal Falls. There is an airfield nearby called Stambaugh Airport. A helicopter will be there in the morning to get us out of here."

Brand searched the map for Crystal Falls. He located it and the airport about fifteen miles west of town.

"It's about three hours away by Fred," he joked with a relieved smile for Madison. "How did you manage a chopper?"

"I called Wes Conklin, my father's personal attorney in New York," she explained. "We can trust him. He and my father have been an item since their twenties."

Brand gave her a confused look.

"Wes and my dad went to school together. They are the best of friends. The story goes that everyone who knew them thought they were gay. My father admitted the only way they could have been closer was if they were."

"What are the odds the FBI has him or his phone under surveillance?"

"It doesn't matter," Madison explained. "I spoke with his daughter. We don't hang out, but we are friendly. She was eating breakfast with her dad when I called. She passed him the phone and I spoke with him in person. We are supposed to be at the airstrip at daylight tomorrow morning."

Brand started the truck's ignition and pulled away from the store parking lot. Once they were on the highway, he looked at her.

"Thank you," he said with the gravity of genuine gratitude. "You saved us, and I owe you one."

Madison looked out the window, pleased by his comment. She watched the snow-covered trees pass by her window, a smile tugging at the corners of her lips.

He gave his attention to his driving, alert for police presence.

32

IT WAS AFTER DARK WHEN CONOLLY entered Crystal falls. He had seen no sign of his targets or the blue truck. His journey was a slow process of visiting every parking lot near the highway, searching for the Ford truck. He suspected they would follow the less travelled highways west as far as they could. His brief departures from the road were merely a measure of caution in case his instincts were wrong.

Iron Mountain was a larger town, but it would take them south of the westward routes they had maintained since leaving the airport at St. Ignace. He doubted they would deviate, particularly to reach a larger town with a larger risk of police presence. They travelled west towards Crystal Falls. They might even enjoy the luxury of a hot meal and a soft bed.

Crystal Falls was the only town of significant size he had encountered since he left the old man at the gas station. Police presence on the route had been light considering there was supposed to be a statewide manhunt in progress. He drove the downtown streets slowly, on the lookout for the blue truck named

Fred. The town was small and easily searched. He concluded they were not near the downtown. He decided to widen his search to smaller rural inns or motels within a short driving distance to restaurants or grocery stores.

A stop at a small boutique near downtown had yielded new clothing for Madison. Brand checked them into a family run inn willing to take cash and requiring no ID. They showered and changed. Although exhausted, Madison agreed eagerly to dinner out. They didn't have to drive far to find a cozy diner.

Brand ate the last of his fries as he watched Madison from across the table, beside a window with a view of the parking lot. At the motel, with a shower and a change of clothes, she shed her disheveled appearance. Once more she was impossible to look away from. The few male patrons near them shared his attraction for her, drawing the ire of jealous spouses.

She was dressed similarly to the other women in the diner, but she had a singular beauty emanating from within, unmatched by anyone there.

Brand drained his coffee and leaned back with a satisfied look. She had nearly cleaned her plate, an unusual feat. She lowered her fork and sipped from a glass half full of diet Coke.

"I'm not sure what will happen once we leave here," Brand said with only enough volume for her to hear. "But I want you to know, I think you are one of the strongest women I have ever met. I wish you weren't in the middle of this, but I feel confident you are going to be okay."

Madison's eyes shone as she returned the glass to the wet ring of its former position. She wanted her response to be adequate to his sentiment without giving too much away about how she felt about him.

She opened her mouth to speak but no words came. She closed her lips and looked towards the long bar lining the back wall of the deli. Several men in work boots, jeans, and heavy jackets drank coffee and ate from filled plates.

"Thank you," she finally managed to say without looking at him.

"If you are almost finished, we need to get back to the room before we are spotted here."

"Brand," she said abruptly, reaching across the table, taking his hand. "I have told you too many times I haven't met anyone like you before."

He nodded, glancing at her hand in his.

"You are the first man I have ever met who cared about what I thought, or what I wanted. You are tough, but not mean. You are one of those guys who runs blindly into a burning building, but you aren't careless. I think you are attracted to me, but you don't let your urges show. So, when you pay me one of the greatest heartfelt compliments I have ever heard, I take it seriously. I take it to heart. Again, thank you."

Brand swallowed. It was his turn to feel off balance. Finally, he nodded.

"You're welcome."

He paid the tab and they returned to the truck. With the night came a noticeable drop in temperature. As he led Madison to the truck, he surveyed the sky but found no clue what was in store for them. He opened the passenger door for her then took his seat behind the wheel.

Their motel was a few blocks east of the deli. He let her into the little room before returning to the truck. He hid it behind the motel, within a tight grove of trees.

He checked the area with a sweeping look before walking back to the motel parking lot, then to their room. He heard Madison in the bathroom changing for bed. There were two double beds in the room. He sat on the bed nearest the door, pulling off his boots and socks. He changed into clean boxers from a new package inside his go bag. He squeezed toothpaste on a toothbrush and moved to the window. He scrubbed his teeth as he looked out the window from behind a slightly open curtain.

He moved to the vanity outside of the closed bathroom door and rinsed his mouth. Returning to the window, he resumed his watch on the parking lot.

He heard the bathroom door open. He turned from the window to see Madison watching him, wearing only one of his tee shirts. She turned off the bathroom light and approached him.

He made no effort to resist her as she wrapped her arms around his neck. When she rose to kiss him, he met her halfway.

She pressed her body into him.

He was a good kisser.

33

CONOLLY ABANDONED HIS SEARCH. He doubted his instincts now. He was more than three hours into the search with no success. He searched every motel, hotel, and inn he could find with no sign of the truck or the rookie. He sat in his car off the main road, in the parking lot of a diner with a Tudor front. He watched a matronly woman lock the front door.

He put the car in gear and rolled down his window. He pulled near the woman, but not near enough to alarm her.

"Sorry to bother you, ma'am," he said with a big smile. "I'm looking for a friend of mine who I was supposed to meet here in town. He is with a pretty blonde girl, driving a blue pickup truck. Have you seen him around?"

The middle-aged woman rested her weight onto one foot and placed a hand on her hip.

"If you see them two, you let them know I'm probably gonna get divorced tomorrow morning because of her! Marvin couldn't keep his damned eyes off of her and I had to send him home before I killed him."

Conolly concealed his surprise at his good fortune.

"Sorry to hear that, ma'am," he said with as much empathy as he could fake. "She has that effect on a lot of people. How long ago were they here?"

"I guess about two or three hours ago. They drove west. As tired as they looked, I doubt they got far."

"Where is the nearest hotel?"

"Hotel?" she repeated with a doubtful tone. "there ain't no hotels nearby. There is a little inn about a quarter mile away."

She gave him general directions and he left her with his sincere thanks. The motel was easy to find. There were three vehicles parked before numbered doors, but none of them was a blue pickup. He stopped before the office and went to the door.

With a hand, he covered the glare from the glass as he looked into the office. The room was dark, a closed sign hanging from the inside of the single window.

Frustrated, he returned to his car, slamming the driver side door. Starting the car, he drove back to the narrow lane in front of the inn. To his left was the highway and a long night of searching. He decided to bed down for the night. The office was closed so he would get no room there, but he was sorely tired and had little patience with locating and checking into a different hotel.

He drove to the back of the motel, searching for a place in the woods to park. He jammed on the brakes. There it was, parked in a grove of trees, the blue truck, the name Fred was plainly visible.

Warily, he searched the area around him. He saw nothing to indicate he was seen, and like most motels, there were no windows in the back wall.

He was in a quandary. There were maybe eight rooms to the motel. He could rule out the rooms with the three cars parked before them. How could he identify the correct room of the remaining five without disturbing the guests, or alerting Brand and the girl to his presence?

The most reasonable choice was also the most unpleasant. He would have to wait out the night in his car. That tactic guaranteed he would not make his presence known by accident and provided him the element of surprise when he moved on the kid. The terrain was not ideal in that there was no choke point or limiting obstacle in which to bottle up the rookie.

Conolly shrugged. He was not worried about it. The kid was a wet-behind-the-ears civilian with a long run of luck on his side. His luck would end at first light.

Conolly drove along the road a short distance until he found a secure hiding place for his car with a good view of the blue truck.

Brand nuzzled Madison's hair, his chest pressed against her back, his arms hugging her close. He listened to her rhythmic breathing, in an exhausted sleep. He carefully lifted his arm off her. She made a small noise of protest as he rolled away from her.

He rose, tucking the blankets around her. He pulled on his boxers and sat on the other bed. He glanced at the red digital readout on the lamp table alarm clock. It read 2:48. He knew he would not be able to sleep. They were supposed to be at the airfield at first light. He didn't want to oversleep. He stood with a shake of his head. The early wake up was not what troubled him. he knew he was resorting to a minor pretense to shield him from the issue troubling him.

Reaching for his pants, he pulled them on and zipped up his DuraShocks. He donned his coat and dropped the Sig in a jacket pocket. He managed to leave the room without waking Madison.

Outside, he leaned against the wall, exhaling a steam cloud as his mind worked at the real problem, his feelings for Madison. He excoriated himself for giving into his weakness for her. He punished himself not for surrendering to his desires, but rather for placing her in danger.

He didn't at all consider himself superstitious, but the facts pointed to a trend promising dire consequences for the women he cared about. This torturously dark pathway of his thoughts was familiar ground for him, particularly lately with his developing feelings for the heiress.

They had no future together. She was from a different world.

He was the hired help, he mused with a grim humor.

He saw she was attracted to him and had strong feelings for him. Her words and manner confirmed this. Would those feelings weather the light of day, in New York, amongst her rich friends?

The only answer was no.

Seeking a new outlet for his attention, he looked at the three cars in the parking lot. Each was parked before a door, the rooms beyond were dark. The night was stiff with the bitter cold, silent in its white blanket, but everything seemed as it was when they arrived from the diner.

Brand placed his hands in his jacket pockets. He found it impossible to distract himself from his thoughts of her. She filled his imagination, leaving no room for caution or doubt. He examined his attraction for her. She was beautiful, but that hackneyed observation was not what piqued his interest in her. From that moment after the party, when she offered to listen to him, then later maintaining her trust in him despite his admission he was not a super trooper, to the phone call she made to arrange the chopper, there was so much to her. A highly intelligent, sensitive, and thoughtful woman abided within a misleading façade of a beautiful, selfishly rich, socialite.

He again pushed these thoughts away. He decided to check on the truck, maybe move it closer for their departure in a couple of hours. He pushed himself away from the wall and walked towards the end of the building. He turned the corner, spotting his truck in the darkness near the grove of trees.

A flash of light caused him to leap to the side, crouching near the back of the motel building. He peered into the darkness beyond the trees shielding his truck from view. The flicker of light had come from that direction.

He waited breathlessly, senses at their highest level of attention. He waited a full three minutes before he saw a dull glow through the trees at some hundred yards beyond his truck.

He surveyed the area nearby. There was little cover behind the motel until the open area he presumed to be a lawn in a warmer season, ended in a region of trees and underbrush.

He hurried across the stark white of the snow-covered lawn, taking cover in a copse of trees. His ears strained to hear any sound from the direction of the light. He heard nothing other than his own breathing and the snow crunching underfoot.

It occurred to him he was being overly suspicious. The light could be a house hidden in the trees beyond. He didn't recall seeing a drive meeting the road beyond where he pulled off into the trees. That didn't preclude a house being there, but he tended to trust his instincts and the alert faculties of his subconscious. He had sensed no house nearby. The thought seemed silly when presented that way, but he had relied upon less with great results.

He eased into the comparatively darker cover under the trees, moving carefully, avoiding branches and brambles. The light glowed once again. The illumination had the distinctive glow of an electronic device. It was probably a cell phone.

What was someone doing in the woods at three in the morning on a cell phone?

Brand eased forward a few more yards, stopping short. He was in the open between trees, but he dared not take another step. He clearly made out the silhouette of an automobile. The glow appeared more regularly. The person inside was using his or her phone.

Brand crept forward until he was no more than twenty feet from the car. Suddenly the door opened, and a large man stepped outside. The dome light gave brand a clear view of Mac Conolly.

The man closed the car door then unzipped, taking a piss on the rear tire of the car. The dome light must have spoiled his night vision because he didn't notice Brand standing no more than five yards away.

Conolly finished emptying his bladder and zipped up. He was about to return to the car when his shoulders stiffened, and he froze where he was.

Brand was unsure of Conolly's relationship with him, other than his hatred of him. Was Riser nearby? Was Sovereign arrayed against him. Brand gripped the Sig inside his jacket pocket.

"Hello Conolly," he said warily. "What are you doing hiding out here in the cold?"

Conolly's shoulders relaxed by degrees. Finally, he turned to face Brand. Surprisingly, he had a strange smile on his face.

"Hey rookie," he returned uncertainly. "Good to see you. You got the girl?"

"Where's Chief?"

"He's in town watching the roads. We have been following you, making sure to keep you safe."

"Why didn't you just knock on the door, instead of sneaking around?"

"Dick said he wasn't sure how you would react to us just showing up out of the blue."

Brand made no rejoinder to Conolly's story. It wasn't adding up.

"Come on kid," Conolly said with a good-natured gesture. "I can see you gripping that gun in your pocket. We're all on the same team. Relax and invite me inside. Now that you found me, there's no reason to hide out here in the freezing cold any longer. I'll call Dick and let him know we're all clear."

Brand made no move to release the gun. Conolly hated him with a passion. This sudden show of good-natured regard was unexpected. If this was a trap, wouldn't Riser be there with a team instead of leaving one man to watch him?

Conolly saw Brand struggling with his doubts. He searched his thoughts for anything that would assuage the kid.

"What you did for Lansch that day, you showed your true colors kid. We weren't very nice to you, and you put that aside. John's a close friend and I appreciate what you did.

"Hell, even Dick has talked me into seeing a side of you I didn't see before."

Conolly took a step forward, his hand extended.

"Here's my apology for the shitty way I treated you. No hard feelings I hope?"

Brand hesitated, looking alternately at the outstretched hand and the man's face. His senses were alive with klaxon bells and sirens. Was his reaction about their unpleasant past and making peace with it, or was Conolly a danger to him still?

"We know all about the FBI's plot and how they are trying to frame you. We are going to help clean up this whole mess. Now how about it? Friends?"

Brand released his grip on the Sig and extended his hand to shake. They exchanged a firm handshake.

"No hard feelings," Brand confirmed. "I need to let her know we have company so she can make herself decent."

He turned to lead the way when he heard the snap of a knife and the rush of feet as Conolly closed on him.

Brand spun to his right as Conolly's blade sliced his coat.

Conolly recovered with unnerving quickness, delivering a hard blow to the side of his head, knocking Brand sprawling in the snow.

Brand's instinct was to reach for the Sig, but Conolly was upon him, his leading hand outstretched, knife clutched close to his body.

Brand threw a handful of snow and dirt into Conolly's face as he rolled away, regaining his feet. He reached for the pistol. It partially cleared his jacket pocket when Conolly struck him in the abdomen with a straight kick, knocking the wind out of him.

Brand fell to the ground again. The Sig falling from his grasp.

Conolly was suddenly above Brand. With a flash of movement, the SEAL's knife shot forward, penetrating Brand's coat, raking his ribs painfully.

Brand felt a searing burn where the blade sliced him. He abandoned his defensive motion with his arms. Instead, he grabbed the older man by the back of the neck, drawing him closer.

The SEAL extended his off arm to stop his descent, leaving his left side exposed.

Brand struck him hard in the ribs with a powerful right-hand blow. His left grasped the knife hand in a vice-like grip. His right drew back before delivering three hard shots to the side of Conolly's head.

The blows stunned Conolly, temporarily delaying his assault as his head swam.

Brand felt a warm flow on his cold skin as blood seeped from the wound. He struggled to regain his breath. Desperately, he brought a knee up, crushing Conolly's testicles.

Conolly rolled off Brand with a groan, the knife gripped in his right hand. Brand kicked him over and over, breaking ribs and damaging internal organs.

Conolly spit blood, trying to protect himself from the attack with impotent slashes of the knife and weak attempts at blocking the kicks with his left arm.

Brand kicked the knife hand, the blade spinning off into the darkness. He was fully engorged with wild rage. He fell heavily upon the man with his knees, bludgeoning his face and head with a flurry of downward blows.

Conolly's face quickly became a mask of torn flesh and dripping blood. The snow beneath and around him grew freckled with blood spatter.

Breathing heavily, drooling blood, Brand stood from the unconscious man. The murderous rage boiled within him still. He wanted to finish Conolly. The hunger for his death was a palpable thing, desperately craving satiety.

Brand's base animal blood lust drew from him a low moan, as he resisted his rage.

He moved to the gun which lay in the snow. He collected it, ineffectually wiping it clean with his hands. His head swam. Either the loss of blood or his receding blood lust caused his head to buzz and a staticky haze clouded his vision. He located the knife and returned to

Conolly's unconscious body. He plunged the blade into the meaty part of the man's leg.

"You won't follow me anymore," he said aloud and turned towards the motel.

He was able to open the driver side door of his truck before he passed out the first time. He came to, lying on the ground below the open door. He stood, then climbed into the cab. He managed to close the door and start the engine before he once more lost consciousness. When he regained his senses, he opened his eyes to a lightening eastern sky. Snow fell in small hard chips. At a distance, he could see the dark spot where Conolly lay on the ground. He had not moved from where Brand had left him.

The heat in the running truck was comforting. The heater blew warm air, dispelling his previous chill. He opened his jacket, revealing a blood-soaked tee shirt beneath. Lightheaded, he put the truck in gear and drove to the parking space before his room. He left the truck running as he moved to the door. He produced the room key, but the key slot eluded his efforts to insert it.

The door opened. Madison paused, his appearance a shock to her slowly awakening senses.

"My god, Brand. What happened?"

He staggered inside the room. With a quick look around outside, she closed and locked the door.

She followed him to the vanity where he removed his coat and shirt. He was bleeding from a long slice across his left side. The area around the wound was covered in dried blood, but the slice oozed when he moved.

He dropped a towel into the sink and turned on the water.

"I'll do this," she said. "I need you to lay down."

Brand's expression softened as he turned to look at her.

"What do you know about field dressing a wound?" he asked with a vacant grin.

"I know enough to see you are going into shock. Lay down here."

She helped him to the bed where earlier they had made love. She pressed him down onto his back.

He resisted her efforts, stubbornly lobbying to take care of the wound himself. She finally convinced him to remain still while she fashioned one of his tee shirts into a makeshift bandage.

"We have to get you to a hospital," she said grimly as she cleaned and bound his wound.

"We have to get to that airfield," he said with a sudden return of serious resolve. "The knife bounced off my ribs. Stop the bleeding for now."

"What knife?" she cried, leaning closer to his face. "Who is out there?"

"I took care of it," he said, his eyes lolled in his head as shock overpowered his reason. His head fell back upon the bed, his eyes closed as his mind swam from his efforts to speak.

"I don't know what else to do for you," she announced after securing the rudimentary bandage.

"Load our stuff in the truck," he said weakly. "You are going to have to drive."

She hurried around the room, packing their belongings, often mixing them into both bags as space and time allowed. She carried the bags to the truck.

She cast a worried look around the parking lot. She saw nothing out of the ordinary that would indicate a life and death struggle. The warm interior of the truck pleased her. Snow was falling and the warmth of the truck offered a welcoming end to her labor of clearing the room.

She helped Brand from the bed. Although he tried, she bore much of his weight as she helped him to the passenger seat of the truck. He was surprisingly heavy.

Once she had him securely inside the cab with seatbelt locked, she took her place in the driver's seat. She backed from the parking slot and drove to the road. She paused at the parking lot entrance to familiarized herself with the route. She studied the map briefly, confirming her route, then drove away from the inn.

She passed through downtown Crystal Falls. The streets were empty in the early morning hour. Like bored bullies, the few signal lights in town delayed her progress at empty intersections.

She turned west and drove the rural highway, the snow flurries increasing. When she finally arrived at the airport, the morning was a dull gray, snow and sleet tapping on the windshield.

Her heart leapt at the sight of blinking red and green lights on the fuselage of the sleek Heli jet waiting on the tarmac, its rotors spinning casually. She parked the truck on the pad near the chopper. One of the pilots helped her with her bags and supported Brand, getting him secured inside the aircraft.

As the chopper gained altitude, she looked down at the blue truck, growing smaller as it retreated into history behind them.

34

BRAND OPENED HIS EYES TO A VASTLY
different world than he last recalled. The cold
gray of rural Michigan was gone. In its place
was a modern glass and steel room with an
expansive view of a downtown cityscape. He
rested in a bedroom high above the ground
amongst the tops of towering skyscrapers.

The room was obviously part of a luxury
apartment in a large city. He touched his face
with a tentative hand. He was clean and
shaved. Next, he carefully probed his left side.
His wound was bandaged and tightly bound.
He felt some discomfort, but none of the sharp
pains he had experienced on the journey to the
airport. He deduced the tightness he felt at the
wound were probably sutures.

He grunted as he sat up, rotating his
position so his feet were over the side of the
bed. He stood carefully. He experienced a
small measure of lightheadedness but was able
to maintain his upright position. He wore
white boxers but no shirt. He made his way to
the adjoining bathroom. He looked at his
reflection in the long mirror.

Overall, other than the wide bandage around his ribs, he looked no worse off for his experiences, although he detected a lingering weariness around the eyes.

He splashed water on his face and dried himself with a hand towel. He returned to the bedroom, moving to the near window wall. He was unable to identify the city with a casual observation. The cloudy sky seemed to indicate he was still in the northern part of the country, maybe Chicago or New York. He wasn't familiar with either place, other than what he had seen on TV.

"You're awake."

He turned at the sound of the familiar female voice. Madison stood in the doorway, dressed in her familiar fashion. She was no longer the victim of a kidnapping, skulking around the wilderness. She looked refreshed.

"You look good," he said with a weak smile. "Thanks for getting us out of there."

"You're welcome," she said, returning the smile. "Hungry?"

He nodded.

"How long?"

"Only a couple of days, but you have missed a lot."

Brand returned to the bed, sitting on the end.

"Are you still a little weak?" she asked, stepping into the room.

"I'm alright," he replied with a grimace.

"You've clothes in the closet. Lunch should be ready by the time you get dressed."

She looked him over appraisingly. Beneath the polish, he saw she still had feelings for him. It shone in her eyes and the concern in her expression.

"Thanks," he said. "I'll be out in a minute."

She left him as he rose with a grimace.

Inside the closet hung two suits and some more casual clothing items. The suits seemed tailored. His go bag was stowed in a large cubby in a built-in wardrobe and chest of drawers. He found socks and expensive shoes in his size.

When he emerged from his room he was dressed in slacks, sweater, and loafers. It wasn't his style, but he appreciated the fit of the fine clothing.

He entered a high-ceilinged flat, consisting of a plush living area and high-tech kitchen. A chef worked busily at food preparation.

Madison appeared through an adjoining doorway.

"Very handsome," she remarked. "Have a seat at the table. Hans will serve."

They sat at the table.

"A chef," Brand said. "Very nice."

"I usually eat out," she explained. "Hans is Daddy's chef. He is on loan until you are well enough to whip up some more of that sturdy Texas fare."

"Is this your place?"

"It is. Welcome to New York."

"We shouldn't be here," Brand warned with a darkening of his features. "The FBI will look here first."

"Calm down, Brand. Like I said, a lot has happened in the past two days."

Hans brought plates, setting them before them.

"Bon appetite," he said with a German accent.

"Thanks," Brand said to the chef, who regarded him with suspicion at the unexpected gratitude.

"You're welcome."

Madison giggled like a schoolgirl.

"You take a bit of getting used to for the unsuspecting."

Brand lifted the water glass, returning it empty to the tabletop. He put his napkin in his lap, digging into the sizzling steak.

"The man you nearly killed behind the inn will survive," she began with the tone of a scolding parent. "But he will never walk without a limp. I can't believe what you did while I slept.

"Your boss, Mr. Riser, was released from the hospital after being shot in the chest by the man you fought. What was his name? Conolly? He was saved by a bullet proof vest and a heavy jacket. Apparently, they fought about you and me and this Conolly shot him, leaving him for dead."

"Riser wasn't after us after all?" he said.

"He was pursuing us, but my dad told me neither of them believed the FBI's story about your role in the kidnapping for long. Conolly was secretly working for some international organization called the Lexicon. They seem to be behind this whole thing. My interview with Sandy Kincaid, a Washington Post reporter, hit the streets this morning. It is all over the news today. You didn't tell me you were part of the group that took down the outgoing FBI and CIA directors. Sandy filled me in on some of your adventures. She said her sources say you are a real problem for the Justice Department and the kidnapping plot was a convenient way to handle it."

Brand shrugged. He had suspected as much. He wondered how much Madison knew about him after her chat with the reporter. Agent Moore didn't seem to value his privacy when it came to Riser. He hoped the information he shared with the Post reporter was more focused upon the plot and its operatives rather than upon him.

"My father released the whole story on his new social media platform. He published a complete recounting of his experiences with the FBI and the DOJ. Even the media outlets that don't usually cover this kind of story can't avoid reporting on this one.

"Daddy tells me he knows a couple of Senators who plan to demand a full investigation into the kidnapping, and Lexicon's role in it. He says this is an international plot of historic proportions."

Brand nodded.

Madison leaned on the table, watching Brand. She gave Hans a look and he excused himself, leaving out the front door.

"What about us?" she asked. "Will you go back to your life and leave me here alone?"

Brand rested his fork on the edge of the plate and wiped his mouth. He gathered his thoughts with difficulty. He was taken aback by her candor about their relationship.

"Where do you see this going?" he asked.

"Where do I see what going?"

He saw the trap being set. He knew innately she was testing him. She had taken the same tact with her father on the plane.

He chose honesty, leaving his pride out of it for now.

"Madison," he explained. "I have feelings for you. I think I have since we agreed to the fake boyfriend ruse. By the way, I have to admit I enjoyed the game. I see so much about you I will miss if you are not in my life, but I don't see how I fit in your life. I know you would not be happy in mine. How do you see us making this work?"

For the first time, Madison was stumped by the conduct of a man. His candor undid the methods she used to divine the intent of the opposite sex. She anticipated obfuscation, instead she was met with unmistakable honesty. He risked vulnerability, leaving himself open for her reprisal, with the faith she would not use it against him.

She paused as the impact of this new and unexpected open discourse washed over her. She realized in an instant she had fortified herself against the pain she guessed he would inflict. As her understanding grew, she basked in the safety and freedom he provided her. He gave her the authority as fearlessly as he faced the dangers they had survived over the past several days.

Those memories flashed before her, reviving experiences she preferred to leave dormant and forgotten, along with the possibilities of outcomes she might have suffered if not for Carson Brand's efforts to thwart them.

"You are right," she admitted. "We are not a fit based upon our lives and experiences. There is no place where our differences would not be apparent."

She rose, moving to his side. She squatted next to his chair, looking up into his face.

"I know only one thing, and that one thing defies any logical or reasonable thought I have. We have a bond that transcends the norms of society. I feel a connection to you that issues from a place I can only describe as the most basic part of me as a living breathing person. We are connected. That connection is undeniable and real. I told you I have never met anyone like you. It sounds silly to bring it up now, except I don't think you know what I mean when I say it. At first, I didn't know either. I do now. You see all of me. You hear me, whether I say it or not. You touch me with your deep caring regard."

Her lips stretched into a thin line, as if she had said too much. She stood, remaining close to him.

He wrapped an arm around her waist, pulling her tightly against him. She buried her hand in his hair. He stood, drawing her to him. He kissed her deeply.

"It's okay to give it time to work itself out," he said, his face close to hers.

She nodded, following him to his room.

Epilogue

RISER TOOK THE PHONE CALL. He had long ago deleted the contact and the number from his cell phone. The area code would have given him a hint of the caller if he had not memorized the number years before. The voice he heard was familiar, but a strained quality made it less rumbling and throatier. He detected age in the timbre of the voice on the other end of the call.

"Dicky," the voice said uncertainly. "Is that you?"

"It's me," Riser replied with the warmth of a bill collector. "What do you want?"

"Everything is gone. They took it all. I need your help."

Riser was genuinely surprised. He would not have expected those words from him. Riser's resentment faded a fraction as his curiosity got the best of him.

"What's happened Dad?" he asked with a level tone.

"They took the ranch. They took our money. They took everything, son."

"Who took it?"

"The federal government did."

"That's ridiculous," Riser scoffed. "You and mom are as straight as they come. What about the church? What about your dude ranch?"

"It wasn't a dude ranch. We called it Nations Under God, and it was a retreat and youth outreach center. They took it."

"How is mom and Bryce?"

"They are fine. Bryce left home after he got a job at the lumber yard. He has a new girlfriend, and they live together."

Riser said nothing although he was certain his half-brother's relationship with him was a thorn in his stepfather's side.

"Tell me the story, Dad. What happened that got the feds on your ass?"

Nations relayed the story of the transformation of their ranch then the email from Bryce. Then he told Riser of the attack upon their church goers and the people planted amongst them who were involved.

"I'll make some calls," Riser promised. "I'll see what I can do."

"You can't do anything, Dicky. This thing is bigger even than you. There is a war going on. The fight is with the United States of America itself. We are the enemy, and we are outgunned."

"We'll see, Dad," Riser said though his teeth. "We'll see."

Brand entered the meeting room where the entire elite force of Sovereign Services was gathered. He took a seat near the doors at the back of the room. Although his status had been elevated greatly by his recent actions, he maintained his habitual low profile within the organization. Missing, however, were the frowns and back of the hand talk from his contemporaries. The others noticed his entry and hailed him with friendly nods and genuine respect.

Moments after Brand entered and settled into a seat, Riser arrived, giving Brand an appreciative nod as he moved to the lectern at the front of the room.

"Thank you all for being here this morning. As you know, Mac Conolly is no longer with Sovereign. Mac killed Davian Williams during his last Op."

The room was awash in silence. Amongst them both men were popular and highly regarded.

"Despite our feelings of regret or grief we move on as a group. As in battle, lost comrades are to be honored. Also in battle, those missing comrades leave a gulf we must attempt to fill as best we can. The time is long overdue that we recognize one amongst us and award him what he deserves. The Ten have voted and we select Carson Brand to join us as a member of The Ten."

Every man rose to his feet. Brand's actions over the past few weeks were well known. He had attained a near hero status amongst them. The announcement was not unexpected, but the moment was an important one for all of them. Many had encountered the roadblocks and pitfalls of lacking SEAL experience. Until Brand, there was no hope of attaining access to the inner sanctum of the prestigious organization. Brand's elevation to the Ten showed it could be done.

Riser beamed at Brand a broad smile.

After Brand's return from New York, their reunion was a short one. Riser was not given to long sentimental speeches. He debriefed Brand, filling him in on his new role within the organization. Even his stoicism could scarcely contain his pride in the young man. He had placed his faith and risked his reputation in support of a most unlikely candidate. He enjoyed the feeling all who believe and are rewarded feel.

Now, Riser allowed himself to share in Brand's moment of victory.

Brand accepted the congratulations of the men around him with single word responses and a constrained smile. He wasn't bashful, but he didn't view his actions as accolade worthy. He felt a sense of loss for his old life. He doubted he would ever grow comfortable or achieve any level of contentment from this new life. He did what he had to do, but the violence and the death were constant companions.

By his estimation, Riser conducted these meetings like a sales manager rewarding top producers rather than the head of a group of soldiers of fortune heaping praise upon a blooded mercenary. Brand again railed against the casual manner with which Sovereign viewed the services they purveyed.

Riser held up his hands for silence.

"To the business at hand, men. I am sure you all have seen the news headlines. There is corruption at the highest levels of the federal government. Our rights as American citizens are under siege by those who are intended to defend them.

"Our mission remains the same. We provide elite protection for those leaders most at risk, those financial giants who are the most vulnerable in this new arena of international finance and monetary uncertainty.

"We are rolling out a new service, a service that will fill the gap between corporate security and private special operational contractors. Our clients are of the same class, but our mission to provide them a more complete offering of protection has evolved. Starting today, you will become an asset to the client, with full authority to do what is required when it is required. Our purview is international in nature. Our base of operations will relocate off continent."

The men in the chairs looked around at one another with confusion. They were thoroughly trained in the laws governing their business. Their code of conduct was specific and inviolate. Riser hinted at a new rule book, and a new and dangerous future. There were few reasons to move their operation out of the United States. Only one of them was good.

Riser brushed away their doubts with a wave of his hand and a reassuring smile.

"The good news is each of you just got a huge raise. Fulfill your current contracts. I will meet with each of you individually to help craft a situation suitable for your skillset and personal needs."

A murmur rose.

Riser raised his hand again.

"If there are no further questions, you are dismissed. Mr. Brand I need a word, please."

Brand rose with the others. He endured a few more congratulations and slaps on the back as he made his way against the tide, towards Riser.

Once the room cleared, Riser cleared his throat.

"Congratulations on the promotion, Brand. You earned it."

"Thanks."

"I wanted to ask a favor. Are you available this weekend?"

Brand thought of Madison. She invited him to New York for the weekend. He was not sure of his place in her life, but he looked forward to seeing her.

"What's up, Chief?"

"I thought you might enjoy a visit to your old stomping grounds – Texas."

"Texas? What's going on there?"

"A situation has arisen, and I need to check on a few things. I could use your help in case I need an extra set of eyes – or a couple of capable hands."

"I'll clear my schedule. Can you give me any details?"

Riser appeared uncomfortable, looking around the room as if someone had sneaked in while he wasn't looking. He cleared his throat again before he spoke.

"My stepdad and I don't speak. He called me yesterday for the first time in fifteen years. He tells me he is under attack, and he asked for my help."

"Under attack by whom?"

Riser considered Brand for a long moment before he replied.

"He is an elder in his church. He and the church created a church camp at my Dad's ranch in southeast Texas. Somehow his church camp was designated a training facility for domestic terrorists. The place was raided. Several church members were killed. Others were arrested and held without bond. His ranch was seized and auctioned. I don't know what we will find, but I would rather have backup while I gather more information."

"I have some experience with this sort of thing," Brand admitted.

"That's why I am asking you to come along."

Brand nodded confidently.

"You can count on me, Chief."

"Thanks, Brand. You don't know how much that helps. I'll email you the details later today."

Brand left the meeting room.

He was headed back to Texas. He should be happy. Why did he feel only foreboding?

ABOUT THE AUTHOR

CRAIG RAINEY (1962 -) IS AN AMERICAN FILM ACTOR, AUTHOR, SCREENWRITER, AND MUSICIAN. HE WAS BORN IN SAN ANGELO, TEXAS, AND LIVES IN AUSTIN. HIS TEXAS ROOTS HAIL BACK TO THE ORIGINAL IMPRESARIO SETTLERS OF COAHUILA Y TEJAS UNDER STEPHEN F. AUSTIN. HE IS A MILITARY VETERAN, AND HE COWBOYED PROFESSIONALLY IN SOUTH TEXAS.